21世纪英语专业系列教材　　　　　　总主编　胡壮麟

英语泛读教程

第 3 册

主　编　李正栓　宋德文
副主编　杨丽华　赵翠华

编　者　葛文词　李海云　彭鲁迁　李金英

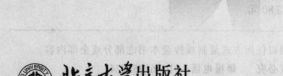

北京大学出版社
PEKING UNIVERSITY PRESS

图书在版编目(CIP)数据

英语泛读教程.第 3 册 / 李正栓,宋德文主编. —北京：北京大学出版社,2008.11
(21 世纪英语专业系列教材)
ISBN 978-7-301-13828-1

Ⅰ.英…　Ⅱ.① 李…② 宋…　Ⅲ.英语—阅读教学—高等学校—教材　Ⅳ.H319.4

中国版本图书馆 CIP 数据核字(2008)第 067922 号

书　　　名：英语泛读教程　第 3 册
著作责任者：李正栓　宋德文　主编
责 任 编 辑：张建民
标 准 书 号：ISBN 978-7-301-13828-1/H·1991
出 版 发 行：北京大学出版社
地　　　址：北京市海淀区成府路 205 号　100871
网　　　址：http://www.pup.cn
电　　　话：邮购部 62752015　发行部 62750672　编辑部 62755217　出版部 62754962
电 子 邮 箱：zbing@pup.pku.edu.cn
印 刷 者：北京飞达印刷有限责任公司
经 销 者：新华书店
　　　　　787 毫米×1092 毫米　16 开本　10.5 印张　263 千字
　　　　　2008 年 11 月第 1 版　2008 年 11 月第 1 次印刷
定　　　价：22.80 元

总 序

　　北京大学出版社自2005年以来已出版《语言与应用语言学知识系列读本》多种，为了配合第十一个五年计划，现又策划陆续出版《21世纪英语专业系列教材》。这个重大举措势必受到英语专业广大教师和学生的欢迎。

　　作为英语教师，最让人揪心的莫过于听人说英语不是一个专业，只是一个工具。说这些话的领导和教师的用心是好的，为英语专业的毕业生将来找工作着想，因此要为英语专业的学生多多开设诸如新闻、法律、国际商务、经济、旅游等其他专业的课程。但事与愿违，英语专业的教师们很快发现，学生投入英语学习的时间少了，掌握英语专业课程知识甚微，即使对四个技能的掌握也并不比大学英语学生高明多少，而那个所谓的第二专业在有关专家的眼中只是学到些皮毛而已。

　　英语专业的路在何方？有没有其他路可走？这是需要我们英语专业教师思索的问题。中央领导关于创新是一个民族的灵魂和要培养创新人才等的指示精神，让我们在层层迷雾中找到了航向。显然，培养学生具有自主学习能力和能进行创造性思维是我们更为重要的战略目标，使英语专业的人才更能适应21世纪的需要，迎接21世纪的挑战。

　　如今，北京大学出版社外语部的领导和编辑同志们，也从教材出版的视角探索英语专业的教材问题，从而为贯彻英语专业教学大纲做些有益的工作，为教师们开设大纲中所规定的必修、选修课程提供各种教材。《21世纪英语专业系列教材》是普通高等教育"十一五"国家级规划教材和国家"十一五"重点出版规划项目《面向新世纪的立体化网络化英语学科建设丛书》的重要组成部分。这套系列教材要体现新世纪英语教学的自主化、协作化、模块化和超文本化，结合外语教材的具体情况，既要解决语言、教学内容、教学方法和教育技术的时代化，也要坚持弘扬以爱国主义为核心的民族精神。因此，今天北京大学出版社在大力提倡专业英语教学改革的基础上，编辑出版各种英语专业技能、英语专业知识和相关专业知识课程的教材，以培养具有创新性思维和具有实际工作能力的学生，充分体现了时代精神。

　　北京大学出版社的远见卓识，也反映了英语专业广大师生盼望已久的心愿。由北京大学等全国几十所院校具体组织力量，积极编写相关教材。这就是说，这套教材是由一些高等院校有水平有经验的第一线教师们制定编写大纲，反复讨论，特别是考虑到在不同层次、不同背景学校之间取得平衡，避免了先前的教材或偏难或偏易的弊病。与此同时，一批知名专家教授参与策划和教材审定工作，保证了教材质量。

当然，这套系列教材出版只是初步实现了出版社和编者们的预期目标。为了获得更大效果，希望使用本系列教材的教师和同学不吝指教，及时将意见反馈给我们，使教材更加完善。

航道已经开通，我们有决心乘风破浪，奋勇前进！

胡壮麟
北京大学蓝旗营

前　言

　　本教材是为了适应新时期高等学校英语专业教学的需要,根据《高等学校英语专业英语教学大纲》的要求而编写的英语专业阅读教材,可供高校英语专业阅读教学使用,也可作为中高级英语学习者的自学书籍。

　　在前两册的基础上,本册进一步突出英语专业阅读教材的特点,广泛收录英美名家在各个时期的作品,旨在扩大学生词汇量,培养英语语感,拓宽学生视野,增强人文素养,提高学生的鉴赏能力和思辨能力。在选择文章时,编者兼顾典藏性和时代性,既有文学巨擘的传世佳作,又不乏颇具前瞻性的商界杂谈;在题材上,力求涵盖社会生活的方方面面,有对生命的考问,有对艺术的追寻,有对爱情的缅怀,也有闪耀智慧光芒的机巧思辨;在体裁上,时评时叙,亦庄亦谐,有的古雅隽永,有的灵异怪诞,有的铺排绚丽,有的朴实无华,于犀利中见幽默,在淡定中显温情,充分体现了本书在选材上时代跨度大,题材范围广,文体多样化的宗旨,从而使学生在徜徉英语语言殿堂的同时,体验中西文化的碰撞,品味跌宕起伏的哲理人生。

　　本书在编排上沿袭了前两册的体例,每个单元有 Text A 和 Text B 两篇阅读材料,对生词、难词加以注释,在注释中编者有意识地给读者提供一定的选择空间,要求学生作出正确的词义选择。为了帮助学生深入理解原文,编者对文中出现的文化现象单独加以注释。考虑到本书是英语专业的基础课教材,编者在每篇文章后都配以阅读练习题,针对性极强,训练学生的略读、寻读、细读、评读等阅读技巧,引导学生去解读、思考、分析和批评。所有练习都围绕阅读展开,回答问题和正误判断部分检测了学生对原文内容的理解程度,解释原文和英汉翻译是对学生的理解能力的更深层次的测试,阅读评述部分旨在训练学生口头和笔头的发挥能力及思维拓展能力,是对原文阅读的进一步延伸。

　　作为英语专业的阅读教材,本书与国内传统的泛读教材有所不同,是一次新的尝试。由于时间仓促以及编者水平有限,纰漏和不周之处在所难免,欢迎使用本书的社会各界人士加以批评指正。

编　者

2008 年 5 月

Contents

Unit One

Text A

The Scroll Marked
(I)
Anonymous

优美的文字和语言,激励人开始新的生活和奋斗。

Today I begin a new life.

Today I shed my old skin, which has too long suffered the bruises of failure and the wounds of mediocrity.

Today I am born anew and my birthplace is a vineyard where there is fruit for all.

Today I will pluck grapes of wisdom from the tallest and fullest vines in the vineyard, for these were planted by the wisest of my profession who have come before me, generation upon generation.

Today I will savor the taste of grapes from these vines and verily I will swallow the seed of success buried in each and new life will sprout within me.

The career I have chosen is laden with opportunity yet it is fraught with heartbreak and despair and the bodies of those who have failed, were they piled one atop another, would cast a shadow down upon all the pyramids of the earth.

Yet I will not fail, as the others, for in my hands I now hold the charts, which will guide through perilous waters to shores, which only yesterday seemed but a dream.

Failure no longer will be my payment for struggle. Just as nature made no provision for my body to tolerate pain neither has it made any

bruise /bruːz/ *n.* injury by a blow or knock to the body, or to a fruit, so that the skin is discolored but not broken

mediocrity /ˌmiːdiˈɔkriti/ *n.* quality of being neither very good nor very bad

vineyard /ˈvɪnjɑːd/ *n.* areas of land planted with grape-vines

pluck /plʌk/ *v.* pick (flower, fruit, etc.)

savor /ˈseɪvə/ *v.* (*lit. or fig.*) appreciate the taste or flavor or character of

verily /ˈverɪli/ *adv.* (*archaic*) really; truly

sprout /spraʊt/ *v.* put out leaves; begin to grow

fraught /frɔːt/ *adv.* involving; attended by; threatening (unpleasant consequences)

atop /əˈtɒp/ *prep.* on top of

perilous /ˈperɪləs/ *adv.* dangerous; full of risk

provision for my life to suffer failure. Failure, like pain, is alien to my life. In the past I accepted it as I accepted pain. Now I reject it and I am prepared for wisdom and principles which will guide me out of the shadows into the sunlight of wealth, position, and happiness far beyond my most extravagant dreams until even the golden apples in the Garden of Hesperides will seem no more than my just reward.

extravagant /ɪksˈtrævəgənt/ *adj.* a. wasteful; (in the habit of) wasting (money, etc.); b. (of ideas, speech, behavior) going beyond what is reasonable, usual or conventional; not properly controlled
eternity /ɪˈtɜːnɪti/ *n.* a. time without end; the future life; b. (*pl.*) eternal truths
allot /əˈlɒt/ *v.* make a distribution of; decide a person's share of
stumble /ˈstʌmbəl/ *v.* a. strike the foot against sth and almost fall; b. move or walk in an unsteady way; c. speak in a hesitating way, with pauses and mistakes
commence /kəˈmens/ *v.* (*formal*) begin; start
unencumbered /ˈʌnɪnˈkʌmbəd/ *adj.* a. get in the way of, hamper, be a burden to; b. crowd; fill up
devour /dɪˈvaʊə/ *v.* a. eat hungrily or greedily; b. be devoured by (curiosity, anxiety, etc.), be filled with, have all one's attention taken up by
diminish /dɪˈmɪnɪʃ/ *v.* make or become less
thou /ðaʊ/ *pron.* used to indicate the one being addressed, esp. in a literary, liturgical, or devotional context

Time teaches all things to him who lives forever but I have not the luxury of eternity. Yet within my allotted time I must practice the art of patience for nature acts never in haste. To create the olive, king of all trees, a hundred years is required. An onion plant is old in nine weeks. I have lived as an onion plant. It has not pleased me. Now I would become the greatest of olive trees and, in truth, the greatest of salesman.

And how will this be accomplished? For I have neither the knowledge nor the experience to achieve the greatness and already I have stumbled in ignorance and fallen into pools of self-pity. The answer is simple. I will commence my journey unencumbered with either the weight of unnecessary knowledge or the handicap of mean ingless experience. Nature already has supplied me with knowledge and instinct far greater than any beast in the forest and the value of experience is overrated, usually by old men who nod wisely and speak stupidly.

In truth, experience teaches thoroughly yet her course of instruction devours men's years so the value of her lessons diminishes with the time necessary to acquire her special wisdom. The end finds it wasted on dead men. Furthermore, experience is comparable to fashion; an action that proved successful today will be unworkable and impractical tomorrow.

Only principles endure and these I now possess, for the laws that will lead me to greatness are contained in the words of these scrolls. What they will teach me more to prevent failure than to gain success, for what is success other than a state of mind? Which two, among a thou and wise men, will define success in the same words; yet failure is always described but one way. Failure is man's inability to reach his goals in life, whatever they may be.

In truth, the only difference between those who have failed and those who have succeed lies in the difference of their habits. Good habits are the key to all success. Bad habits are the unlocked door to failure. Thus, the first law I will obey, which precede all the others is—I will form good habits and become their slave.

As a child I was slave to my impulses; now I am slave to my habits, as are all grown men. I have surrendered my free will to the years of accumulated habits and the past deeds of my life have already marked out a path which threatens to imprison my future. My actions are ruled by appetite, passion, prejudice, greed, love, fear, environment, habit, and the worst of these tyrants is habit. Therefore, if I must be a slave to habit, let me be a slave to good habits. My bad habits must be destroyed and new furrows prepared for good seed.

I will form good habits and become their slave.

And how will I accomplish this difficult feat? Through these scrolls, it will be done, for each scroll contains a principle which will drive a bad habit from my life and replace it with one which will bring me closer to success. For it is another of nature's laws that only a habit can subdue another habit. So, in order for these written words to perform their chosen task, I must discipline myself with the first of my new habits which is as follows:

I will read each scroll for thirty days in this prescribed manner, before I proceed to the next scroll.

First, I will read the words in silence when I arise. Then, I will read the words in silence after I have partaken of my midday meal. Last, I will read the words again just before I retire at day's end, and most important, on this occasion I will read the words aloud.

On the next day I will repeat this procedure, and I will continue in like manner for thirty days. Then, I will turn to the next scroll and repeat this procedure for another thirty days. I will continue in this manner until I have lived with each scroll for thirty days and my reading has become habit.

And what will be accomplished with this habit? Herein lies the hidden secret of all man's accomplishments. As I repeat the words daily they will soon become a part of my active mind, but more important, they will also seep into my other mind, that mysterious source which never sleeps, which creates my dreams, and often makes me act in ways I do not comprehend.

As the words of these scrolls are

impulse /'ɪmpʌls/ *n.* a. push or thrust; impetus; b. sudden inclination to act without thought about the consequences; c. state of mind in which such inclinations occur; tendency to act without reflection

surrender /sə'rendə/ *v.* a. give up; b. yield under pressure or from necessity; abandon possession of; yield or give way to (a habit, emotion, influence, etc.)

accumulate /ə'kjuːmjʊleɪt/ *v.* make or become greater in number or quality; come or gather together; heap up

prejudice /'predʒ,ʊdɪs/ *n.* a. opinion, like or dislike, formed before one has adequate knowledge or experience; instance of this; b. (*legal*) injury that may or does arise from some action or judgment

feat /fiːt/ *n.* sth difficult well done, esp. sth showing skill, strength or daring

subdue /səb'djuː/ *v.* a. overcome; bring under control; b. make quieter, softer, gentler

prescribe /prɪs'kraɪb/ *v.* a. advise or order the use of; b. say, with authority, what course of action is to be followed

partake /pɑː'teɪk/ *v.* (*dated formal*) a. take a share in; b. have some of (the nature or characteristic of)

seep /siːp/ *v.* (of liquids) ooze out or through; trickle

consumed by my mysterious mind I will begin to awake, each morning, with a vitality I have never known before. My vigor will increase, my enthusiasm will rise, my desire to meet the

vitality /vaɪˈtælɪti/ n. vital power; capacity to endure and perform functions

confront /kənˈfrʌnt/ n. a. bring face to face; b. be or come

world will overcome every fear I once knew at sunrise, and I will be happier than I ever believed it possible to be in this world of strife and sorrow.

Eventually I will find myself reacting to all situations which confront me as I was commanded in the scrolls to react, and soon these actions and reactions will become easy to perform, for any act with practice becomes easy.

Thus a new and good habit is born, for when an act becomes easy through constant repetition it becomes a pleasure to perform and if it is a pleasure to perform it is man's nature to perform it often. When I perform it often it becomes a habit and I become its slave and since it is a good habit this is my will.

Today I begin a new life.

Cultural Notes

Garden of Hesperides—It was Hera's orchard in the west, where either a single tree or a grove of immortality-giving golden apples grew. The apples were planted from the fruited branches that Gaia gave to Hera as a wedding gift when she accepted Zeus. The Hesperides were given the task of tending to the grove, but occasionally plucked from it themselves. Not trusting them, Hera also placed in the garden a never-sleeping, hundred-headed dragon, named Lado, as an additional safeguard.

Hesperides—They were the daughters of Hesperus, or Night (brother of Atlas), and fabled possessors of a garden producing golden apples, in Africa, at the western extremity of the known world.

Thou—The word "thou" is a second person singular pronoun in English. It is now largely archaic, having been replaced in almost all contexts by you. "Thou" is the nominative form; the oblique/objective form is "thee" (functioning as both accusative and dative), and the possessive is "thy" or "thine". Almost all verbs following "thou" have the endings "-st" or "-es"t; e.g. "thou goest". In Middle English, "thou" was sometimes abbreviated by putting a small "u" over the letter thorn.

Exercises

I. Answer the following questions based on the text.

1. What do you think is the most critical quality for a man who wants to achieve his goal in life?

2. Why does the author assume that "failure no longer will be my payment for struggle"?

3. Could we rely only on time and experience we get in life as a guidance or resource from which we can draw instructions and know where to go?

4. Do you consider principles something more important than any other factors mentioned in the text?

5. Why will the author read each scroll for thirty days in that prescribed manner? What could be the result of this?

II. Text Review. Write T for true and F for false in the brackets before each of the following statements.

( ) 1. According to the text, grapes are used as an image here because they taste sweet, so compared to the pain of failure, they supply us a feeling of satisfaction.

( ) 2. Pain to the body is what failure to the life.

( ) 3. Time is the most important to a man and it determines everything for a mortal human being.

( ) 4. Experience is of absolutely no value for a man because old men always nod wisely but speak stupidly.

( ) 5. A man must learn, first of all, how to prevent failure rather than gain success, since success is only a state of mind.

( ) 6. A man must try to conquer all and could not be the slave of everything or everybody then he could be successful.

( ) 7. Habits will make one lazy because he just does everything accordingly without thinking, so before long one will become stupid and ridiculous.

( ) 8. If one wants to succeed, one must read each of the scrolls for thirty days and the reading itself will ensure the success of anybody.

( ) 9. Habit and will are widely different from each other because will calls for our perseverance yet habit is something natural and random in daily life.

( ) 10. Everybody is born with a certain habit and he will live with it in his future existence, which can never be changed.

III. Paraphrase the following sentences in English.

1. The career I have chosen is laden with opportunity yet it is fraught with heartbreak and despair and the bodies of those who have failed...

2. Failure no longer will be my payment for struggle.

3. Just as nature made no provision for my body to tolerate pain neither has it made any provision for my life to suffer failure.

4. Yet within my allotted time I must practice the art of patience for nature acts never in haste.

5. I have surrendered my free will to the years of accumulated habits and the past deeds of my life have already marked out a path which threatens to imprison my future.

IV. Translate the following sentences into Chinese.

1. I have neither the knowledge nor the experience to achieve the greatness and already I have stumbled in ignorance and fallen into pools of self-pity.

2. The Church of England tried to suppress the individual in their spiritual beliefs, their private domain, the seat of life where all people inquire about their own existence.

3. This phenomenon where noble ideals continue to rise up even from the ashes of our own indignities is uniquely American.

4. The colonists were an independent lot and there was no way they accepted the Church of England or the aristocratic social structure as something they could embrace.

5. Jefferson stated in the past people were never empowered to censure or punish their leaders and those that would even raise their voice in protest were considered traitors.

V. Respond to each of the following statements.

1. People tend to believe more of their own experience in life, with or without knowing whether any personal experience is not enough.

2. As a salesman, if he wants to be successful, he must have some qualities, such as character, professional knowledge and various abilities.

3. That time could do all for man is a generally accepted assumption by most people, yet they always neglect that nobody could live as long as time.

4. Grapes are used as a metaphor because the wine, in some way the same with human wisdom, is made as the collective work of many.

5. Principle is a guide to one's success, because the power of daily discipline is huge.

VI. Provide a text which can support your viewpoint on one of the statements in *Exercise V*. Make your comment on the text you choose.

Text B

The Scroll Marked
(II)

Anonymous

优美的文字和语言,激励人开始新的生活和奋斗。

I will greet this day with love in my heart.

For this is the greatest secret of success in all ventures. Muscle can split a shield and even destroy life but only the unseen power of love can open the hearts of men and until I master this art I will remain no more than a peddler in the market place. I will make love my greatest weapon and none on whom I call can defend against its force.

My reasoning they may counter; my speech they may distrust; my apparel they may disapprove; my face they may reject; and even my bargains may cause them suspicion; yet my love will melt all hearts liken to the sun whose rays soften the coldest clay.

I will greet this day with love in my heart.

And how will I do this? Henceforth will I look on all things with love and I will be born again. I will love the sun for it warms my bones; yet I will love the rain for it cleanses my spirit. I will love the light for it shows me the way; yet I will love the darkness for it shows me the stars. I will welcome happiness for it enlarges my heart; yet I will endure sadness for it opens my soul. I will acknowledge rewards for they are

venture /'ventʃə/ a. *n.* undertaking in which there is risk; b. *v.* take the risk of, expose to, danger or loss; c. *v.* go so far as, presume, dare

peddler /'pedlə/ *n.* person who travels about selling small articles

apparel /ə'pærəl/ *v.* (*old use or lit.*) dress or clothing

suspicion /səs'pɪʃən/ *n.* a. feeling that a person has when he suspects; suspecting or being suspected; feeling that sth is wrong; b. slight taste or suggestion

liken /'laɪkən/ *v.* point out the likeness of one thing (to another)

henceforth /hens'fɔːθ/ *adv.* from this time on; in future

my due; yet I will welcome obstacles for they are my challenge.

I will greet this day with love in my heart.

And how will I speak? I will laud my enemies and they will become friends; I will encourage my friends and they will become brothers. Always will I dig for reasons to applaud; never will I scratch for excuses to gossip. When I am tempted to criticize I will bite on my tongue; when I am moved to praise I will shout from the roofs.

obstacle /'ɒbstəkə/ *n.* sth in the way that stops progress or makes it difficult
laud /lɔːd/ *v.* (*formal*) praise; glorify
ambitious /æm'bɪʃəs/ *adv.* a. full of ambitions (strong desire to be or do sth); b. showing or needing ambitions
repulse /rɪ'pʌls/ *v.* a. repel; drive back (the enemy); resist (an attack) successfully; b. (not replaceable by repel) refuse to accept (sb's help, friendly offers, etc.); discourage (a person) by unfriendly treatment
sustain /sə'steɪn/ *v.* a. keep from falling or sinking; b. (enable to) keep up; maintain; c. suffer; undergo; d. (*legal*) uphold; give a decision in favor of
exultation /ˌegzʌl'teɪʃən/ great joy (at); triumph (over)
unwrinkle /ˌʌn'rɪŋkl/ *v.* make less of the wrinkles

Is it not so that birds, the wind, the sea and all nature speaks with the music of praise for their creator? Cannot I speak with the same music to his children? Henceforth will I remember this secret and it will change my life.

I will greet this day with love in my heart.

And how will I act? I will love all manners of men for each has qualities to be admired even though they be hidden. With love I will tear down the wall of suspicion and hate which they have built round their hearts and in its place will I build bridges so that my love may enter their souls.

I will love the ambitious for they can inspire me! I will love the failures for they can teach me. I will love the kings for they are but human; I will love the meek for they are divine. I will love the rich for they are yet lonely; I will love the poor for they are so many. I will love the young for the faith they hold; I will love the beautiful for their eyes of sadness; I will love the ugly for their souls of peace.

I will greet this day with love in my heart.

But how will I react to the actions of others? With love. For just as love is my weapon to open the hearts of men, love is also my shield to repulse the arrows of hate and the spears of anger. Adversity and discouragement will beat against my new shield and become as the softest of rains. My shield will protect me in the market place and sustain me when I am alone. It will uplift me in moments of despair yet it will calm me in time of exultation. It will become stronger and more protective with use until one day I will cast it aside and walk unencumbered among all manners of men and, when I do, my name will be raised high on the pyramid of life.

I will greet this day with love in my heart.

And how will I confront each whom I meet? In only one way. In silence and to myself I will address him and say I Love You. Though spoken in silence these words will shine in my eyes, unwrinkle my brow, bring a smile to my lips, and echo in my voice; and his heart will be opened. And who is there who will say nay to my goods when his heart feels my love?

I will greet this day with love in my heart.

And most of all I will love myself. For when I do I will zealously inspect all things which enter my body, my mind, my soul, and my heart. Never will I overindulge the requests of my flesh, rather I will cherish my body with cleanliness and moderation. Never will I allow my mind to be attracted to evil and despair, rather I will uplift it with the knowledge and wisdom of the ages. Never will I allow my soul to become complacent and satisfied, rather I will feed it with meditation and prayer. Never will I allow my heart to become small and bitter, rather I will share it and it will grow and warm the earth.

I will greet this day with love in my heart.

Henceforth will I love all mankind. From this moment all hate is let from my veins for I have no time to hate, only time to love. From this moment I take the first step required to become a man among men. With love I will increase my sales a hundredfold and become a great salesman. If I have no other qualities I can succeed with love alone. Without it I will fail though I possess all the knowledge and skills of the world.

I will greet this day with love, and I will succeed.

I will persist until I succeed.

In the Orient young bulls are tested for the fight arena in a certain manner. Each is brought to the ring and allowed to attack a picador who pricks them with a lance. The bravery of each bull is then rated with care according to the number of times he demonstrates his willingness to charge in spite of the sting of the blade. Henceforth will I recognize that each day I am tested by life in like manner. If I persist, if I continue to try, if I continue to charge forward, I will succeed.

I will persist until I succeed.

I was not delivered unto this world in defeat, nor does failure course in my veins. I am not a sheep waiting to be prodded by my shepherd. I am a lion and I refuse to talk, to walk, to sleep with the sheep. I will hear not those who weep and complain, for their

zealously /ˈzeləsli/ adv. full of, acting with, showing energy and enthusiasm

overindulge /ˌəʊvərɪnˈdʌldʒ/ v. a. indulge gratify; give way to and satisfy (desires, etc.); overlook the faults of; b. allow oneself the pleasure of

moderation /ˌmɒdəˈreɪʃən/ n. a. quality of being moderate; freedom from excess; b. (pl.) (shortened to Mods) first public examination for a degree in classical studies at Oxford

complacent /kəmˈpleɪsənt/ adj. self-satisfied

meditation /medɪˈteɪʃən/ n. the act or time of thinking seriously or deeply (about)

hundredfold /ˈhʌndrədfəʊld/ n. one hundred times as much or as many

arena /əˈriːnə/ n. central part, for games and fights, of a Roman

picador /ˈpɪkədɔː/ n. man (mounted on a horse) who uses a lance to incite and weaken bulls in the sport of bull-fighting

demonstrate /ˈdemənstreɪt/ v. a. show clearly by giving proofs or examples; b. take part in a demonstration

prod /prɒd/ n. push or poke with sth pointed

shepherd /ˈʃepəd/ a. n. a man who takes care of sheep; b. v. take care of; guide or direct

disease is contagious. Let them join the sheep. The slaughterhouse of failure is not my destiny.

> contagious /kən'teɪdʒəs/ *adj.* a. (of disease) spreading by contact; b. (of a person) in such a condition that he may spread a disease; c. (*fig.*) spreading easily by example
>
> slaughterhouse /'slɔːtəhaʊs/ *n.* place where animals are butchered for food

I will persist until I succeed.

The prizes of life are at the end of each journey, not near the beginning; and it is not given to me to know how many steps are necessary in order to reach my goal. Failure I may still encounter at the thousandth step, yet success hides behind the next bend in the road. Never will I know how close it lies unless I turn the corner.

Always will I take another step. If that is of no avail I will take another, and yet another. In truth, one step at a time is not too difficult.

I will persist until I succeed.

Cultural notes

Pyramid—A pyramid is any three-dimensional structure where the upper surfaces are triangular and converge on one point (apex). The bases of pyramids are usually quadrilateral or trilateral (but generally may be of any polygon shape), meaning that a pyramid usually has four or three sides. The measurements of these triangles uniformly classify the shape as isosceles and sometimes equilateral. Pyramid-shaped structures were built by many ancient civilizations, such as in China, Egypt, France, Greece, India and Rome and so on, to contain the bodies and possessions of the dead.

The Orient—It is a term traditionally used in Western culture to refer to the Middle East (Southwest Asia and Egypt), South Asia, Southeast Asia and East Asia. It is opposite with "the Occident".

Exercises

I. Answer the following questions based on the text.

1. Do you agree with the author that love is the greatest in this world?

2. How could one show his love when others counter his reasoning and distrust his speech and disapprove his apparel?

3. Is it possible to love all manners of men though each has qualities to be admired?

4. People generally consider love is selfish. Could love be so generous and be shared with so many?

5. What is more important in one's life and career according to the text, love or perseverance?

II. Text Review. Write T for true and F for false in the brackets before each of the following statements.

(　) 1. Love is one of the greatest power, thus no one can defend against it.

(　) 2. All things, sadness, happiness, rewards, obstacles, aren't very helpful in one's life, and some of them can only bring negative effects to people.

(　) 3. In the author's opinion, one must always be ready to praise rather than to criticize if one is filled with love.

(　) 4. According to the author, since love can tear down the wall of suspicion and hate, we should love our enemies.

(　) 5. The sun can soften the coldest clay, therefore, love, just like the sun, will melt the coldest heart.

(　) 6. Only those who have a high social status are respectable, while others are not for various reasons.

(　) 7. Giving love is completely from one's heart, no one can be compelled to love.

(　) 8. Love can bring happiness to a person when he knows the enemies become friends because of love.

(　) 9. The author thinks that his soul shouldn't be satisfied with what he has, he should desire more and request more.

(　) 10. It is self-contradictory when the author says that all can offer a person with different advantages, and that he was not delivered unto this world in defeat.

III. Paraphrase the following sentences in English.

1. Always will I dig for reasons to applaud; never will I scratch for excuses to gossip.

2. Adversity and discouragement will beat against my new shield and become as the softest of rains.

3. Never will I overindulge the requests of my flesh, rather I will cherish my body with cleanliness and moderation.

4. I was not delivered unto this world in defeat, nor does failure course in my veins.

5. Failure I may still encounter at the thousandth step, yet success hides behind the next bend in the road.

IV. Translate the following sentences into Chinese.

1. For this is the greatest secret of success in all ventures. Muscle can split a shield and even destroy life but only the unseen power of love can open the hearts of men.

2. I will love the sun for it warms my bones; yet I will love the rain for it cleanses my spirit. I will love the light for it shows me the way; yet I will love the darkness for it shows me the stars.

3. I will love the ambitious for they can inspire me! I will love the failures for they can teach me. I will love the kings for they are but human; I will love the meek for they are divine. I will love the rich for they are yet lonely; I will love the poor for they are so many. I will love the young for the faith they hold; I will love the beautiful for their eyes of sadness; I will love the ugly for their souls of peace.

4. Never will I allow my mind to be attracted to evil and despair, rather I will uplift it with the knowledge and wisdom of the ages. Never will I allow my soul to become complacent and satisfied, rather I will feed it with meditation and prayer. Never will I allow my heart to become small and bitter, rather I will share it and it will grow and warm the earth.

5. The prizes of life are at the end of each journey, not near the beginning; and it is not given to me to know how many steps are necessary in order to reach my goal. Failure I may still encounter at the thousandth step, yet success hides behind the next bend in the road. Never will I know how close it lies unless I turn the corner.

V. Respond to each of the following statements.

1. Love is one aspect of human nature.

2. Love doesn't exist there naturally of itself but love can be everywhere when and only when we get rid of the prejudice against others.

3. Which is the stronger force, love or evil?

4. Love is prevailing everywhere in nature, what men need to do is to be gentle and sensitive enough to feel it.

5. Success may be given various definitions: Success is making loads of money; success is achieving your goals; success is fulfilling your potential. What does success mean to you?

VI. Provide a text which can support your viewpoint on one of the statements in *Exercise V*. Make your comment on the text you choose.

Unit Two

Language and Culture Differences in Daily Life
Anonymous

语言和文化的差异在世界全球化的今天日益凸现出来，了解这些已经成了当务之急。

In many aspects of our life, we often divide the world into two parts: the eastern one and the western one. The former usually refers to Asia and the latter includes mainly Europe, North Africa and America. We divide like this not only because of the geographical location differences, but also due to the cultural differences to a large extent. In the following parts, you'll see such differences, from the causes to the customs of the two sides nowadays.

Part I   What leads to the cultural difference?

The cultures of the East and the West really distinguish each other a lot. This is because the culture systems are two separate systems on the whole.

The origin of the eastern cultures is mainly from two countries: China and India. Both of the two cultures are gestated by rivers. In China, the mother river is the Yellow River while the Indian one is the Hindu River. These two cultures were developed for several thousand years and formed their own styles. Then in the Tang Dynasty of China, the Chinese culture gradually went overseas to Japan, mixed into the Japanese society and shaped the Japanese culture. Though a bit different from the Chinese one, it belongs to the same system.

When the two mother rivers gave birth to the

geographical /ˌdʒiəˈɡræfikəl/ *adj.* of geography (science of the earth's surface, physical features, divisions, climate, products, population, etc.)
location /ləʊˈkeɪʃən/ *n.* a. position or place; b. place, not a film studio, where (part of) a film is photographed
origin /ˈɒrɪdʒɪn/ *n.* starting-point
gestate /ˈdʒesteɪt/ *v.* a. to carry in the uterus during pregnancy; b. to conceive and gradually develop in the mind

eastern culture, another famous culture was brought up on the Mesopotamian Plain—the Mesopotamian Civilization. This civilization later on developed into the cultures of the Ancient Greece and Ancient Rome. And these two are well-known as the base of the European culture. Like the Chinese culture, the European one also crossed waters. When the colonists of England settled down in America, their culture went with them over the Atlantic Ocean. So the American culture doesn't distinguish from the European one a lot.

Mesopotamian Civilization ancient civilization developed in Mesopotamian Plain

distinguish /dɪsˈtɪŋgwɪʃ/ v. a. see, hear, recognize, understand well the difference; b. make out by looking, listening, etc. c. be a mark of character, difference; d. behave so as to bring credit to oneself

pictographic /ˌpɪktəˈgræfik/ adj. a. consisting of an ancient or prehistoric drawing or painting on a rock wall; b. consisting of one of the symbols belonging to a pictorial graphic system

count /kaʊnt/ v. a. say or name (e.g. numerals) in order; b. find the total of; c. include; be included; in the reckoning; consider (sb or sth) to be

interference /ˌɪntəˈfɪərəns/ n. (of persons) breaking in upon (other persons' affairs) without right or invitation

typical /ˈtɪpɪkəl/ adj. serving as a type; representative or characteristic

individual /ˌɪndɪˈvɪdjuəl/ a. adj. (opp. of general)special for one person or thing; b. n. characteristic of a single person, animal, plant or thing; c. n. any one human being (contrasted with society)

community /kəˈmjuːnɪti/ n. a. the people living in one place, district or country, considered as a whole; b. group of persons having the same religion, race, occupation, etc, or with common interests; c. condition of sharing, having things in common, being alike in some way

At the same time, the difference of the language systems adds to the cultural differences. In the East, most languages belong to the pictographic language while the Western languages are mostly based on the Latin system, for example, the one I'm using to write this paper.

Other factors like human race difference count as well. But what's more, due to the far distance and the steep areas between the East and West, the two cultures seldom communicate until in recent centuries. So they grew up totally in their own ways with almost no interference from the other.

Part II　How differently do people behave in daily life?

The differences are everywhere. They affect people's ways of thinking and their views of the world. Even in everyday life, the cultural differences show up from the moment the eyes are opened to the minute the dreams are invited.

In the following, I'll give some typical example of the differences.

Section 1: Greeting

Greeting is the first step to form a culture, because people begin to communicate with others. The individuals become a community.

How do Chinese greet each other? Informally, if we meet an friend in the street, we are used to say: "Hi, have you had your meal?" or "Where are you going?" When it is the case of two gentlemen, they tend to shake hands.

However, in the western countries, the above questions are just questions, not greeting at all. They may think you're inviting them to dinner if you ask about their meals. Usually, they'll just give each other a smile or greet with a "Hi." They'll shake hands only in some formal situations. By the way, Westerners can leave a party or meeting halls without a formal conge, nor should they shake hands with every attendee as most of us will do in China.

Section 2: Expressing gratitude

Think of the situations below. Your mother is busy in the kitchen. She suddenly asks you to fetch a bowl for her. You do so. What'll your mother's response be? Probably she'll just continue doing the cooking. After a while, the dinner is ready. Your mother hands you your bowl of rice. What's your response? Probably just begin to eat.

That's what I want to say. In Chinese families, we rarely say "Thank you" to other family members for receiving help or service. Neither will we say so between good friends. It's such an unpopular response that if you say it, the counterpart will think you are treating him as a stranger, otherwise you are lacking of intimacy.

But in the West, "thank you" is one of the most frequently used sentences. Teachers will thank a student for answering a question; husbands will thank his wife for making a coffee.

However, as an interesting phenomenon, it's a custom to say "thank you" in Japan. Whether in family or among friends, Japanese chronically use it all the day. This is probably the aberrance of the culture.

Section 3: Dining

The ways people eat, that is, the table manner, really distinguish a lot. The reason for this is probably because of the different dining tools and menus.

Easterners use chopsticks, or sometimes even grasp rice straightly with hands as Indians do. The thin and long chopsticks cannot be used to cut food, so we usually use our teeth to act as knives. We hold our food, meat or vegetable, with the chopsticks, send them to the mouths, bite off a part of it and remain the other part on the chopsticks. That's the usual way we eat. We are also used to hold up our bowls when having rice or soup. Japanese hold bowls to have miso soup without spoons. But all these habits are considered rude in the Western countries.

conge /'kɔːnʒeɪ/ *n.* a. formal permission to depart; b. abrupt and unceremonious dismissal

attendee /ə,ten'diː/ *n.* a person who is present on a given occasion or at a given place

gratitude /'ɡrætɪtjuːd/ *n.* thankfulness; being grateful

counterpart /'kaʊntəpɑːt/ *n.* person or thing exactly like, or closely corresponding to another

intimacy /'ɪntɪməsi/ *n.* a. the state of being intimate; close friendship or relationship; (*euphemism*) sexual relations; b. (*pl.*) intimate actions, e.g. caresses or kisses

chronically /'krɒnɪkəli/ *adv.* (of a disease or condition) continually, lasting for a long time

aberrance /æ'berəns/ *n.* straying away from what is normal, expected or usual; being not true to type

chopsticks /'tʃɒpstɪks/ *n.* (*pl.*) pair of tapering sticks (wood, ivory, etc.) used by the Chinese and Japanese for lifting food (placed on the thinnest ends) to the mouth

miso soup Japanese soup made of a high-protein fermented paste consisting chiefly of soybeans, salt, and usually grain (as barley or rice) and ranging in taste from very salty to very sweet

The etiquette in the West requests that when eating, bowls and plates cannot leave the tables. Food should be cut by knives to fit into the mouths. Of course your mouth cannot touch the plates or bowls. So the regular process is like this. You cut your steak on the plate with fork and knife, send the meat cube into the mouth with fork and nothing will be returned back but the fork alone.

etiquette /'etɪket/ *n.* rules for formal relations or polite social behavior among people, in a class of society or profession
symbolize /'sɪmbəlaɪz/ *v.* be a symbol of; make use of a symbol or symbols for
preference /'prefərəns/ *n.* a. act of preferring; b. that which is preferred; the favoring of one person, country, etc. esp. by admitting imports at a lower import duty
lantern /'læntən/ *n.* case (usu. metal and glass) protecting a light from the wind, etc., outdoors
node /nəʊd/ *n.* a. (*bot.*) point on the stem of a plant where a leaf or bud grows out; b. (*phy.*) point or line of rest in a vibrating body; c. (*fig.*) point at which the parts of something begin or meet
banger /'bæŋə/ *n.* a. (*sl.*) sausage; b. noisy firework; c. old dilapidated car

Section 4: Symbolizing

Symbolization is how people imagine or regard something. It actually reflects the way people think. Here I'll only discuss some symbolization that frequently appears in daily life.

The first is about the colors. We often give each color some meanings, because we feel differently when facing different colors. So people always have preference when choosing colors of clothes, decorations, etc. In the APEC summit held in Shanghai several years ago, on the last day, the presidents from all over the world wore the traditional Chinese Tang suits and took a photo together. The colors of the suits were chosen by themselves freely. However, it's quite interesting to find that most Easterners chose red while most of the westerners preferred blue. To explain this, it's easy to realize that what red means is almost opposite in the East and the West. Red means luck, fortune here. We Chinese often use this color to decorate in festivals, such as red lanterns, red Chinese nodes, and red bangers. But red stands for blood, revolutions in the West. So the presidents avoided wearing this unlucky color.

Cultural Notes

Mesopotamian Plain—It is a region in west Asia between the River of Tigris and the River of Euphrates extending from the mountains of east Asia Minor to the Persian Gulf.

Ancient Rome—In the early half of the first century BC, the rise of Rome, from provincial settlement to imperial power, is an epic story that reads like fiction rather than fact. A fable goes like this: Romulus is said to have slain his twin brother Remus and founded the future city-state, both infants having survived abandonment on the banks of the Tiber thanks to the nurturing milk of a she-wolf. Ancient Rome traces all facets of one of the world's greatest civilizations, from the legends surrounding Rome's foundation to the strife that precipitated the Empire's collapse. It describes a remarkable imperial power that left an indelible mark on the lands it occupied. The face of Europe today would be radically different, were it not for the rich cultural, technological, linguistic, and administrative legacy bequeathed it by the Romans.

Ancient Greece—The ancient Greece civilization lasted from about 800 BC, when the Greeks began to set up city states, to 146 BC when the Romans invaded and conquered Greece.

Latin system—It is the italic language of ancient Latium and of Rome and until modern times. It is still the dominant language of school, church, and state in Western Europe.

APEC summit—Ninth Asia-Pacific Economic Cooperation summit was held on October 20 to 21, 2001, in Shanghai. The theme of the conference was "New Century, New Challenge: participation, cooperation, and promote common prosperity."

In April 1992, the Australian Prime Minister first advocated APEC summit for the time, the Asia-Pacific region to hold a summit meeting. On November 19—20, 1993, the first informal summit meeting was held in Seattle in the United States of Black Island. Apart from Malaysia, the other 14 members of the Organization attended the meeting. There are 21 member countries (or districts) now: Australia, Brunei, Canada, Chile, China, Chinese Hong Kong, Indonesia, Japan, Korea, Malaysia, Mexico, New Zealand, Papua New Guinea, Peru, Philippines, Russia, Singapore, Chinese Taipei, Thailand, United States and Vietnam.

Exercises

I. Answer the following questions based on the text.

1. What has caused the division of eastern and western worlds in your opinion?
2. Please tell the role China or Chinese culture plays in eastern cultures.
3. What is the part of language in culture? Please give some examples.
4. Do you insist your mother should say thank you as a western mother does when you have done something for her?

5. Do any two eastern countries (or western countries) have the same tradition or cultural characteristics?

II. Text Review. Write T for true and F for false in the brackets before each of the following statements.

(　) 1. The division of east and west concerns both the location and cultural aspects in countries.

(　) 2. Chinese culture is longer than that of India as everybody can see.

(　) 3. Japanese develops more rapidly because its culture is splendid by itself.

(　) 4. Western and eastern cultures are different also because European culture originates from a plain, not along rivers like eastern ones.

(　) 5. Language systems exert significant influence on the difference of culture.

(　) 6. The author has given a thorough statement of the different aspects in the two cultural traditions.

(　) 7. Greeting is the first step to communicate with others, thus its role is not to be neglected.

(　) 8. Both in Chinese and English families, people have different ways to express their gratitude.

(　) 9. Rudeness and politeness are not to be divided according to a certain tradition only, to some extent it is only something conventional.

(　) 10. Color is something most natural which has nothing to do with cultures.

III. Paraphrase the following sentences in English.

1. The cultures of the East and the West really distinguish each other a lot.

2. These two cultures were developed for several thousand years and formed their own styles.

3. Whether in family or among friends, Japanese chronically use it all the day. This is probably the aberrance of the culture.

4. The etiquette in the West requests that when eating, bowls and plates cannot leave the tables.

5. We often give each color some meanings, because we feel differently when facing different colors.

IV. Translate the following sentences into Chinese.

1. We divide like this not only because of the geographical location differences, but also due to the cultural differences to a large extent.

2. Then in the Tang Dynasty of China, the Chinese culture gradually went overseas to Japan, mixed into the Japanese society and shaped the Japanese culture.

Though a bit different from the Chinese one, it belongs to the same system.

3. Like the Chinese culture, the European one also crossed waters. When the colonists of England settled down in America, their culture went with them over the Atlantic Ocean. So the American culture doesn't distinguish from the European one a lot.

4. Other factors like human race difference count as well. But what's more, due to the far distance and the steep areas between the East and West, the two cultures seldom communicate until in recent centuries.

5. We Chinese often use this color to decorate in festivals, such as red lanterns, red Chinese nodes, and red bangers. But red stands for blood, revolutions in the West. So the presidents avoided wearing this unlucky color.

V. Respond to each of the following statements.

1. Cultural differences are there definite and sure even though sometimes we don't feel it strongly.

2. Japanese culture is deeply rooted in Chinese culture, which is obvious in many respects.

3. Culture is changing with history, while some facets remain relatively stable in the course of the developing.

4. No matter how hard one could try, the influence of culture couldn't be so easily rooted out from one's life.

5. Respecting difference in cultures will be our best choice when we are communicating with people from other cultures or touring in other countries.

VI. Provide a text which can support your viewpoint on one of the statements in *Exercise V*. Make your comment on the text you choose.

Text B

Different Ethical Values in Chinese and American Cultures

Anonymous

《中美文化中的不同伦理观》对于不同民族的伦理观念的对比,初步确立一个较为清晰的印象。

I. Cases across Chinese and American cultures

A young American woman went to Hong Kong to work, and at the time of her arrival she knew nothing about the Chinese culture or language. On her way to school one day, she went to the bank to get some money. Unexpectedly, the bank clerk asked her if she had had her lunch. She was extremely surprised at such a question because in the American culture it would be regarded as an indirect invitation to lunch. Between unmarried young people it can also indicate the young man's interest in dating the girl. Since this bank clerk was a complete stranger to the girl, she hastily commented that she had eaten already. After this she proceeded to school and was even more surprised when one of the teachers asked her the same question. In the following days she was asked the same question again and again, and she spent many hours trying to work out why so many people kept asking her this. Eventually she came to a conclusion: the people must be concerned about her health. She was somewhat underweight at the time, and so she concluded they must worry that she was not eating properly! Only much later did she discover that the question had no real significance at all—it was merely a greeting.

Misunderstanding like this can easily occur. Some more cases are given below:

1) In Chinese greetings, you will often hear "Have you eaten yet/had your lunch" (asked after meal time), "What have you done", "Where have you been", "Where are you going" (asked on the way), "Are you going to work",

ethical /'eθɪkəl/ *adj.* of morals or moral questions
unexpectedly /ˌʌnɪk'spektɪdli/ *adv.* unseen, not expected
indicate /'ɪndɪkeɪt/ *v.* point to; point out; make known; be sign of; show the need of; state briefly
hastily /'heɪstɪli/ *adv.* said, made or done quickly
proceed /prə'siːd/ *v.* **a.** go forward, go on; **b.** come, arise from; **c.** take legal action; **d.** go on from a lower university degree
eventually /ɪ'ventjuəli/ *adv.* in the end
significance /sɪg'nɪfɪkəns/ *n.* meaning; importance

"Are you going home", "Are you taking a walk" (asked when meeting a neighbor), "Are you full / hungry" (asked around meal time), "Are you going shopping / doing sport" (asked when a certain thing is being done). In America, people usually greet each other by saying "Hi / Hello", "Good morning / afternoon / evening", "How are you", "How do you do".

relatively /ˈrelətɪvli/ *adv.* comparatively; in proportion to

abrupt /əˈbrʌpt/ *adj.* a. unexpectedly sudden; b. (of speech, writing, behavior) rough; brusque; disconnected

compliment /ˈkɒmplɪmənt/ *n.* a. expression of admiration, approval, etc., either in words or by action, e.g. by asking sb for his advice or opinions, or by imitating him; b. (*formal*) greetings

joint /dʒɔɪnt/ a. *adj.* (*attrib only*) held or done by, belonging to, two or more persons together; b. *n.* place, line or surface at which two or more things are joined; c. *n.* device or structure by which things, e.g. lengths of pipe, bones are joined together; d. *n.* (*sl.*) place visited by people for gambling, drinking or drug-taking; e. *n.* (*sl.*) cigarette containing a drug; f. *v.* provide with a joint or joints; g. *v.* divide at a joint or into joints

considerate /kənˈsɪdərɪt/ *adj.* thoughtful (of the needs, etc., of others)

maintain /meɪnˈteɪn/ *v.* a. keep up; remain; continue; b. support; c. assert as true; d. keep in good repair or working order; e. defend

2) In Chinese partings, the Chinese way of leave-taking is relatively brief or even seems too abrupt. "Chinese visitors often stand up suddenly and say 'I'm leaving now'. As they move to the door, they use phrases like 'I'm sorry to have wasted your time' or ' I'm sorry to have taken up so much of your time'". When the guest is about to leave, it is polite for the host to insist on the guest's staying a little longer. Moreover, the host generally sees his guest off to the door and usually even further. When the host is not going to accompany the guest for a distance, he may say to the guest, "I'm not going to see you off afar" or "Please walk slowly". And the guest will respond as "Don't see me off" or "Please go back". In American partings, a guest must hint several times that he is leaving as the preparation for leaving. Then, just before he leaves, he must say something like "Thank you for a lovely afternoon" or "Thank you, I enjoyed this beautiful evening". After saying goodbye to each other, the host usually shows the guest to the door and sees him off there.

3) As for compliment responses, when being complimented by "Your shoes are very pretty", a Chinese may reply with "No, they are not as pretty as yours" or "Really? I got them very cheap", while an American may reply with a simple "Thanks" or "Oh, they are ancient. I've had them for years". When being complemented by "You have done a great job", a Chinese may respond with "Oh, that is the result of joint efforts of my leaders and colleagues", while an American with a simple "Thank you for your compliment".

II. Different ethical values

When a Chinese speaker makes such greetings as those in Case 1 on meeting, he is not really concerned about or interested in whether you have eaten, what you have done, where you have been, and whether you are really doing a certain thing, but intends to make you feel that he is considerate and thoughtful towards you and to maintain a good relationship with you. These greetings are not to be answered, you may nod or smile and then pass; moreover, he will always go away before you answer. Such Chinese greetings sound very strange to Americans and often make them feel very uncomfortable. They feel that their own privacy is interfered with. To them, it has nothing to do with others whether they have eaten, what they have done, where they have been, and whether they are really doing a certain thing.

It is well illustrated in Chinese parting expressions that Chinese always keep in mind friendship, familiarity and amicability, and tend to show consideration and concern for others. But Americans never do so. Even they may think "Why did you bother yourself wasting my time since you think it was a waste of my time".

With regard to compliment responses, Chinese always show modesty and value solidarity, and emphasize co-operation among group members. They believe that individual success is due to the collective effort of the staff in a unit, an organization or a community, and they belittle their own efforts by owing successes to others just to keep the harmonious world going. But Americans always show pride and value independence, and emphasize personal happiness and achievements. They believe that individual success is due to personal effort. That is why most American heroes (in art or history) are independent and tend to accomplish their goals with little or no assistance from others, which can be illustrated from Abraham Lincoln's endeavor (to be a president) to make himself an idol of most Americans.

Chinese people value family so much that they always try to be amicable and show much concern for others just as they do within a family. Not surprisingly, in their conversations they always talk of personal stuffs like age, income, marriage and so on. Americans worship privacy so much that they would like to be able to do certain things unobserved by others. They believe that each person has his own separate identity and personality, which should be recognized and reinforced. Therefore, conversations with others' personalstuffs and activities involved are not advocated.

As far as social ethical value is concerned, Chinese people do value and

interfere /ˌɪntəˈfɪə/ *v.* **a.** (of person) break in upon (other persons' affairs) without right or invitation; **b.** (of person) meddle; tamper (with); **c.** (of events, circumstances, etc.) come into opposition; hinder or prevent

illustrate /ˈɪləstreɪt/ *v.* **a.** explain by examples, pictures, etc.; **b.** supply a book, article, lecture, etc. with pictures, diagrams, etc.

amicability /ˌæmɪkəˈbɪliti/ *n.* peaceability; being done in a friendly way

modesty /ˈmɒdɪsti/ *n.* state of being modest

solidarity /ˌsɒlɪˈdærɪti/ *n.* unity resulting from common interests or feelings

emphasize /ˈemfəsaɪz/ *v.* put emphasis on; give emphasis to

belittle /bɪˈlɪtl/ *v.* cause to seem unimportant or of small value

harmonious /hɑːˈməʊnɪəs/ *adj.* **a.** pleasingly or satisfactorily arranged; **b.** in agreement; free from ill feeling; **c.** sweet-sounding; tuneful

amicable /ˈæmɪkəbəl/ *adj.* peaceable; done in a friendly way

reinforce /ˌriːɪnˈfɔːs/ *v.* make stronger by adding or supplying more men or material; increase the size, thickness, of sth so that it supports more weight, etc.

involve /ɪnˈvɒlv/ *v.* **a.** (sb or sth) to be caught or mixed up (in trouble, etc.); get (sb or sth) into a complicated or difficult condition; **b.** have as a necessary consequence

advocate /ˈædvəkeɪt/ **a.** *n.* person who speaks in favor of sb or sth (esp. a cause); **b.** *n.* (*legal*) person who does this professionally in a court of law in Scotland (=barrister in England and Wales) **c.** *v.* to suppovt or recommend publicly

emphasize the interests of the people, the community and the whole nation. They even sacrifice the interests of individuals for those of the collective, as is sufficiently and clearly incarnated in those like "Serve the people" (from Mao Zedong), "Common wealth" (from Deng Xiaoping) and "Power for the people" (from Jiang Zemin). Unlike Chinese, Americans emphasize and focus on the interests of the individual rather than those of the collective. They even believe that there must be something wrong with someone who fails to demonstrate individualism, which can be seen from American Grand Elections and some sayings like "God helps those who help themselves" and "He travels the fastest who travels alone."

sacrifice /'sækrɪfaɪs/ a. n. the offering of sth precious to a god; instance of this; the thing offered; b. n. the giving up of sth of great value to oneself for a special purpose, or to benefit sb else; sth given up in this way; c. v. make a sacrifice; d. v. give up as a sacrifice

sufficiently /sə'fɪʃəntli/ adv. enough

incarnate /'ɪnkɑːnɪt/ a. adj. having a body; (esp.) in human form; b. adj. (of an ideal, ideal, etc.) appearing in human form; c. v. make incarnate; d. put (an idea, etc.) into a real or material form; e. v. (of a person) be a living form of (a quality)

individualism /ɪndɪ'vɪdjuəlɪzəm/ n. a. social theory that favors the free action and complete liberty or belief of individuals (contrasted with the theory favoring the supremacy of the state); b. feeling or behavior of a person who puts his own private interests first; egoism

collectivism /kə'lektɪvɪzəm/ n. a. a political or economic theory advocating collective control especially over production and distribution; also a system marked by such control; b. emphasis on collective rather than individual action or identity

welfare /'welfeə/ n. a. condition of having good health, comfortable living and working conditions, etc; b. (US) social security

thoughtfulness /θɔːtfulnɪs/ n. given to or chosen or made with heedful anticipation of the needs and wants of others

hospitality /ˌhɒspɪ'tælɪti/ n. friendly and generous reception and entertainment of guests, esp. in one's own home

priority /praɪ'ɒrɪti/ n. a. right to have or do sth before others; b. claim to consideration; high place among competing claims

self-reliance /'selfrɪ'laɪəns/ n. having or showing confidence in one's own powers, judgment, etc.

Through the above case studies, we can see that what obviously attracts our attention to differences in values between Chinese culture and American culture is the emphasis on whether to perform individualism or collectivism. Chinese stress the importance of the whole nation and community, tend to emphasize the interests and welfare of the collective over those of the individual, value considerations, concerns and thoughtfulness for others, attach much importance to co-operation and collective efforts, and think much of friendship and amicability and hospitality, which we call collectivism. Americans, on the contrary, emphasize the importance of human individuals in contrast to the social wholes, such as families, classes or societies, to which they belong, stress the priority of individual needs, interests and welfare over those of a group, value individual rights and freedom, prefer the virtue of self-reliance and personal independence and loosely knit social relationships and think more of individual roles than of collective efforts, which we call individualism.

Cultural Notes

Privacy—Privacy has no definite boundaries and it has different meanings for different people. It is the ability of an individual or group to keep their lives and personal affairs out of public view, or to control the flow of information about themselves. Privacy can be seen as an aspect of security — one in which trade-offs between the interests of one group and another can become particularly clear.

The right against unsanctioned invasion of privacy by the government, corporations or individuals is part of many countries' privacy laws, and in some cases, constitutions. Almost all countries have laws which in some way limit privacy; an example of this would be law concerning taxation, which normally require the sharing of information about personal income or earnings. In some countries individual privacy may conflict with freedom of speech laws and some laws may require public disclosure of information which would be considered private in other countries and cultures.

Countries such as France protect privacy explicitly in their constitution (France's *Declaration of the Rights of Man and of the Citizen*), while the Supreme Court of the United States has found that the US constitution contains "penumbras" that implicitly grant a right to privacy against government intrusion, for example in *Griswold v. Connecticut* (1965). Other countries without constitutional privacy protections have laws protecting privacy, such as the United Kingdom's *Data Protection Act 1998* or Australia's *Privacy Act 1988*. The European Union requires all member states to legislate to ensure that citizens have a right to privacy, through directives such as *Directive 95/46*.

American Grand Elections—It is the US presidential election campaign. American presidents are elected every four years in the Election Day, the first Tuesday after the first Monday in November in even years, which is legally chosen for national election.

Individualism—It is a term used to describe a moral, political, or social outlook that stresses human independence and the importance of individual self-reliance and liberty. Individualists promote the exercise of individual goals and desires. They oppose most external interference with an individual's choices—whether by society, the state, or any other group or institution. The concept of "individualism" was first used by the French Saint-Simonian socialists to describe what they believed was the cause of the disintegration of French society after the 1789 Revolution. The term was however already used (pejoratively) by reactionary thinkers of the French Theocratic School, such as Joseph de Maistre, in their opposition to political liberalism. In the English language, the word was first introduced in the English translation of the second volume of *Alexis de Tocquevilles Democracy in America,* which was published in 1835. A more positive use of the term in Britain came to be used with the writings of James Elishama Smith.

Collectivism—It is a term used to describe any moral, political, or social outlook, which stresses human interdependence and the importance of a collective, rather than the importance of separate individuals. Collectivists focus on community and society, and seek to give priority to group goals over individual goals. The philosophical underpinnings of collectivism are for some related to holism or organicism, the view that the whole is greater than the sum of its parts. Specifically, a society as a whole can be seen as having more meaning or value than the separate individuals that make up that society. Collectivism is widely seen as the antipole of individualism.

Exercises

I. Answer the following questions based on the text.

1. Do you think Hong Kong should be more English or American rather than Chinese since English has long been their daily usage?
2. Do you think Chinese leave-taking is abrupt when your visitors stand up and go?
3. Which way of seeing the guests off is better in your opinion, the Chinese way or the American one?
4. What is the bigger difference—the difference in understanding or expressing?
5. Do you think American independence is so great as to dwarf the Chinese cooperation?

II. Text Review. Write T for true and F for false in the brackets before each of the following statements.

( ) 1. People care about the young American woman's health so they asked about her lunch.

( ) 2. All Chinese people will insist their guests stay longer when they are to take leave.

( ) 3. The Chinese are always sincere when they say that is the joint efforts of their leaders and colleagues.

( ) 4. Chinese people tend to show more consideration and concerning about others in daily addressing.

( ) 5. Abraham Lincoln's endeavor was an idol of most Americans because of his heroic independence.

( ) 6. Chinese people are inclined to extend their concern for family members to others because they value family as a tradition.

( ) 7. The Chinese have many ways of greetings which have no significant meaning.

( ) 8. Not all Americans worship privacy very much and they don't want others to know much of their life and personal affairs.

( ) 9. Americans would think the demonstrating of individualism is very important.

( ) 10. In the text, the word individualism has a negative meaning, which is quite same with the meaning in Chinese.

III. Paraphrase the following sentences in English.

1. She was somewhat underweight at the time, and so she concluded they must worry that she was not eating properly!

2. With regard to compliment responses, Chinese always show modesty and value solidarity, and emphasize co-operation among group members.

3. As far as social ethical value is concerned, Chinese people do value and emphasize the interests of the people, the community and the whole nation.

4. Chinese people value family so much that they always try to be amicable and show much concern for others just as they do within a family.

5. Americans, on the contrary, emphasize the importance of human individuals in contrast to the social wholes, such as families, classes or societies.

IV. Translate the following sentences into Chinese.

1. He is not really concerned about or interested in whether you have eaten, what you have done, where you have been, and whether you are really doing a certain thing, but intends to make you feel that he is considerate and thoughtful towards you and to maintain a good relationship with you.

2. It is well illustrated in Chinese parting expressions that Chinese always keep in mind friendship, familiarity and amicability, and tend to show consideration and concern for others.

3. Chinese stress the importance of the whole nation and community, tend to emphasize the interests and welfare of the collective over those of the individual, value considerations, concerns and thoughtfulness for others, attach much importance to co-operation and collective efforts, and think much of friendship and amicability and hospitality, which we call collectivism.

4. Americans value individual rights and freedom, prefer the virtue of self-reliance and personal independence and loosely knit social relationships and think more of individual roles than of collective efforts, which we call individualism.

5. Americans emphasize and focus on the interests of the individual rather than those of the collective. They even believe that there must be something wrong with someone who fails to demonstrate individualism.

V. Respond to each of the following statements.

1. Individualism is an impressive characteristic of the Americans.
2. Sometimes too much hospitality will bring trouble to people.
3. National customs tend to change more or less under the global influence.
4. National glory is less important than that of an individual, as everybody has only one life.
5. Self-reliance doesn't conflict with collectivism, and emphasis on both aspects is necessary in our culture.

VI. Provide a text which can support your viewpoint on one of the statements in *Exercise V*. Make your comment on the text you choose.

Unit Three

Successful New Year

Anonymous

《成功的新年》如何安排好生活？如何过好新的一年？本文将试图给您一个建议，希望对您或有裨益。

Now that the Christmas festivities are over, the next order of Business is the New Year. That means resolutions.

Frankly, I'm tired of New Year's resolutions. I make them every year. I break them every year, often forgetting the resolutions by Martin Luther King Day. On the other hand, there are plenty of bad habits I'd like to get rid of before my next birthday in September. So here I am, finalizing my New Year's resolutions strategy. Let's see if we can break the losing streak in naught seven.

I have two lofty goals for 2007:

* Get some exercise
* Quit smoking

I agonized before typing those words. I'm an introvert, super lazy and smoke like a chimney. Trust me when I tell you I'm scared as hell sharing these resolutions. Given my track record of not finishing what I start, there's a good chance of failure.

But if I'm serious about growing as a person, not smelling like Uncle Joe's burnt ribs all the time, and not having to sit down every 10 feet, putting these resolutions out in public is the best thing I can do.

So here's the game plan...

streak /striːk/ *n.* **a.** a long stripe or mark on a surface which contrasts with the surface; **b.** a particular type of behaviour of a person; **c.** a continuous series of successes or failures in gambling or sport

lofty /ˈlɒ(ː)fti/ *adj.* **a.** (of thoughts, aims, etc.) noble; **b.** high; **c.** (derog.) seeming to be proud or superior

agonize /ˈægənaɪz/ *v.* to suffer great anxiety or worry intensely

introvert /ˌɪntrəˈvɜːt/ *n.* person who is shy, quiet and unable to make friends easily cf. extrovert

as hell (*infml*) used after adjectives or some adverbs to emphasize the adjective or adverb

Smokey's 8 sure-fire tips for successful New Year's resolutions:

(If you have tips to make New Year's resolutions more sure-firely successful, please share in the comments!)

sure-fire (*infml*) sure to succeed

factor in include a particular thing in the calculations about how long sth will take, how much it will cost, etc.

consecutive /kən'sekjʊtɪv/ *adj.* following in regular unbroken order

kinda /'kaɪndə/ kind of

accountable /ə'kaʊntəbəl/ *adj.* responsible; having to justify one's actions

1. Aim for something you can track

"Lose weight" or "get more exercise" are nice resolutions and all, but without specifics to focus on, they're doomed from the get-go.

Can you aim for a number or other measurable goal? The more focused the resolution, the easier it is to succeed.

Instead of "be healthier", how about one of these more specific resolutions?

* Take a 20-minute walk everyday after lunch.

* Run a 7-minute mile.

* Finish the company 10k in an hour.

* Lose 20 pounds.

For the exercising resolution, my trackable goal is 120 days in the gym. I want to be generally healthier, get more exercise, and have more energy. Factoring in my schedule and overall laziness, an average of 3 times a week at the gym is a hard, but achievable goal.

For the quit-smoking resolution, my trackable goal is to have 30 consecutive smoke-free days within 3 months.

2. Set a deadline, the sooner the better

A deadline far off in the distance is quickly forgotten. Without a deadline, you may find yourself making the same resolutions year after year.

For my goal of exercising at least 3 days a week, I need to get 120 days in the gym in a whole year (365 days). Hmm, looking at that big 1-2-0 number is kinda scary and having a deadline so far away (Dec 31, 2007) makes it easy to ignore the resolution for just another day.

That really increases my chances of failure. I think I need to add a 3-month milestone of 30 days in the gym by April 1. Doesn't seem so hard now, and hopefully by April, getting some exercise has become an indispensable habit that I'll continue for the rest of the year and beyond.

3. Be accountable to someone you don't want to let down

Having to tell someone whose opinion you respect when you've succeeded (or failed) is a big incentive.

Remember that deadline? You can combine tips 2 and 3 into one "I finally accomplished a resolution!" party. Make that date at the beginning of the year!

For me, I'm being accountable to you, the Internet. I figure you, dear Internet, are the scariest person I can be accountable to. God help me.

Health Top Tips Nutrition Lifestyle

4. Use the buddy system

The buddy system works for keeping us safe. It also works for keeping us motivated.

Find a friend who wants what you want. Both of you now have a fighting chance of keeping this year's resolution.

I have a buddy for both resolutions. There're plenty of people looking to quit smoking and/or get more exercise.

5. Do a 30-day challenge

I learned about the 30-day challenge from Steve Pavlina. "It's a way to trick yourself into not being scared of the commitment." Steve says.

It seems too overwhelming to think about making a big change and sticking with it every day for the rest of your life when you're still habituated to doing the opposite. The more you think about the change as something permanent, the more you stay put.

That summarizes how I feel about the quit-smoking challenge. I love smoking. It's great after a meal. Or in the mornings with a soy latte and the *New York Times*. Trade that in for mood swings and cravings so strong I want to claw my eyes out. That's crazy talk.

I'm using the 30-day challenge to track the nicotine intake. To break it down into a manageable chunk. I'm not going to be smoke-free every day, but 30 consecutive smoke-free days within the first 3 months is doable. 1 month, 4 weeks, 30 days. No biggie.

6. Visualize the result

Why are you making this resolution? It's not because you suddenly hate chocolate and all things sugary. It's because you want to fit into those jeans. More than that, it's because you want the sweet ego-boosting adulation from all those around. Think about the sweet adulation, not the velvety sweetness of cheesecake.

For me, the goal is to not be out of breath walking from my car up the stairs to my apartment. That's not a very sexy goal to visualize, so I imagine myself chasing down a purse snatcher and being everybody's hero. And not coughing up a lung every morning.

7. Reward yourself

Ruth's Chris Filet gives you something awesome to look forward to.

buddy /'bʌdi/ *n.* companion, partner

commitment /kə'mɪtmənt/ *n.* a. an obligation, responsibility, or promise that restricts freedom of action; b. dedication to a cause or principle

soy latte latte is a strong coffee with frothy steamed milk. soy latte is one type of coffee beverage which is combined with soy milk.

chunk /tʃʌŋk/ a. a roughly cut lump; b. (*infml*) a part, esp. a large part

No biggie. (*AmE*) not particularly important or serious

adulation /ˌædjʊ'leɪʃən/ *n.* praise and admiration for someone that is more than they really deserve

velvety /'velvɪti/ *adj.* soft and smooth in a way that suggests the feel of velvet

filet /fi'leɪ/ *n.* a piece of meat or fish without bones

If you're quitting smoking, calculate how much money you saved and splurge on yourself.

I spent roughly $700 on cigarettes a year. At the end of the year, I'm going to take that money and buy my friends a nice meal. (I seem to have Andrea's selfish need to be selfless.)

I'm picturing a fat, juicy Filet, medium rare, and a side of sweet potato casserole (with pecan crust) at Ruth's Chris.

8. Start right away

If you don't start on January 1, your chance of success drops from 74% to 37%. (source: Bureau of Fake Statistics) So start immediately!

I think starting on the 2nd is okay. We'll need a day off to recover from the hangover. Don't put it off too long, or you'll be making the same resolution next year.

I have a sneaking suspicion I have some kind of attention deficit disorder, though never formally diagnosed. If I put something off for a couple of days, forget about it. Seriously, just forget about it. It's gone forever.

If you need some ideas, here are the Top 10 New Year's Resolutions, according to 10 Million Resolutions.

1. Lose Weight and Get in Better Physical Shape
2. Stick to a Budget
3. Debt Reduction
4. Enjoy More Quality Time with Family & Friends
5. Find My Soul Mate
6. Quit Smoking
7. Find a Better Job
8. Learn Something New
9. Volunteer and Help Others
10. Get Organized

splurge /splɜːdʒ/ v. to spend more money than one can usually afford

medium rare medium (of meat) partly cooked but still slightly pink inside, cf. rare, well-done

casserole /ˈkæsərəʊl/ n. a. a dish made by cooking meat, vegetables or other foods in liquid inside a heavy container at low heat; b. the heavy, deep container with a lid used in cooking such dishes

pecan /pɪˈkæn/ n. a long thin sweet nut with a dark red shell

crust /krʌst/ n. a hard outer covering of sth

sneaking /ˈsniːkɪŋ/ adj. a. secret, not openly expressed; b. (of a feeling or belief) not proved but probably right

attention deficit disorder (AmE) attention deficit hyperactivity disorder (BrE) a condition in which someone, esp. a child, is often in a state of activity or excitement and unable to direct their attention towards what they are doing

quality time the time that one focuses on or dedicates oneself to a cherished person or activity

soul mate a person with whom one has a strong affinity

Cultural Notes

Martin Luther King Day—Martin Luther King Day is a national holiday observed each year in the United States on the third Monday in January, commemorating the birthday (Jan.15) of Martin Luther King, Jr. Dr. King (1929—1968) was an African-American clergyman who shaped the American civil rights movement. His nonviolent demonstrations against racial inequality led to civil rights legislation. King was an eloquent speaker and delivered his famous speech "I Have a Dream" at 1963 march on Washington. He was awarded the Nobel Peace Prize in 1964 and became not only the symbolic leader of American blacks but also a world figure. On the evening of April 4, 1968, he was assassinated while leading a protest march in Memphis, Tennessee.

Joe—Some common names in English sometimes have special meanings. For example, "By George" means "Oh, dear". The name "Joe" means an ordinary man or sometimes it refers to the typical person who can represent a group of people of the same kind. One of the other expressions concerning the name is "a Joe job", which is a boring task.

Smokey—a. Smokey Bear, fictional character, whose mission is to raise public awareness to protect America's forests. Smokey's message now is "Only You Can Prevent Wildfires." b. The word "Smokey" also refers to "the highway police (*slang*)".

God help me—May God help me. It is used to give force to a statement of the danger or seriousness of a situation or action.

The *New York Times*—The flagship publication of the *New York Times* Company, the *New York Times* is one of the most influential newspapers in the world. The *New York Times* Company got its start in 1851 when Henry Jarvis Raymond and George Jones produced their first paper, the *New York Daily Times*, which quickly became a success. The word *Daily* was dropped in 1857. Now the company has become a major newspaper publisher and media company, which owns newspapers, television and radio stations, and electronic information services.

Exercises

I. Answer the following questions based on the text.

1. Why does the author write the article?

2. What does the author intend to achieve in the coming new year?

3. Why does he put his resolutions out in public this time?

4. Who is Smokey here?

5. What resolutions are easier to be carried out according to the author?

II. Text Review. Write T for true and F for false in the brackets before each of the following statements.

( ) 1. The author is tired of New Year's resolutions because he doesn't think it significant.

( ) 2. The author doesn't think he will have a big change after a chain of failure in the past.

( ) 3. In comparison with "Lose 20 pounds", the resolution of "Lose weight" is not bad.

( ) 4. "Run a 7-minute mile" is equal to "Run a mile in 7 minutes".

( ) 5. Working out in the gym about 4 weeks before April is acceptable for the author.

( ) 6. The Internet won't let down the author.

( ) 7. The author has a very bad cough.

( ) 8. The author will have a meal with his friends at Ruth's Chris at the end of the year.

( ) 9. Many people are careful in spending money.

( ) 10. People are most concerned about their weight and physical shape.

III. Paraphrase the following phrases or sentences in English.

1. Let's see if we can break the losing streak in naught seven.

2. Given my track record of not finishing what I start, there's a good chance of failure.

3. I think I need to add a 3-month milestone of 30 days in the gym by April 1.

4. It's a way to trick yourself into not being scared of the commitment.

5. The more you think about the change as something permanent, the more you stay put.

IV. Translate the following sentences into Chinese.

1. But if I'm serious about growing as a person, not smelling like Uncle Joe's burnt ribs all the time, and not having to sit down every 10 feet, putting these resolutions out in public is the best thing I can do.

2. Hmm, looking at that big 1-2-0 number is kinda scary and having a deadline so far away (Dec 31,2007) makes it easy to ignore the resolution for just another day.

3. Trade that in for mood swings and cravings so strong I want to claw my eyes out.

4. More than that, it's because you want the sweet ego-boosting adulation om all those around.

5. I'm picturing a fat, juicy Filet, medium rare, and a side of sweet potato casserole (with pecan crust) at Ruth's Chris.

V. Respond to each of the following statements.

1. It seems so easy to make changes in our lives until we actually begin to do the work.

2. Be clear about what you really want before setting goals.

3. Confidence, commitment and patience ensure success.

4. Be tight on your goals but flexible on your plans.

5. Failure is your friend.

VI. Provide a text which can support your viewpoint on one of the statements in *Exercise V.* Make your comments on the text you choose.

Text B

A Winning Way to Handle New Ideas
Azriel Winnett

《处理新想法的成功之路》改变一种思维和行为的习惯,从另一个角度看待同一个问题,这是我们对于新的观念所应该持有的态度,也是我们面对未来应该持有的态度。观念指导我们的行为,因此处理好这些新的想法就显得尤为重要。

Janet DiClaudio, who was in charge of medical records at two large American hospitals, had an unusual problem. But, the past master in finding creative solutions to work related problems that she was, she found an equally unusual solution.

Of course, proper record keeping is critically important in any hospital. Moreover, if it is run on a commercial basis, medical records will determine how and what the institution gets paid. On the other hand, filling out medical records is not the most exciting pastime in the world. It can be a big pain, in fact. Doctors would prefer to do other things with their time.

But records have to be completed, properly and promptly. So what do you do about it? Janet DiClaudio got down to work and developed a highly "sophisticated system".

Janet called her system "Tootsie Roll Pops". Every time a doctor completed a medical record on time, he or she was awarded a Tootsie Roll Pop—apparently a cheap candy you buy by the bagful—and his or her name went into a drawing for a magnum of champagne.

Now, you don't have to feel sorry for most of these worthy doctors, thanks very much. Some of them can afford to buy a Tootsie Roll Pop factory. Many have case loads of the best champagne in the world back Home in their cellars.

Yet Janet's system worked like a charm. The "Tootsie Roll Pop" campaign led to a doubling in record-completion productivity at the General Hospital in Buffalo, New York, where Janet was working.

She then took a new position at a hospital in Savannah, Georgia, and found that her new institution had a backlog of about 300 medical records. No problem! In Savannah, she rewarded each doctor who completed a record from the backlog with a handful of animal crackers.

Two weeks later, the hospital had gone through twenty pounds of animal crackers, but the record backlog had been all but eliminated. As a result, the hospital was able to collect more than four million dollars. For that return, I hardly think the accounts department would have complained about the expenditure on the crackers!

A basic need moves the most sophisticated. Roger Firestien recounts this delightful medical saga in his *Leading on the Creative Edge* which I quoted in a previous article. What has it do with us? Well, I bring it here not only because it is such a beautiful illustration of creativity in problem solving, but also—and this is what really concerns us—it forcefully demonstrates the power of praise and recognition.

After all, the doughty physicians in our story weren't children; it couldn't have been the handout of a few measly goodies that motivated them. There's a more basic need, however, that apparently doesn't fail to move even the most sophisticated amongst us.

magnum /'mægnəm/ n. a large wine bottle that holds approximately 1.5 liters

champagne /ʃæm'peɪn/ n. an expensive white or pink fizzy wine made in the Champagne area of Eastern France, or, more generally, any similar wine. Champagne is often drunk to celebrate sth

case load caseload the number of cases handled (as by a court or clinic) usu. in a particular period

cellar /'selə/ n. a room under the ground floor of a building, usually used for storage

backlog /'bæklɒg/ n. a large amount of things that one should have done before and must do now

animal crackers animal-shaped cookies

saga /'sɑːgə/ n. a. a long and complicated series of events, or a description of this; b. a long story about events that happen over many years

doughty /'daʊti/ adj. resolute and without fear

measly /'miːzli/ adj. very small and disappointing in size, quantity, or value

goody /'gʊdi/ n. a. sth that is nice to eat; b. sth attractive, pleasant, or desirable

amongst /ə'mʌŋst/ among

In a landmark work *In Search of Excellence* researchers Tom Peters and Robert Waterman ask readers to imagine that they are sales assistants in a store who are being punished for failing to treat a customer well.

If you are in this situation, you might feel yourself to be in a frustrating dilemma, because you still don't know what to do to receive approval. In fact, you might well react by avoiding customers altogether, since you have come to associate customers with punishment.

landmark /'lændmɑːk/ *n.* a. sth prominent that identifies location; b. important new development; c. sth preserved for historic importance; d. boundary marker

altogether /ˌɔːltə'geðə/ a. *adv.* completely or in total; b. with everything included

live up to fulfill the requirements or expectations of

macho /'mætʃəu/ *adj.* having or showing characteristics conventionally regarded as male, esp. physical strength and courage, aggressiveness, and lack of emotion

disservice /'dɪˈsɜːvɪs/ *n.* an action that causes harm or difficulty

inhibition /ˌɪnhɪ'bɪʃən/ *n.* a feeling of fear or embarrassment that stops one from behaving naturally

to the winds to the wind aside, away

discerning /dɪ'sɜːnɪŋ/ *adj.* showing the ability to make good judgments, esp. about art, music, beauty, style, etc.

Now, supposes a manager would tell you that a "mystery shopper" has complimented you on your outstanding courtesy and helpfulness. What would you do now? Most likely, you'd rush back to the floor to find more customers to treat well, for now you have associated them with praise and recognition. Your self-esteem has been enhanced immeasurably, and you want to keep living up to expectations of you.

I would have thought that you don't need to be a university professor to work this one out, but Peters and Waterman report:

"Our general observation is that most managers know very little about the value of positive reinforcement. Many either appear not to value it at all, or consider it beneath them, undignified, or not very macho. The evidence from the excellent companies strongly suggests that managers who feel this way are doing themselves a great disservice..."

But positive reinforcement should be dispensed not only when someone whom we lead does something we wanted him to do. Encouragement is also the appropriate response when someone suggests a novel idea or solution to a problem. And this brings me back to a subject we have discussed before.

Inhibitions to the winds...

About 30 years ago, a creativity consulting firm on the American East Coast was conducting creativity seminars for large corporations. The leaders urged participants to throw inhibitions to the winds, unleash the power locked up in their minds, and to throw up all the ideas they could manage, however wild they might appear to be. Their peers were then asked to evaluate the proposals and see if they could be used to solve company problems.

Inevitably, seminar participants could only see negative aspects in most of the suggestions, and swiftly tore them to pieces. As the sessions ended, the more discerning amongst them sometimes confided in the organizers: "You know, we had the beginnings of some pretty powerful ideas in this session. But by the time we got done evaluating them, all we had left was the same worn-out, old concepts."

Then it happened that at one seminar, several people from the same company noticed the idea slaughtering. They approached the two leaders conducting the session and suggested they talk to the president of their company.

"This man," they explained, "has a unique way of dealing with ideas. And it seems to pay off. Our company is growing by leaps and bounds, has excellent relationships with customers and suppliers, and is a great place to work."

Of course, the two consultants were intrigued. They asked for a meeting with the company president. "I obviously must be doing something right," he told them, "but I'm darned if I know what it is... I'd love to find out."

In short, the consultants shadowed the president for a week. They sat in on meetings and strategic conversations and walked through the plant with the president.

The visitors soon realized that when someone approached the president with a new idea, the latter became very conscious of what was about to occur. Someone in the company was about to present an idea they thought might improve the organization, smooth out the work flow, or make more money. The president became all ears. In contrast to his counterparts in many other companies who perceived new ideas as threats, he saw them as opportunities. He knew that this was the stuff that made his Business better.

When someone proposed an idea, the president would respond by enumerating the PLUSES (strengths or advantages) of the idea. He would then discuss its POTENTIALS (possible spin-offs or future gains which could be realized if the idea were implemented). Finally, he would address CONCERNS posed by the idea.

Even when addressing concerns, however, instead of saying: "This idea will cost too much", he would throw out a challenge by asking: "How might you reduce the cost?" or "How might you raise the money to develop this idea?" Instead of offering a prophecy of doom by saying: "Management will never accept this idea" he would inquire: "How might you get management's support?"

The seed which was planted in the minds of this corporate president's "shadows" that week led to the development and fine-tuning of a tool that was to have far reaching effects in the Business and organizational world. The PPC (Pluses, Potentials, Concerns) Technique was developed by Dr. Firestien and two colleagues, Dianne Foucar-Szocki and Bill Shepard.

confide /kən'faɪd/ *v.* to tell sth secret or personal to someone whom you trust not to tell anyone else

by leaps and bounds in leaps and bounds, extremely rapidly

darned /dɑːnd/ *adj.* (*infml*) used instead of a swearword to express annoyance, surprise, or refusal

spin-off /'spɪnɒf/ a product made during the manufacture of sth else

prophecy /'prɒfisi/ *n.* a prediction uttered under divine inspiration

If you were to propose an idea to this company president, and he evaluated it together with you in the manner outlined above, how would you react? Wouldn't you be inspired by the friendly challenge thrown out at you to find a way of overcoming even the smallest concerns?

It makes you think, doesn't it?

Cultural Notes

Azriel Winnett—A writer, editor and the creator of Hodu.com—Your Communication Skills Portal, a free website helping people improve their communication and relationship skills in their business or professional life, in the family unit and on the social scene. Most of the publications in the website are his works. A former South African, Mr. Winnett presently lives in Israel.

Tootsie Roll Pop—A hard candy lollipop with a Tootsie Roll filling at its center. The Tootsie Pop was invented in 1931 by The Sweets Company of America, which changed its name to Tootsie Roll Industries, Inc. in 1966. In addition to chocolate (the original flavor), Tootsie Pops come in a variety of flavors including raspberry, cherry, orange and grape, etc.

Exercises

I. Answer the following questions based on the text.

1. What distinguishes Janet DiClaudio from others?
2. Why does the author tell her story here?
3. What problem do most managers share according to Waterman?
4. Why did the two consultants shadow the president of the company?
5. How did the president respond to the idea proposed by his men?

II. Text Review. Write T for true and F for false in the brackets before each of the following statements.

( ) 1. If a doctor keeps the medical records properly, he can get a good pay.

( ) 2. Many doctors working at the Buffolo General Hospital possess great wealth.

( ) 3. The accounts department of the hospital in Savannah, Georgia, where Janet worked was not satisfied with the large expenses for the animal crackers.

( ) 4. Simple methods may possibly be the most effective.

( ) 5. Janet knew the magic of the positive reinforcement very well.

( ) 6. Peterson and Waterman points out that many managers don't value praise and recognition because it doesn't have much influence on their work.

( ) 7. The seminar participants were expected to raise constructive ideas.

( ) 8. To acquire sound advice, the president invited the two leaders of the session to his company.

( ) 9. Many managers suffer from fear of novel ideas.

( ) 10. The creativity seminars held 30 years ago inspired Dr. Firestien and his colleagues to develop the PPC technique.

III. Paraphrase the following phrases or sentences in English.

1. But, the past master in finding creative solutions to work related problems that she was, she found an equally unusual solution.

2. There's a more basic need, however, that apparently doesn't fail to move even the most sophisticated amongst us.

3. Your self-esteem has been enhanced immeasurably, and you want to keep living up to expectations of you.

4. Then it happened that at one seminar, several people from the same company noticed the idea slaughtering.

5. Finally, he would address CONCERNS posed by the idea.

IV. Translate the following sentences into Chinese.

1. Moreover, if it is run on a commercial basis, medical records will determine how and what the institution gets paid.

2. Two weeks later, the hospital had gone through twenty pounds of animal crackers, but the record backlog had been all but eliminated.

3. But positive reinforcement should be dispensed not only when someone whom we lead does something we wanted him to do.

4. The leaders urged participants to throw inhibitions to the winds, unleash the power locked up in their minds, and to throw up all the ideas they could manage, however wild they might appear to be.

5. The seed which was planted in the minds of this corporate president's "shadows" that week led to the development and fine-tuning of a tool that was to have far reaching effects in the Business and organizational world.

V. Respond to each of the following statements.

1. Healthy relationships help us enjoy a happier and more productive life.

2. Lack of recognition can have a profoundly negative impact on productivity.

3. The solutions are within ourselves to reduce the stress in our workplace.

4. Work only with people you like and believe in.

5. Don't get discouraged if your boss is criticizing you.

VI. Provide a text which can support your viewpoint on one of the statements in *Exercise V*. Make your comments on the text you choose.

Unit Four

Text A

What Is True Freedom?

Ashok Kumar Gupta

《什么是真正的自由》自由是一个热点甚至敏感的话题，因此认清什么是真正的自由就显得愈发重要。本文着意论述什么是真正的自由。

Freedom is the cherished goal of humanity throughout its history.

No society has ever been happy under the rule of people of some other society. History, from one perspective, is nothing but a struggle between two groups—one attempting to enslave or keeping enslaved the other and the other fighting incessantly to ward off this slavery. All wars are nothing but a manifestation of this ancient phenomenon. It seems we cannot tolerate losing our freedom and at the same time we cannot allow others to be free. When we are under the rule of someone else we fight to throw off the shackles and when we are free we strive to enslave others.

It is true not only for political or social groups but also for individuals. Just have a look at the kind of relationships we have built. Don't we try to dominate all persons we come across? We can see parents trying to dominate children, husbands trying to dominate wives, bosses trying to dominate subordinates and vice versa. Even friends try to dominate each other. It seems life is nothing but a struggle to dominate the other.

It can be said that there are nations, societies, groups or individuals who are free. Today, in the modern world, autonomy seems to be the norm. We can see autonomous entities all around, but this autonomy is superficial. Such autonomy remains in existence only till such a

ward off prevent from happening

shackle /ˈʃækəl/ *n.* **a.** metal band on prisoner; **b.** U-shaped fastener **c.** restraint on freedom

autonomy /ɔːˈtɒnəmi/ *n.* **a.** the right of a group of people to govern itself, or to organize its own activities; **b.** personal independence and the capacity to make decisions and act on them

norm /nɔːm/ *n.* **a.** a standard or model or pattern regarded as typical; **b.** the usual or normal situation, way of doing sth, etc.

time when a more powerful entity decides to take it away. A behind-the-scene power struggle is going on everywhere. Human beings are not left untouched by all this. They can feel it subconsciously. As a result, modern man is continuously trying to defy authority or any force which makes him feel bound in any sense. To take a small example, individual human beings, these days, are preferring not to marry at all. Even after marriage, the

entity /'entɪti/ *n.* sth that exists as a single and complete unit
defy /dɪ'faɪ/ *v.* a. openly resist sb or sth; b. challenge sb
curtail /kɜː'teɪl/ *v.* a. to cut short; b. to restrict
encroach /ɪn'krəʊtʃ/ *v.* a. to intrude gradually or stealthily, often taking away sb's authority, rights, or property; b. exceed proper limits
inkling /'ɪŋklɪŋ/ *n.* a slight suggestion or vague understanding
mirage /'mɪrɑːʒ/ *n.* a. an optical illusion in which atmospheric refraction by a layer of hot air distorts or inverts reflections of distant objects; b. sth that appears to be real but is unreal or merely imagined
mire /'maɪə/ *v.* a. to get stuck in mud; b. to involve sb or sth in difficulties
tenuous /'tenjuəs/ *adj.* a. thin and fine, and therefore easily broken; b. weak and unconvincing
fragility /frə'dʒɪlɪti/ *n.* a. quality of being easily damaged or destroyed; b. lock of physical strength

moment one feels that his/her freedom is being curtailed, one walks away. Religious, legal or social pressures are proving inadequate in preserving the institution of marriage.

In my opinion, freedom is one of the greatest values in life. It is in our very nature and that is the reason every one resents if his/her freedom is encroached upon. The only trouble is that most of us are not even aware of our shackles. We do not even have a faint inkling of the numerous ways our freedom is denied to us. On the surface it appears that modern man has certainly acquired a degree of freedom unimaginable in the past. But it is only a mirage. There exists no freedom at all. There is a subtle and vicious system of slavery which has become all pervading. You need to ask one question only to see through the mist we are all mired in. The question is: can I identify the person, group or element who can take away my freedom?

If you cannot identify a single element, let me congratulate you. You are fortunate in the sense that you are not aware of the tenuousness and fragility of the so called freedom of yours. It means that you have not really had any brush with authorities (in any sense of the word). It is only a matter of time and if you are fortunate enough the time of realization may not come in your life at all and you will depart happily from this world thinking that you lived a free life. If you can identify even one force on this earth which can curtail your freedom in any way, let me congratulate you too. For it means that you can see things if you wish to. Our freedom can maintain its status only as long as someone more powerful than us doesn't see us as a threat to his interests. Step in his way and he will force you to open your eyes. It is not at all difficult to conclude that the so called freedom we have lasts only as long as someone else (who is more powerful than us) allows us.

This article does not intend to discuss our freedom in political or social sense. It can be shown that freedom does not exist in this sense anywhere on this earth. It is easy to see that the moment your interests, however personal, go against some authority you are subdued by the powers whose interests collide with yours. It is almost futile to aspire for freedom at such a level simply because at this level it is "power" which defines freedom. The more the power, the more the freedom. And since ordinary human beings like us, who are not politicians or officials or priests, cannot wield much power, we should not hope for freedom in this sense.

All this relates to the world outside of us. What about freedom at a much deeper and personal level? I want to talk of a certain level where all human beings are equally powerful. Where guns or jails or police do not come into play at all. Where, if you can recognize and earn your freedom, such powers of the world would not matter at all. This is purely at the level of an individual, where there is no one else to take away or grant you some freedom. Where it is only you who can decide whether you want freedom or not.

Just as there are various degrees of freedom, there are various degrees of slavery too. At a certain level, there exists the most vicious form of slavery. It is at the existential level. While political slavery curtails political freedom, existential slavery curtails the most profound form of freedom. Humanity has recognized the superficial levels of freedom but is almost unaware of the ultimate or true freedom. We are not even aware that we are not free at all.

One of my favorite Zen story goes like this:

A Zen Guru was going somewhere with his disciples. They saw a man who was coming towards them with a cow. The cow had a rope tied around its neck and the man was holding the other end of the rope. The Guru asked his disciples, "Who is the slave, the man or the cow?" The disciples said, "The cow is the slave. It is tied with the rope. The man is the master since he is controlling the cow." The Guru smiled and said, "No! You are wrong. If the rope slips from the man's hands and the cow starts running away you will find that the man will run after the cow. The man is also tied down with the cow, only his rope is invisible."

We are also tied down with so many invisible ropes. We are not free. We want to be happy but can we? Does it depend on us? No, our Happiness and sorrow depend on someone else. Anyone can make you angry anytime he wishes. You might have vowed many times that you will not get angry, but all your vows come to naught time and again. Anyone can make you unhappy anytime he wishes. You have no

subdue /sʌb'djuː/ v. a. to bring a person or group of people under control using force; b. soften sth; c. repress or control feelings repress or control feelings

aspire /ə'spaɪə/ v. have an ambitious plan or a lofty goal

guru /'guruː/ n. a. a religious leader or teacher in Hinduism and Šikhism; b. someone who has a reputation as an expert leader, teacher, or practitioner in a particular field

disciple /dɪ'saɪpəl/ n. a. someone who believes in the ideas of a great teacher or leader, esp. a religious one; b. one of the first 12 men to follow Christ

vow /vaʊ/ v. to promise or decide solemnly

naught /'nɔːt/ n. a. the number zero; b. nothing

time and again time and time again, very often

control over your own emotions. You have control over other people's emotions and they

irrespective /ˌɪrɪ'pektɪv/ *adj.* in spite of everything

have control over yours. You are their slave and they are yours. You are not even free to choose your own emotions. It seems that the switches, which control our emotions, are not accessible to us while being fully accessible to others. You can switch on or off any emotion in me and I can do the same to you. But your own emotional switches are out of your reach.

This is the deepest form of slavery. We have become slaves by nature. At least, we should have freedom to choose our own feelings and emotions. If I wish to remain happy, why should someone else be able to take my Happiness away so easily? If one wants to remain peaceful why should he not be able to maintain his peace irrespective of the outside disturbances?

Cultural Notes

Ashok Kumar Gupta—An Indian engineer by profession, a programmer by hobby, and a thinker by nature. His other major writings include *What is destiny? Is there a free will? Astrology: A Science or Superstition? What is Happiness and How to achieve it? How India lost its Glory?* etc.

Zen—Buddhist school that developed in China and later in Japan as the result of a fusion between the Mahayana form of Buddhism originating in India and the Chinese philosophy of **Daoism** (Taoism). **Zen** (**Buddhism**) derives from **Chinese Chan** (**Buddhism**) and emerged in Japan in the 12th century. **Zen** and **Chan**, respectively, the Japanese and Chinese ways of pronouncing the Sanskrit term **dhyana** which designates a state of mind roughly equivalent to contemplation or meditation. **Dhyana** denotes specifically the state of consciousness of a **Buddha**, one whose mind is free from the assumption that the distinct individuality of oneself and other things is real. **Zen** or **Chan** asserts that enlightenment can come through meditation and intuition rather than faith. The way of **Zen** or **Chan** is an intriguing one. Its predilection for paradox and intuition—as opposed to reason and logic—challenges our innate assumptions about the world and our own minds. As a major school of Buddhism, **Zen** or **Chan** has a tremendous influence on Chinese philosophy and people's life attitude. Besides, it influences various areas of Chinese culture in a profound way. Down the centuries, the **Zen** or **Chan** way has found unique expression in Chinese architecture, literature, music, painting, gardening, tea ceremonies and so on. The inconceivable value of **Zen Buddhism** enables it to continue playing an active role on the cultural stage of China and even the whole world in the present day.

 Exercises

I. Answer the following questions based on the text.

1. What is the essence of wars, according to the author?
2. Why is modern autonomy superficial?
3. For how long can one's freedom maintain its status?
4. Why does the author tell a Zen story?
5. What is the deepest form of slavery?

II. Text Review. Write T for true and F for false in the brackets before each of the following statements.

( ) 1. History is a fight against slavery.

( ) 2. People tend to enslave others.

( ) 3. Some people can enjoy absolute freedom while others can't.

( ) 4. It was quite unusual for people to keep their independence in the past.

( ) 5. In the modern world one can enjoy complete freedom to end his marriage and nothing can prevent him from doing it.

( ) 6. Compared with those in the past, modern people acquire more freedom and also have the initiative to keep the freedom as long as possible.

( ) 7. It is impossible to find political or social freedom on the earth.

( ) 8. Power defines freedom.

( ) 9. People cannot remain happy as they wish because their happiness depends on someone else.

( ) 10. The target readers of this article include politicians, officials, priests and ordinary people.

III. Paraphrase the following phrases or sentences in English.

1. Today, in the modern world, autonomy seems to be the norm.
2. A behind the scene power struggle is going on every where.
3. You need to ask one question only to see through the mist we are all mired in.
4. Step in his way and he will force you to open your eyes.
5. You might have vowed many times that you will not get angry, but all your vows come to naught time and again.

IV. Translate the following sentences into Chinese.

1. History, from one perspective, is nothing but a struggle between two groups—one attempting to enslave or keeping enslaved the other and the other fighting incessantly to ward off this slavery.

2. It is in our very nature and that is the reason every one resents if his/her freedom is encroached upon.

3. It is almost futile to aspire for freedom at such a level simply because at this level it is "power" which defines freedom.

4. Humanity has recognized the superficial levels of freedom but is almost unaware of the ultimate or true freedom.

5. It seems that the switches, which control our emotions, are not accessible to us while being fully accessible to others.

V. Respond to each of the following statements.

1. Freedom means many things to many people.

2. The idea of freedom in modern China has broadened.

3. The focuses of Western and Chinese philosophy are radically different.

4. When we have children, they are not ours to own.

5. If you are open to the world, honest to yourself and proud of yourself, you're really yourself.

VI. Provide a text which can support your viewpoint on one of the statements in *Exercise V*. Make your comments on the text you choose.

Text B

I'm Too Busy for Me
Dawn Fields

《我忙得没空做自己》在这个高速发展的时代,似乎每个人都在为自己忙碌。但是每个人又都忙得没有时间做自己:在这个生活的悖论中我们如何找到自己,不妨我们细读此文。

Everyone is busy nowadays. It's hard to find time for anything. From the time we wake up in the morning until the time we go to bed, it's hard to find 30 minutes to simply be by yourself. If you are married with children, I know you can relate to what I am saying.

I have a girlfriend who is single and we were having the discussion about how the grass is always greener on the other side. I said I would love to have a few days when I come Home to an empty house with peace and quiet. She said she would love to put the key in the door, knowing that someone is on the other end.

I had to laugh because although that sounds great, once it is a reality there are days when you wish everyone on the other side of the door would simply disappear for about an hour so you can come home and relax without having to start dinner, do Homework, bathe children, iron clothes for the next day or prepare lunch for everyone to take to school and work the following day. I know I sure wish that would happen and I believe that most married women with children can relate to what I am saying.

Don't get me wrong! I love my family with all of my heart and all of my soul. But if they disappeared for an hour or two, I would probably love them even more. If I had just one day when no one was yelling, "Mommy!" or "Honey!" I wouldn't be mad.

In fact, finding time to be by yourself is totally necessary if you wish to live a happy, prosperous and purpose-driven life. If there is noise going on around you 24/7 it's impossible to hear the quiet voice that speaks inside of us—that guides us and gives us direction on which path we should take. If that voice is not used to being heard, eventually, it would quiet itself and that is no good.

I know how <u>hectic</u> life can be. Trust me.

I know what it feels like to wish there were 35 hours each day and be willing to spend only 3 of those hours sleeping so you can get all the other things that you need to get done done.

But the problem is most of the stuff that we need to get done, does nothing towards working towards our personal development.

If you simply let life <u>dictate</u> to you what you do with your life, you will find that there is never time to take simply for yourself. Yes, you can schedule a vacation every now and then and that is great. But, generally, on vacation you still are not spending time by yourself. You have planned an exhausting schedule that takes you here and there and everywhere. You are trying to get in all the sites and events that you can over a

hectic /'hektɪk/ *adj.* constantly busy and hurried
dictate /dɪk'teɪt/ *v.* a. say out loud for the purpose of recording; b. tell someone what to do, give orders c. control or influence sth

5-to-7-day period.　Most of us actually need a vacation after coming back from a vacation with all the activities that we've covered during that time period.

No matter how hectic your life may be IT IS IMPERATIVE THAT YOU SPEND TIME EACH AND EVERY DAY BY YOURSELF TO THINK AND REFLECT ON LIFE AND LISTEN TO THAT INNER VOICE.

The same way each day you make sure that you have enough time to take a shower each morning or the same way you make sure that you eat lunch each day, make it a part of your daily routine to spend time with and by yourself.

When I say by yourself—that's exactly what I mean—by yourself.　Go somewhere you won't be disturbed by the children,　the spouse,　the phone,　the television,　the radio,　or your emails.　Go somewhere you can have total peace and quiet.

Pick a time that is convenient for you.

I like the early morning.　The reason I pick early morning is because everyone else is asleep.　No one calls me early in the morning.　There isn't any television or radio on or children or husband calling my name for any reason. I have total peace and quiet.

But it is entirely up to you as to what time works best with your schedule.

Once you find a quiet place and a quiet time try your best to be consistent in both the time and the location.　Meaning,　try to make sure you have your quiet time the same time and place each and every day.

And simply SIT and BE STILL.

I always start by saying a little prayer to God asking Him for His guidance on whatever it is that I am trying to overcome in my life. Right now, I am asking Him to help me be more like Him.　I am asking that I am always mindful of the way that I speak and treat people—especially those that are closest to me.

I don't know about you,　but I have the tendency sometimes to be more short-tempered with the people who are closest to me than I am with strangers.　I am asking God to help me with this and to help me be more like Him in every way possible.

You can ask for whatever it is that you want to work on in your life.

Then, simply sit and relax. Pay attention to any thoughts that come to you.

These thoughts that we receive during our quiet "meditation" periods, are God's guidance.　Our spirits are communicating with us and giving us direction on things to do in our life that will bring us the results that we are seeking.

mindful /'maindfəl/ adj. bearing in mind; attentive to

short-tempered /ʃɔːt ' tempəd/ easily made angry or impatient

meditation /medɪ'teɪʃən/ n.　a.　the practice of emptying your mind of thoughts and feelings,　in order to relax completely or for religious reasons;　b. the act of thinking deeply and seriously about sth

You can achieve anything that you desire once you take the time to listen to that inner voice, that guiding light inside of you and TRUST it.

second-guess a. attempt to anticipate or predict; b. to criticize sth after it has already happened

This is important. You must TRUST that voice and do as it says. Don't second-guess it. There is no need to second-guess because those directions are coming directly to you from God. Just LISTEN, TRUST and ACT.

ACTION POINT: For the next 30 days, find 30 minutes each day for quiet time. Whether it is in the morning, afternoon, or evening, doesn't matter. What matters is that you pick a time and be consistent. Find a quiet place. You can decide to go walking each morning in the park; or the bathroom might be the only place you can get peace and quiet, it doesn't matter. Perhaps you can only find time during your lunch break so you decide to spend 30 minutes sitting in your car in the back of the parking lot. Be creative. It doesn't matter where or when you do this, just make sure that you do.

Think of something that you would like to change about yourself, your life or your situation to make it better. And go into your quiet time with the impression on your mind and listen to your inner voice—that guiding voice.

Listen. Trust. Act. It will never steer you wrong.

Cultural Notes

Dawn Fields—A motivational speaker, life coach and author. She teaches how to discover your life's purpose and incorporate it into a career, in a really, down-to-earth, no nonsense sort of approach. Her other major writings include *Can a Little Faith Move Mountains? What You Sow, So Shall You Reap, Don't Be Afraid-Just Believe, What's Missing In Your Life, Jesus Tells the Secret of How to Get Everything You Desire In Life, A Burning Desire,* etc.

Uppercase Letters and Lowercase Letters—The shape of lowercase letters (or "small letters") varies roughly in three ways. Some of them ascend (e.g. b, h, d, k, l, etc.) or descend (e.g. g, j, p, q, y, etc.) and the left have no ascenders or descenders (e.g. a, c, e, i, o, m, n, r, s, etc.) at all. Because lower-case letters are characteristic of going up and down and sometimes just staying in the middle, the words or phrases in the small form can be recognized and understood more easily and quickly. Uppercase letters (or "capital letters"), in contrast, do not have any "shape" for they are of the same height. That's probably why people find it difficult to read the words in capitals. They have to slow down and read the capitalized part very carefully if they intend to figure out the meaning.　To focus readers' attention on the essential points, the author, obviously taking advantage of the features of uppercase letters for emphasis, capitalizes all the letters of quite a few words and even a whole long sentence here in this article.

 Exercises

I. Answer the following questions based on the text.

1. What did the author's girlfriend want to do?

2. Why did the author have a different idea from her girlfriend?

3. How can we make our life happy, prosperous and purpose-driven according to the author?

4. When is the best time for the author to enjoy total peace and quiet?

5. What should we think of in our quiet "meditation" periods?

II. Text Review. Write T for true and F for false in the brackets before each of the following statements.

(　) 1. The author has at least one child.

(　) 2. The author is sure that all married women with children can understand her words.

(　) 3. The author has got tired of the housework and her family.

(　) 4. It is impossible to enjoy a happy life unless we set aside some time to be by ourselves.

(　) 5. Housework has nothing to do with one's personal development.

(　) 6. Going on vacation is a good way for us to spend time by ourselves.

(　) 7. It is necessary for us to spend some time each day listening to the quiet voice inside of us.

(　) 8. The author is more patient with others than her family.

(　) 9. The inner voice functions as a guiding light.

(　) 10. It's really important we choose a right place at a right time to listen to our inner voice which is actually God's direction.

III. Paraphrase the following phrases or sentences in English.

1. If you are married with children, I know you can relate to what I am saying.

2. Don't get me wrong!

3. I am asking God to help me with this and to help me be more like Him in every way possible.

4. And go into your quiet time with the impression on your mind and listen to your inner voice—that guiding voice.

5. Listen. Trust. Act. It will never steer you wrong.

IV. Translate the following sentences into Chinese.

1. She said she would love to put the key in the door, knowing that someone is on the other end.

2. If there is noise going on around you 24/7 it's impossible to hear the quiet voice that speaks inside of us—that guides us and gives us direction on which path we should take.

3. If you simply let life dictate to you what you do with your life, you will find that there is never time to take simply for yourself.

4. No matter how hectic your life may be IT IS IMPERATIVE THAT YOU SPEND TIME EACH AND EVERY DAY BY YOURSELF TO THINK AND REFLECT ON LIFE AND LISTEN TO THAT INNER VOICE.

5. Our spirits are communicating with us and giving us direction on things to do in our life that will bring us the results that we are seeking.

V. Respond to each of the following statements.

1. Our jobs or careers seem to cause constant stress.

2. "I'm too busy" doesn't mean that you are.

3. You should always listen to your body, your mind, and your emotions.

4. Life can be stressful and at times you'll have to take steps to deal with ongoing stress in a positive way.

5. Adjusting to a new job quickly or not depends on what efforts you make and how you learn it.

VI. Provide a text which can support your viewpoint on one of the statements in *Exercise V*. Make your comments on the text you choose.

Unit Five

Middle Age, Old Age

W.S Maugham

《中年,老年》本文作者通过对人生中不同阶段的思考,将每个年龄阶段的优劣进行对照,深沉的思索和细致入微的笔触结合,给人无穷的教益。

I think I have been more than most men conscious of my age. My youth slipped past me unnoticed and I was always burdened with the sense that I was growing old. Because for my years I had seen much of the world and traveled a good deal, because I was somewhat widely read and my mind was occupied with matters beyond my years, I seemed always older than my contemporaries. But it was not until the outbreak of the war in 1914 that I had an inkling that I was no longer a young man. I found then to my consternation that a man of forty was old. I consoled myself by reflecting that this was only for military purposes, but not so very long afterwards I had an experience which put the matter beyond doubt. I had been lunching with a woman whom I had known a long time and her niece, a girl of seventeen. After luncheon, we took a taxi to go somewhere or other. The woman got in and then her niece. But the niece sat down on the strapontin leaving the empty seat at the back beside her aunt for me to sit on. It was the civility of youth (as opposed to the right of sex) to a gentleman no longer young. I realized that she looked upon me with the respect due to age.

It is not a very pleasant thing to recognize that for the young you are no longer an equal. You belong to a different generation. For them your race is run. They can look up to you; they can admire you; but you are apart from them,

consternation /ˌkɒnstəˈneɪʃən/ *n.* fear resulting from the awareness of danger

strapontin /strəˈpɒntin/ *n.* tip-up seat in the theatre or car

civility /sɪˈvɪlɪti/ *n.* a. polite or courteous behaviour; b. (*pl.*) polite words or actions

and in the long run they will always find the companionship of persons of their own age more grateful than yours.

But middle age has its compensations. Youth is bound hand and foot with the shackles of public opinion. Middle age enjoys freedom. I remember that when I left school I said to myself, "henceforward I can get up when I like to and go to bed when I like." That of course was an exaggeration, and I soon found that the trammeled life of the civilized man only permits of a modified independence. Whenever you have an aim you must sacrifice something of freedom to achieve it. But by the time you have reached middle age you have discovered how much freedom it is worth while to

grateful /ˈɡreɪtfəl/ adj. a. feeling or expressing thanks; b. giving pleasure or comfort

compensation /kɒmpənˈseɪʃən/ n. a. money in payment for loss, damage or work done; b. the act of giving money or sth else to pay for loss, damage, or work done; c. amends

henceforward /hensˈfɔːwəd/ adv. from now on

trammel /ˈtræməl/ v. to hinder or restrict

mortify /ˈmɔːtɪfaɪ/ v. a. to make someone feel ashamed or embarrassed; b. (Christianity) to subdue one's emotions, the body, etc., by self-denial

play a scratch game of golf a scratch golfer is one whose handicap is zero, such as a professional. The handicap in golf is simply the number of strokes by which a player's averaged score exceeds par for the course. To play a scratch game of golf here means to play skillfully like a golf professional

be (all) to the good to be to someone's benefit

reconciliation /ˌrekənsɪliˈeɪʃən/ n. a. the ending of conflict or renewing of a friendly relationship between disputing people or groups; b. the process of making two opposite beliefs, ideas or situations agree

succeed /səkˈsiːd/ v. a. to achieve an aim; b. to do well in a specified field; c. to come next in order after (someone or sth)

threshold /ˈθreʃhəʊld/ n. a. the lower horizontal part of an entrance or doorway, esp. one made of stone or hardwood; b. any doorway or entrance; c. the starting point of an experience, event, or venture; d. the point at which sth begins to take effect or be noticeable

sacrifice in order to achieve any aim that you have in view. When I was a boy I was tortured by shyness, and middle age has to a great extent brought me a relief from this. I was never of great physical strength and long walks used to tire me, but I went through them because I was ashamed to confess my weakness. I have now no such feeling and I save myself much discomfort. I always hated cold water, but for many years I took cold baths and bathed in cold seas because I wanted to be like everybody else. I used to dive from heights that made me nervous. I was mortified because I played games worse than other people. When I did not know a thing I was ashamed to confess my ignorance. It was not till quite late in life that I discovered how easy it is to say: "I do not know." I find with middle age that no one expects me to walk five and twenty miles, or to play a scratch game of golf, or to dive from a height of thirty feet. This is all to the good and makes life pleasant: but I should no longer care if they did. That is what makes middle age tolerable, the reconciliation with oneself.

Yesterday I was seventy years old. As one enters upon each succeeding decade it is natural, though perhaps irrational, to look upon it as a significant event. When I was thirty my brother said to me, "Now you are a boy no longer, you are a man and you must be a man." When I was forty I told myself, "That is the end of youth." On my fiftieth birthday I said, "It's no good fooling myself, this is middle age and I may just as well accept it." At sixty I said, "Now it's time to put my affairs into order, for this is the threshold of old age and I must settle my accounts." I decided to withdraw from the theatre and I wrote *The Summing Up*, in which I tried to review for my own comfort what I had learnt of life and literature, what I had done and what satisfaction it had brought me. But of all anniversaries I think the seventieth is the most momentous. One has reached the three scores and ten which one is accustomed to accept as allotted span of man, and one can but look upon such years as remain to one as uncertain contingencies stolen while old Time with his scythe has his head turned the other way. At seventy one is no longer on the threshold of old age. One is just an old man.

On the continent of Europe they have an amiable custom when a man who has achieved some distinction

momentous /məʊˈmentəs/ *adj.* of great significance

allot /əˈlɒt/ *v.* to assign as a share or for a particular purpose

span /spæn/ *n.* a. distance between limits; b. the period of time that sometimes exists or happens; c. a unit of length based on the width of a stretched hand, usu taken as nine inches (23 cms)

contingency /kənˈtɪndʒənsi/ *n.* a. an unknown or unforeseen future event or condition; b. dependence upon chance or factors and circumstances that are presently unknown

scythe /saɪð/ *n.* a long-handled tool for cutting grass or grain, with a curved sharpened blade that is swung parallel to the ground

amiable /ˈeɪmiəbəl/ *adj.* having a pleasant nature, friendly

eminent /ˈemɪnənt/ *adj.* well-known and well-respected

solitary /ˈsɒlɪtəri/ *adj.* a. done without the company of other people; b. of plants and animals; not growing or living in groups or colonies; c. single, alone; d. (of a place) without people, empty

game of patience patience (game) is a British term applied to any of various games of cards that can be played by one person. The American term for such games is solitaire (game)

colored /ˈkʌləd/ *n.* a United States term for Blacks that is now considered offensive

muse /mjuːz/ *v.* to think about sth deeply and carefully for a long time

sting /stɪŋ/ *n.* a. a pointed part of an insect, plant or animal that goes through a person's or animal's skin and leaves behind poison; b. a mental pain; c. the sharp pointed organ of certain animals or plants used to inject poison

reaches that age. His friends, his colleagues, his disciples (if he has any) join together to write a volume of essays in his honor. In England we give our eminent men no such flattering mark of our esteem. At the utmost we give dinner, and we do not do that unless he is very eminent indeed...

My own birthday passed without ceremony. I worked as usual in the morning and in the afternoon went for a walk in the solitary woods behind my house.

I went back to my house, made myself a cup of tea and read until dinner time. After dinner I read again, played two or three games of patience, listened to the news on the radio and took a detective story to bed with me. I finished it and went to sleep. Except for a few words to my colored maids I had not spoken to a soul all day. So I passed my seventieth birthday and so I wished to pass it. I mused.

Two or three years ago I was walking with Liza and she spoke, I do not know why, of the horror with which the thought of old age filled her. "Don't forget," I told her, "That when you're old you won't have the desire to do various things that make life pleasant to you now. Old age has its compensations."

"What?" she asked.

"Well, you need hardly ever do anything you don't want to. You can enjoy music, art and literature, differently from when you were young, but in that different way as keenly. You can get a good deal of fun out of observing the course of events in which you are no longer intimately concerned. If your pleasures are not so vivid your pains also have lost their sting."

Cultural Notes

W.S Maugham (1874—1965)—William Somerset Maugham was an English playwright, novelist, and short story writer. He was one of the most popular authors of his era. Maugham's first novel, *Liza of Lambeth*, published in 1897, turned out a great success but his masterpiece is generally agreed to be *Of Human Bondage*, a semi-autobiographical novel, which came out in 1915. His other memorable novels are *The Moon and Sixpence* (1919), *Cakes and Ale* (1930), *The Razor's Edge* (1944). Not only a successful playwright and a short story writer, Maugham was also one of the significant travel writers of the inter-war years (1918—1939). His famous travel books include *On a Chinese Screen* (1922) and *The Gentleman In the Parlour*. Maugham once traveled through China and Hong Kong for around four months in 1920 and produced some impressive stories after that, one of which, for example, *The Painted Veil*, has been adapted for film three times. The essay here is from *A Writer's Notebook* (1949), one of his autobiographical books.

The Summing Up—One of Maugham's major autobiographical books, published in 1938.

Liza—The author's daughter.

Exercises

I. Answer the following questions based on the text.

1. Why did the woman's niece leave the empty seat at the back beside her aunt for the author?
2. What advantage does middle age have over youth?
3. Why did the author feel relieved and comfortable as a middle-aged man?
4. How did people on the continent of Europe celebrate the seventieth birthday of a man who has some achievement?
5. How did the author pass his seventieth birthday?

II. Text Review. Write T for true and F for false in the brackets before each of the following statements.

( ) 1. When the World War I broke out the author was in his forties.

( )　2. When he was young the author used to have long walks because he was a strong man.

( )　3. The author often took cold baths and bathed in cold seas because he thought it good to his health.

( )　4. The author was not a good golf player when he was young.

( )　5. When the author was young his life was not pleasant because he was critical of himself.

( )　6. The author wrote this essay in his seventies.

( )　7. The age of thirty is the end of youth according to the author.

( )　8. A man in his fifties is still middle-aged in the eyes of the author.

( )　9. The author began to write his The Summing Up at sixty because he saw the sixtieth as the most important.

( ) 10. On his seventieth birthday the author played cards by himself.

III. Paraphrase the following phrases or sentences in English.

1. I consoled myself by reflecting that this was only for military purposes, but not so very long afterwards I had an experience which put the matter beyond doubt.

2. For them your race is run.

3. Youth is bound hand and foot with the shackles of public opinion.

4. In England we give our eminent men no such flattering mark of our esteem.

5. So I passed my seventieth birthday and so I wished to pass it.

IV. Translate the following sentences into Chinese.

1. Because for my years I had seen much of the world and traveled a good deal, because I was somewhat widely read and my mind was occupied with matters beyond my years, I seemed always older than my contemporaries.

2. That of course was an exaggeration, and I soon found that the trammeled life of the civilized man only permits of a modified independence.

3. Now it's time to put my affairs into order, for this is the threshold of old age and I must settle my accounts.

4. One has reached the three scores and ten which one is accustomed to accept as allotted span of man, and one can but look upon such years as remain to one as uncertain contingencies stolen while old Time with his scythe has his head turned the other way.

5. You can get a good deal of fun out of observing the course of events in which you are no longer intimately concerned.

V. Respond to each of the following statements.

1. Aging is a fact of life.

2. Death is a different experience at different times in life.

3. Kinship terms reflect the Chinese traditional system of respect.

4. Time cannot wrinkle our heart.

5. If popularity in school can really change you on the inside, you should be careful.

VI. Provide a text which can support your viewpoint on one of the statements in *Exercise V*. Make your comments on the text you choose.

Text B

Golden Wedding

Ruth Suckow

《金婚》一次金婚仪式的经过,以及当事人切身的感受和在场者的表现,让我们与当事人一起体味那种似乎年轻重新来过的感觉经历。普通,精彩,感人。

Mrs. Willie turned to her husband and said, "Pa, you are to change your clothes."

"Why are you in such a hurry?"

"Well," she answered, "you want to be ready when George comes, don't you?"

"Oh, he will not come. How can he get his car through all this snow?"

Mrs. Willie quickly answered, "Yes, yes he will, Pa. They invited us to their home, didn't they? So you go now and put on your good clothes."

Mr. Willie said something under his breath, he still looked angry, but he obeyed his wife. She watched him go and thought, "Why does he do this?"

He always acted this way, ever since they got married fifty years ago. Every time he knew he ought to do something, he protested. So it was every time they had to go somewhere.

George will not come today. It was just like Pa to say that. If he knew his wife was depending on something, he had to be against it. He never wanted to agree that

under one's breath quietly so that other people can not hear exactly what one is saying

anything was going to be right. He was always tearing down her hopes. If she felt that something would turn out right, he was sure it would turn out wrong. She was always pulling forward, he pulling back. But in fifty years of marriage, this pulling usually ended with his doing what she asked.

Mrs. Willie looked out of the window at the quiet white street. The snow was still falling. For a moment, she became fearful that perhaps this time Pa was right. George would not be able to get through the snow. But then she said softly, "He will come. George will come."

As she watched for her son-in-law George, her husband came back into the room. She looked up and said, "Oh, Pa, why did you have to put on that old necktie?"

"What old necktie?"

"Oh, you know what I mean," she answered, "I should think you would be ashamed to wear that tie at all. Just think of where we are going today. You go and put on the nice one, the one Jenny sent you for Christmas. Just try and look nice for once today. You don't know who maybe there and see us."

Again the angry look, "Just who do you think is going to be there?"

"Well, you know the dinner is for us," she answered.

"Oh, there won't be many people who would come out in all this snow just to eat dinner with us!" But he went back and put on the other tie.

She felt like crying. Her hands shook as she sewed. Oh, why did he have to hurt her and why today? They knew each other so well, each knew without even thinking just what little things could hurt the other. Now he was saying that this dinner was nothing special! Today—their golden wedding anniversary! Married for fifty years! Nothing special? That was what he meant by wearing that old necktie. He always talked to her about their age, how nobody cared about them. But to do it today on such a special day! Yet, after all if you looked at it one way, he was right. Here they were in their old house, two old people living alone! Maybe he was right, and may be she was a fool to want to celebrate her fifty-year marriage to him. They had had enough bad luck as he always said they would. Still, she hoped for the best. He wanted to, but was afraid. She felt her grace silk dress. It looked so nice, and then she called to him, "Pa, here comes George! Hurry and get ready."

Pa was ready, in fact it was she who had to run back to her bedroom to comb her hair. And it was time to go! Pa turned to George, "I didn't think you get here," he said.

"Oh," his son-in-law answered, "there is more than one way of getting here." And there in front of the house was a big sled. Pa and ma followed George to

anniversary /ˌænɪˈvɜːsəri/ n. the day on which an important event happened in a previous year

grace /greɪs/ n. a. elegance and beauty of movement, form, or expression; b. a pleasing or charming quality

sled /sledʒ/= sledge, n. small vehicle sliding over snow

it. They wore heavy wool coats.

Mrs. Willie looked up and saw two of their friends in the sled. They were the minister reverent Baxter and his wife. They helped the old couple to get in. Mrs. Baxter smiled. Her cheeks and nose were red from the cold and her eyes were bright.

"Well," she said, "How's the bride and groom?"

"All are right, I guess," said Mrs. Willie.

And then George looked around and called "Get up!" And the two big brown horses ran quickly. The snow was beautiful. The road and the trees were like silver. It was warm under the furs in the sleigh. It felt like a holiday already. After a time, they arrived at a big farmhouse, standing behind trees that looked blue-brown in the snow.

They got out of the sleigh and went up to steps and into the kitchen, there was their daughter Clara. She looked happy. Her fat arms were bare and she was pink from the heat of the ovens. What good smells came from those ovens! Roasting chickens and biscuits and there were dishes everywhere. Clara took Mrs. Baxter and Mrs. Willie to a bedroom. There they took off their coats and gloves.

Clara said, "Now mama, you don't have to help me. You go into the parlor and talk to Mrs. Baxter. Minnie will help me." Minnie was Mrs. Willie's daughter-in-law. So she was there too with Mrs. Willie's son John. Mrs. Willie was glad she had worn her best dress. It wasn't a big party, but there was Clara, and George and their daughters, John and Minnie and the Baxters too.

Mrs. Willie sat in a chair and folded her hands. It was a party! The smells in the kitchen, all those dishes, even the bedroom was very clean. And she could hear children's voices in another room, laughing and shouting. Now she looked around and she remembered. She remembered how this same house had looked when she had come to it fifty years earlier! Then it looked different. It seemed smaller and very empty with a feeling of open space around it.

Suddenly, noises broke into her thoughts. Shouts came from outside. Mrs. Willie turned quickly to the window and a great sleigh came up to the house. People were in it and they were calling and waving. Again, Mrs. Willie's hands shook. But this time it was from happiness. She and her husband stood up and a great crowd of people came in crying, "Where is the bridal couple? Look at the happy groom. Well, well, congratulations!"

Then, the door of the dining room opened. Everyone said that Ma and Pa must go in first. They were gently

minister /'mɪnɪstə/ n. one who is authorized to perform religious functions in a Christian church, esp. a Protestant church

reverent /'revərənt/ adj. (formal.) showing great respect and admiration

bride /braɪd/ n. a woman on her wedding day, or just before or just after it

groom /grʊm/ n. a. a person whose job is to feed and take care of horses, esp. by brushing and cleaning them; b. = bridegroom, a man on his wedding day, or just before or just after it

sleigh /sleɪ/ n. a sledge, esp. one pulled by horses over snow

parlor /'pɑːlə/ n. a. reception room in an inn or club where visitors can be received; b. a room in a private house or establishment where people can sit and talk and relax

bridal /'braɪdl/ adj. of or relating to a wedding or bride

pushed forward by the others. They sat at the head of the table. Mr. Willie looked almost afraid. He seemed

plate /pleɪt/ *v.* coat with a layer of metal

to be thinking, "All of this for two old people?" But Mrs. Willie was happy. She saw the room as one great light glasses plated silver, white and yellow all around. There were laughs and calls everywhere, then all stood quietly while Mr. Baxter said a prayer. It was all very quiet and serious. Only a child's voice broke the silence. They sat and the laughter began again. "Oh, isn't this lovely?" someone said. "Well, grandma," said one of the children, "what do you think of it?" Mrs. Willie turned pink and said slowly, "I don't know what to say!" Here was the celebration she had dreamed about and now it was real! So real it was actually happening!

Cultural Notes

Ruth Suckow (1892—1960)—American writer. She was born in Hawarden, Iowa, and lived most of her life in that State. Suckow began her writing career as a poet but established her fame as a writer of novels and short stories. The most successful years of her career was the 1920s when she was ranked as one of the top 10 American fiction writers by H.L. Mencken, a noted critic and publisher. Suckow's novels and short stories reflected her Iowa background. She wrote about ordinary farmers, small-town Iowans, and also independent women. Her works center on family and church affairs. Suckow's major works include *Country People* (1924), *Iowa Interiors* (1926), *The Kramer Girls* (1930), *The Folks* (1934), *Some Others and Myself* (1952). The story Golden Wedding is from her novel *Iowa Interiors*.

Golden Wedding—A wedding anniversary is an anniversary of the date on which a wedding took place. Married persons regard the day of their marriage as important, and therefore always celebrate their wedding anniversary in some special way. Golden wedding is the 50th anniversary of marriage and other important wedding anniversaries are, for example, China wedding (20 yrs), Silver wedding (25 yrs), Pearl wedding (30 yrs), Ruby wedding (40 yrs), Diamond wedding (60 yrs), Platinum wedding (70 yrs), etc. Spending half a century in love with each other is a wonderful thing in married life, which makes golden wedding one of the most celebrated wedding anniversaries. Celebrations of this event is traditionally made by all the friends and family. Holding a party is the most common way to celebrate it. Traditional and modern 50th wedding anniversary gifts have a theme of gold.

Pa/Ma—The informal vocative expressions for a father or a mother, probably derived from baby talk. They sometimes are used as forms of direct address between the husband and the wife, who have had at least one child.

Exercises

I. Answer the following questions based on the text.

1. Why did Mrs. Willie ask her husband to change his clothes?
2. Who was George?
3. Why did Mrs. Willie feel like crying before George came?
4. How many children did Mrs. Willie have?
5. Why did Mrs. Willie's hands shake for the second time?

II. Text Review. Write T for true and F for false in the brackets before each of the following statements.

( ) 1. Mr. Willie didn't think George would come that day.
( ) 2. When George came Mrs. Willie was already well prepared.
( ) 3. The celebration of the golden marriage was held before Christmas.
( ) 4. Mrs. Willie was doing the needle work before George came.
( ) 5. Mr. Willie always did what his wife asked him to do because he didn't like quarrelling with her.
( ) 6. They went to their daughter's house on a sled pulled by big dogs.
( ) 7. Mr. Willie didn't like the idea of celebrating their fifty-year marriage.
( ) 8. Clara and George didn't have sons.
( ) 9. Mr. Baxter was a pious Christian.
( ) 10. Mrs. Willie never dreamed about such a lovely party before.

III. Paraphrase the following phrases or sentences in English.

1. If he knew his wife was depending on something, he had to be against it.
2. I should think you would be ashamed to wear that tie at all.
3. They had had enough bad luck as he always said they would.
4. It seemed smaller and very empty with a feeling of open space around it.
5. She saw the room as one great light glasses plated silver, white and yellow all around.

IV. Translate the following sentences into Chinese.

1. Mr. Willie said something under his breath, he still looked angry, but he obeyed his wife.
2. But in fifty years of marriage, this pulling usually ended with his doing what she asked.
3. They knew each other so well, each knew without even thinking just what little things could hurt the other.
4. Her cheeks and nose were red from the cold and her eyes were bright.
5. After a time, they arrived at a big farmhouse, standing behind trees that looked blue-brown in the snow.

V. Respond to each of the following statements.

1. Being married for all your life has become so difficult in modern age.
2. Maintain a commitment to the marriage.
3. Chinese people value the close family relationship.
4. If you really care your parents, it's not so hard to show your love.
5. What points may help you finalize your decision to get married?

VI. Provide a text which can support your viewpoint on one of the statements in *Exercise V*. Make your comments on the text you choose.

Unit Six

The Bridges of Madison County
Robert James Waller

The Beginning

　　《廊桥遗梦》是一个著名的爱情故事,古老的廊桥,孤独的远游者,两颗中年人的心渐渐贴近,撞出火花,寻觅已久的灵魂找到了永恒的归宿。这段不了情缘,应该有一个美丽的缘起。让我们顺着作者的笔触,缓缓回溯⋯⋯

　　There are songs that come free from the blue-eyed grass, from the dust of a thousand country roads.　This is one of them. In late afternoon,　in the autumn of 1989,　I'm at my desk, looking at a blinking cursor on the computer screen before me, and the telephone rings.

　　On the other end of the wire is a former Iowan named Michael Johnson. He lives in Florida now. A friend from Iowa has sent him one of my books. Michael Johnson has read it; his sister, Carolyn, has read it; and they have a story in which they think I might be interested. He is circumspect, refusing to say anything about the story, except that he and Carolyn are willing to travel to Iowa to talk with me about it.

　　That they are prepared to make such an effort intrigues me,　in spite of my skepticism a bout such offers. So I agree to meet with them in Des Moines the following week. At a Holiday Inn near the airport,　the introductions are made, awkwardness gradually declines,　and the two of them sit across from me,　evening coming down outside, light snow falling.

　　They extract a promise: If I decide not

blue-eyed grass a substantial group of flowering plants of the iris family,　all native to the America.　The flowers are relatively simple and often grow in clusters.　In addition to blue, flower colors also include white, yellow, purple, etc.

cursor /'kɜːsə/ *n.*　a moving marker on a computer screen that marks the point at which keyed characters will appear or be deleted

circumspect /'sɜːkəmspekt/ *adj.* cautious and careful not to take risks

intrigue /ɪn'triːg/ *v.　a.* to make interested or curious; *b.* to plot secretly or dishonestly

skepticism /'skeptɪsɪzəm/ *n.*　an attitude of doubting that claims or statements are true or that sth will happen

extract /ɪks'trækt/ *a. v.* to pull out or uproot by force; *b.* to remove from a container; *c.* to derive (pleasure, information, etc.) from some source; *d.* to obtain information, money, etc., often by taking it from sb who is unwilling to give it

to write the story, I must agree never to disclose what transpired in Madison County, Iowa, in 1965 or other related events that followed over the next twenty-four years. All right, that's reasonable. After all, it's their story, not mine.

So I listen. I listen hard, and I ask hard questions. And they talk. On and on they talk. Carolyn cries openly at times, Michael struggles not to. They show me documents and magazine clippings and a set of journals written by their mother, Francesca.

transpire /træns'paɪə/ v. a. to happen; b. give off (water) through the skin; c. come to light, become known

clipping /'klɪpɪŋ/ n. a. a piece that has been cut off sth; b. an article cut from a newspaper

tangentially /tæn'dʒenʃəli/ adj. (formal) having only a slight or indirect connection with sth

tawdry /'tɔːdri/ adj. a. intended to be bright and attractive but cheap and of low quality; b. involving low moral standards, extremely unpleasant or offensive

gossip /'gɒsɪp/ n. a. idle talk, usu. about other people's private lives, esp. of a disapproving or malicious nature; b. an informal conversation, esp. about other people's private lives; c. a person who habitually talks about other people, usually maliciously

debasement /dɪ'beɪsmənt/ n. reduce of the quality or value of sth

commitment /kə'mɪtmənt/ n. a. an obligation, responsibility, or promise that restricts freedom of action; b. dedication to a cause or principle

shatter /'ʃætə/ v. a. to break suddenly into many small pieces; b. to damage badly or destroy; c. to upset (someone) greatly

Room service comes and goes. Extra coffee is ordered. As they talk, I begin to see the images. First you must have the images, then come the words. And I begin to hear the words, begin to see them on pages of writing. Sometime just after midnight, I agree to write the story—or at least attempt it.

Their decision to make this information public was a difficult one for them. The circumstances are delicate, involving their mother and, more tangentially, their father. Michael and Carolyn recognized that coming forth with the story might result in tawdry gossip and unkind debasement of whatever memories people have of Richard and Francesca Johnson.

Yet in a world where personal commitment in all of its forms seems to be shattering and love has become a matter of convenience, they both felt this remarkable tale was worth the telling. I believed then, and I believe even more strongly now, they were correct in their assessment.

In the course of my research and writing, I asked to meet with Michael and Carolyn three more times. On each occasion, and without complaint, they traveled to Iowa. Such was their eagerness to make sure the story was told accurately. Sometimes we merely talked; sometimes we slowly drove the roads of Madison County while they pointed out places having a significant role in the story.

In addition to the help provided by Michael anal Carolyn, the story as I tell it here is based on information contained in the journals of Francesca Johnson; research conducted in the northwestern United States, particularly Seattle and Bellingham, Washington; research carried out quietly in Madison County, Iowa; information gleaned from the photographic essays of Robert Kincaid; assistance provided by magazine editors; detail supplied by manufacturers of photographic films and equipment; and long discussions with several wonderful elderly people in the county home at Barnesville, Ohio, who remembered Kincaid from his boyhood days.

In spite of the investigative effort, gaps remain. I have added a little of my own imagination in those instances, but only when I could make reasoned judgments flowing from the intimate familiarity with Francesca Johnson and Robert Kincaid I gained through my research. I am confident that I have come very close to what actually happened.

One major gap involves the exact details of a trip made across the northern United States by Kincaid. We knew he made this journey, based on a number of photographs that subsequently were published, a brief mention of it by Francesca Johnson in her journals, and handwritten notes he left with a magazine editor. Using these sources as my guide, I retraced what I believe was the path he took from Bellingham to Madison County in August of 1965. Driving toward Madison County at the end of my travels, I felt I had, in many ways, become Robert Kincaid.

Still, attempting to capture the essence of Kincaid was the most challenging part of my research and writing. He is an elusive figure. At times he seems rather ordinary. At other times ethereal, perhaps even spectral. In his work he was a consummate professional. Yet he saw himself as a peculiar kind of male animal becoming obsolete in a world given over to increasing amounts of organization. He once talked about the "merciless wail" of time in his head, and Francesca Johnson characterized him as living "in strange, haunted places, far back along the stems of Darwin's logic."

Two other intriguing questions are still unanswered. First, we have been unable to determine what became of Kincaid's photographic files. Given the nature of his work, there must have been thousands, probably hundreds of thousands, of photographs. These never have been recovered. Our best guess—and this would be consistent with the way he saw himself and his place in the world—is that he destroyed them prior to his death.

The second question deals with his life from 1975 to 1982. Very little information is available. We know he earned a sparse living as a portrait photographer in Seattle for several years and continued to photograph the Puget Sound area. Other

---

essence /'esə ns/ *n.* a. the most important and distinctive feature of sth, which determines its identity; b. a liquid taken from a plant, etc. that contains its smell and taste in a very strong form

elusive /ɪ'luːsɪv/ *adj.* difficult to find, define, or achieve

ethereal /ɪ'θɪə rɪəl/ *adj.* a. extremely delicate or refined; b. seeming to belong to another, more spiritual, world

spectral /'spektrəl/ *adj.* a. connected with a spectrum; b. (liter) like a ghost, connected with a ghost

consummate /'kɒnsəmɪt/ *adj.* (*formal*) extremely skilled

obsolete /'ɒbsəliːt/ *adj.* no longer used, out of date

wail /weɪl/ *n.* a prolonged high-pitched cry of pain or sorrow

haunt /hɔːnt/ *v.* a. to visit (a person or place) in the form of a ghost; b. to remain in the memory or thoughts of; c. to visit (a place) frequently

prior to before

sparse /spɑːs/ *adj.* small in amount and spread out widely

than that, we have nothing. One interesting note is that all letters mailed to him by the Social Security Administration and Veterans Administration were marked "Return to Sender" in his handwriting and sent back.

Preparing and writing this book has altered my world view, transformed the way I think, and, most of all, reduced my level of cynicism about what is possible in the arena of human relationships. Coming to know Francesca Johnson and Robert Kincaid as I have through my research, I find the boundaries of such relationships can be extended farther than I previously thought. Perhaps you will have the same experience in reading this story.

That will not be easy. In an increasingly callous world, we all exist with our own carapaces of scabbed-over sensibilities. Where great passion leaves off and mawkishness begins, I'm not sure. But our tendency to scoff at the possibility of the former and to label genuine and profound feelings as maudlin makes it difficult to enter the realm of gentleness required to understand the story of Francesca Johnson and Robert Kincaid. I know I had to overcome that tendency initially before I could begin writing.

If, however, you approach what follows with a willing suspension of disbelief, as Coleridge put it, I am confident you will experience what I have experienced. In the indifferent spaces of your heart, you may even find, as Francesca Johnson did, room to dance again.

Summer 1991

cynicism /'sinisizəm/ *n.* the beliefs or philosophy of the ancient Greek Cynics. cf. cynic *a.* a person who believes that people only do things to help themselves, rather than for good or sincere reasons *b.* a person who does not believe that sth good will happen or that sth is important

arena /ə'riːnə/ *n.* *a.* a seated enclosure where sports events take place; *b.* a sphere of intense activity; *c.* the area of an ancient Roman amphitheatre where gladiators fought

callous /'kæləs/ *adj.* showing no concern for other people's feelings

carapace /'kærəpeɪs/ *n.* the hard shell on the back of some animals such as crabs and tortoises, that protects them

scabbed-over a coined word by the writer, which means "having scabs all over sth" in the context. cf. scab crust over healing wound

mawkish /'mɔːkɪʃ/ *adj.* foolishly or embarrassingly sentimental

scoff /skɒf/ *v.* *a.* (at) to speak in a scornful and mocking way about (sth); *b.* (*infml*) to eat (food) fast and greedily

maudlin /'mɔːdlɪn/ overly or tearfully sentimental, esp. because affected by alcohol

Cultural Notes

The *Bridges of Madison County*—A best-selling novel by Robert James Waller. The novel is presented as a novelization of a true story, but it is in fact completely fiction. The famous compelling story tells about an Italian woman, Francesca, who lived on a farm in Iowa with her husband and children, once met a National Geographic photographer, Robert, and they fell in love with each other and found the promise of perfect personal happiness. They understood, with sadness, that the most important things in life were not always about making yourself happy, though. The most moving part of the story for the reader may be to see how they struggled to decide not to spend the rest of their lives together in the end. The novel was successfully made into a film of the same name in 1995, directed by Clint Eastwood. The film stars are Eastwood and Meryl Streep.

Robert James Waller (1939—)—American author, photographer and musician. He was born in Rockford, Iowa and currently resides in Texas. Waller received his Ph D in business in 1968 and later taught at the University of Northern Iowa. Several of his books have been on the *New York Times* bestseller list including 1992's *The Bridges of Madison County* which was the top best-seller in 1993. Both that novel and his 1995 novel, *Puerto Vallarta Squeeze*, have been made into motion pictures.

Madison County—A county in the state of Iowa, which is located in the Midwest of the U S Madison County is famous for being the birthplace of John Wayne, a former American film star, and for a number of covered bridges (or "roofed bridge", a bridge with a roof and walls that protect it against the weather).

Coleridge (1772—1834)—Samuel Taylor Coleridge was an English poet, critic, and philosopher, who was one of the founders of the Romantic Movement in England and one of the Lake Poets. His best-known poems are perhaps *The Rime of the Ancient Mariner and Kubla Khan*. His major prose work is *Biographia Literaria*.

Puget Sound—A deep inlet of the Pacific Ocean, in northwestern Washington.

Exercises

I. Answer the following questions based on the text.

1. Where did the author get the story?
2. How did Michael and Carolyn know their mother's story?
3. Who was Robert Kincaid and what did he do for a living?
4. What else did the author exert to accomplish the story except his investigative effort?

5. According to the author, what made Francesca's story extraordinary and impressive?

II. Text Review. Write T for true and F for false in the brackets before each of the following statements.

(　) 1. Both Michael and Carolyn cried as they told their mother's story to the writer.

(　) 2. The author didn't decide whether or not to write Francesca's story until the next day.

(　) 3. Michael and Carolyn had to travel to Iowa from northern America to meet the writer.

(　) 4. Michael and Carolyn were worried that their mother's story was not remarkable, which might result in people's bad comments on their parents.

(　) 5. The author is under the impression that modern people don't take personal responsibility seriously.

(　) 6. The author met Michael and Carolyn five times altogether before completing the novel.

(　) 7. Seattle lies in the southwestern United States.

(　) 8. Robert Kincaid grew up in Ohio.

(　) 9. Penetrating Francesca was the most difficult part for the author to write.

(　) 10. Robert Kincaid lived in Bellingham ten years after he left Madison County.

III. Paraphrase the following phrases or sentences in English.

1. On the other end of the wire is a former Iowan named Michael Johnson.

2. First you must have the images, then come the words.

3. Yet in a world where personal commitment in all of its forms seems to be shattering and love has become a matter of convenience, they both felt this remarkable tale was worth the telling.

4. First, we have been unable to determine what became of Kincaid's photographic files.

5. In an increasingly callous world, we all exist with our own carapaces of scabbed-over sensibilities.

IV. Translate the following sentences into Chinese.

1. In late afternoon, in the autumn of 1989, I'm at my desk, looking at a blinking cursor on the computer screen before me, and the telephone rings.

2. Michael and Carolyn recognized that coming forth with the story might result

in tawdry gossip and unkind debasement of whatever memories people have of Richard and Francesca Johnson.

3. I am confident that I have come very close to what actually happened.

4. Yet he saw himself as a peculiar kind of male animal becoming obsolete in a world given over to increasing amounts of organization.

5. Preparing and writing this book has altered my world view, transformed the way I think, and, most of all, reduced my level of cynicism about what is possible in the arena of human relationships.

V. Respond to each of the following statements.

1. The most important things in life are not always about making yourself happy.

2. We divorce because we married the "wrong" people.

3. Chinese and American people have shared plenty of similar family values, but differences still exist in various forms.

4. What should you do if your parents fight?

5. Only do you understand what marriage entails and clarify your expectations, you can finally enjoy a happy life after marriage.

VI. Provide a text which can support your viewpoint on one of the statements in *Exercise V*. Make your comments on the text you choose.

Text B

Letter in the Wallet

Anonymous

《钱包里的信》爱情总是能够打动我们,这是一种永恒的,使人心灵净化的感情。但是苦苦期盼的爱情较之那些从最初就很顺利的爱情更令我们感动,因为这种等待里有一种切实的纯粹。

It was a freezing day, a few years ago, when I stumbled on a wallet in the street. There was no identification inside. Just three dollars, and a crumpled letter that looked as if it had been carried around for years. The only thing legible on the torn envelope was the return address. I opened the letter and saw that it had been written in 1924-almost 60 years ago. I read it carefully, hoping to find some clue to the

stumble /'stʌmbəl/ v. a. to walk unsteadily; b. to miss a step and fall or nearly fall; c. to encounter by chance; d. to make a mistake
crumple /'krʌmpəl/ v. a. to crease and wrinkle; b. to collapse; c. look upset or disappointed
legible /'ledʒəbəl/ adj. (of written or printed words) clear enough to read

identity of the wallet's owner.

It was a "Dear John" letter. The writer, in a delicate script, told the recipient, whose name was Michael, that her mother forbade her to see him again. Nevertheless, she would always love him. It was signed Hannah.

script /skrɪpt/ n. a. a written text of a play, film/movie, broadcast, talk, etc; b. writing done by hand; c. a set of letters in which a language is written; d. series of commands in computer program
recipient /rɪ'sɪpiənt/ n. (formal) a person who receives sth
party /'pɑːti/ n. a. a person or group participating in an action or affair; b. a group of people sharing a common political aim; c. a social gathering for pleasure; d. a particular individual
take a chance take a risk in the hope of a favorable outcome

It was a beautiful letter. But there was no way, beyond the name Michael, to identify the owner. Perhaps if I called information the operator could find the phone number for the address shown on the envelope.

"Operator, this is an unusual request. I'm trying to find the owner of a wallet I found. Is there any way you could tell me the phone number for an address that was on a letter in the wallet?"

The operator gave me her supervisor, who said there was a phone listed at the address, but that she could not give me the number. However, she would call and explain the situation. Then, if the party wanted to talk, she would connect me. I waited a minute and she came back on the line. "I have a woman who will speak with you."

I asked the woman if she knew a Hannah.

"Oh, of course! We bought this house from Hannah's family thirty years ago." "Would you know where they could be located now?" I asked.

"Hannah had to place her mother in a nursing home years ago. Maybe the home could help you track down the daughter."

The woman gave me the name of the nursing home. I called and found out that Hannah's mother had died. The woman I spoke with gave me an address where she thought Hannah could be reached.

I phoned. The woman who answered explained that Hannah herself was now

living in a nursing home. She gave me the number. I called and was told, "Yes, Hannah is with us."

I asked if I could stop by to see her. It was almost 10 p.m. The director said Hannah might be asleep. "But if you want to take a chance, maybe she's in the day room watching television."

The director and a guard greeted me at the door of the nursing home. We went up to the third floor and saw the nurse, who told us that Hannah was indeed watching TV. We entered the day room. Hannah was a sweet, silver-haired old-timer with a warm smile and friendly eyes. I told her about finding the wallet and showed her the letter. The second she saw it, she took a deep breath. "Young man," she said, "This letter was the last contact I had with Michael." She looked away for a moment, then said pensively, "I loved him very much. But I was only sixteen and my mother felt I was too young. He was so handsome. You know, like Sean Connery, the actor."

We both laughed. The director then left us alone. "Yes, Michael Goldstein was his name. If you find him, tell him I still think of him often. I never did marry," she said, smiling through tears that welled up in her eyes. "I guess no one ever matched up to Michael..."

I thanked Hannah, said good-bye and took the elevator to the first floor. As I stood at the door, the guard asked, "Was the old lady able to help you?"

I told him she had given me a lead. At least I have a last name. But I probably won't pursue it further for a while. I explained that I had spent almost the whole day trying to find the wallet's owner.

While we talked, I pulled out the brown-leather case with its red-lanyard lacing and showed it to the guard. He looked at it closely and said, "Hey, I'd know that anywhere. That's Mr. Goldstein's. He's always losing it. I found it in the hall at least three times."

"Who's Mr. Goldstein?" I asked. "He's one of the old-timers on the eighth floor. That's Mike Goldstein's wallet, for sure. He goes out for a walk quite often."

I thanked the guard and ran back to the director's office to tell him what the guard had said. He accompanied me to the eighth floor. I prayed that Mr. Goldstein would be up.

"I think he's still in the day room," the nurse said. "He likes to read at night...a darling old man."

We went to the only room that had lights on, and there was a man reading a book. The director asked him if he had lost his wallet. Michael Goldstein looked up, felt his back pocket and then said, "Goodness, it is missing."

"This kind gentleman found a wallet. Could it be yours?"

The second he saw it, he smiled with relief. "Yes," he said, "that's it.

old-timer a. someone who has been or worked in a place for a long time; b. an old or elderly person

pensive /ˈpensɪv/ adj. thinking deeply about sth, esp. in a sad or serious manner

well up a. (of a liquid) to rise to the surface of sth and start to flow; b. (lit.) (of an emotion) to become stronger

match up to (usu. used in negative sentences) to be as good, interesting, successful as sb/sth

give (sb) a lead a. encourage others by doing first; b. provide a hint towards the solution of a problem

lanyard /ˈlænjəd/ n. a. a cord worn round the neck to hold a whistle or knife; b. a short rope or cord used to hold or fasten sth on a ship

lacing /ˈleɪsɪŋ/ n. a. lace that fastens; b. a small amount of alcohol or a drug added to a drink or to food

accompany /əˈkʌmpəni/ v. a. to travel or go somewhere with someone; b. to happen or appear with sth else; c. to play a musical instrument, esp. a piano, while someone else sings or plays the main tune

Must have dropped it this afternoon.　I want to give you a reward."

"Oh, no, thank you," I said.　"But I have to tell you something.　I read the letter in the hope of finding out who owned the wallet."

The smile on his face disappeared. "You read that letter?"

"Not only did I read it,　I think I know where Hannah is."

He grew pale.　"Hannah? You know where she is? How is she? Is she still as pretty as she was?"

I hesitated.

"Please tell me!" Michael urged.

"She's fine, and just as pretty as when you knew her."

"Could you tell me where she is? I want to call her tomorrow."

He grabbed my hand and said, "You know something? When that letter came, my life ended. I never married. I guess I've always loved her."

"Michael," I said.　"Come with me." The three of us took the elevator to the third floor. We walked toward the day room where Hannah was sitting, still watching TV. The director went over to her.

"Hannah," he said softly.　"Do you know this man?" Michael and I stood waiting in the doorway.

She adjusted her glasses, looked for a moment, but didn't say a word.

"Hannah, it's Michael. Michael Goldstein. Do you remember?"

"Michael? Michael? It's you!"

He walked slowly to her side.　She stood and they embraced.　Then the two of them sat on a couch,　held hands and started to talk.　The director and I walked out, both of us crying.

"See how the good Lord works," I said philosophically.　"If it's meant to be, it will be." Three weeks later, I got a call from the director who asked. "Can you break away on Sunday to attend a wedding?" He didn't wait for an answer. "Yup (=yes), Michael and Hannah are going to tie the knot!"

It was a lovely wedding,　with all the people at the nursing home joining in the celebration.　Hannah wore a beige dress and looked beautiful.　Michael wore a dark blue suit and stood tall. The home gave them their own room, and if you ever wanted to see a 76- year-old bride and a 78-year old groom acting like two teen-agers,　you had to see this couple.

A perfect ending for a love affair that had lasted nearly 60 years.

elevator /'elɪveɪtə/ *n.* lift = (*AmE*) (*BrE*) a machine that carries people or goods up and down to different levels in a building or a mine. cf. **escalator** (moving stairs that carry people between different floors of a large building)

embrace /ɪm'breɪs/ *v.* **a.** to clasp (someone) with one's arms as an expression of affection or a greeting; **b.** to accept eagerly; **c.** to include or be made up of

break away **a.** leave or get away; **b.** to escape suddenly from sb who is keeping you prisoner; **c.** to change or depart from established customs or procedures

tie the knot (*infml*) to get married

beige /beɪʒ/ *adj.* light yellowish-brown in color

Cultural Notes

"Dear John" letter—The term "Dear John letter" refers to a letter written by a woman to her husband or boyfriend to inform him their relationship is over, usually because she has found another man. While the exact origins of the phrase are unknown, it is commonly believed to have been coined by Americans during World War II. Large numbers of American troops were stationed overseas for many months or years, and as time passed many of their wives or girlfriends decided to begin a relationship with a new man rather than wait for their old one to return. As letters to servicemen from wives or girlfriends back home would typically contain affectionate language, a serviceman receiving a note beginning with a curt "Dear John" (as opposed to the expected "Dear Johnny", "My dearest John", or simply "Darling", for example) would instantly be aware of the letter's purpose. In more recent times, women have come to be subjected to such impersonal break-up letters as well. These are referred to as "Dear Jane" letters.

Nursing home—Skilled nursing facility (SNF), or skilled nursing unit (SNU), also known as a rest home. It's a place of residence for people who require constant nursing care and have significant deficiencies with activities of daily living. Residents include the elderly and younger adults with physical disabilities. Adults 18 or older can stay in a skilled nursing facility to receive physical, occupational, and other rehabilitative therapies following an accident or illness. In the United States, nursing homes are required to have a licensed nurse on duty 24 hours a day, and during at least one shift each day, one of those nurses must be a Registered Nurse.

Sean Connery (1930—)—British movie superstar. Sir Thomas Sean Connery is a Scottish actor and producer who is perhaps best known as the first actor to portray James Bond in cinema, starring in seven Bond films. In 1987 he won the Academy Award for Best Supporting Actor for his role in *The Untouchables*. His other successful films include *The Name of the Rose* (1986), *The Hunt for Red October* (1990), *The Russia House* (1990), *The Rock* (1996), *Entrapment* (1999), etc. Connery has repeatedly been named as one of the most attractive men alive by various magazines, though he is older than most sex symbols. Sir Sean Connery was knighted by Queen Elizabeth II in July 2000.

Exercises

I. Answer the following questions based on the text.

1. What happened to the author on a freezing day?
2. Who was Hannah?
3. Where did the author find Hannah and Michael?
4. Who finally helped the author find the owner of the wallet and why?
5. How did the story about Hannah and Michael go after the author helped them meet again 60 years later?

II. Text Review. Write T for true and F for false in the brackets before each of the following statements.

(   ) 1. The author read the letter in the wallet because he was curious about it.

(   ) 2. The author called the operator to find the address of the owner of the wallet.

(   ) 3. The operator helped the author find the phone number of the address.

(   ) 4. Hannah didn't marry Michael because her mother didn't like him.

(   ) 5. Michael was around eighteen years old when he fell in love with Hannah.

(   ) 6. Young Michael was so handsome that no one could match up to him.

(   ) 7. It took the author two days to find the owner of the wallet.

(   ) 8. The guard knew the wallet very well because he had found it several times before.

(   ) 9. Mr. Goldstein always put his wallet in his coat pocket.

(   ) 10. Hannah and Michael continued to live in the nursing room after getting married.

III. Paraphrase the following phrases or sentences in English.

1. The only thing legible on the torn envelope was the return address.
2. The operator gave me her supervisor, who said there was a phone listed at the address, but that she could not give me the number.
3. Then, if the party wanted to talk, she would connect me.
4. The second she saw it, she took a deep breath.
5. "See how the good Lord works," I said philosophically. "If it's meant to be, it will be."

IV. Translate the following sentences into Chinese.

1. Perhaps if I called information the operator could find the phone number for the address shown on the envelope.

2. Hannah was a sweet, silver-haired old-timer with a warm smile and friendly eyes.

3. "Yes, Michael Goldstein was his name. If you find him, tell him I still think of him often. I never did marry," she said, smiling through tears that welled up in her eyes.

4. The second he saw it, he smiled with relief. "Yes," he said, "that's it. Must have dropped it this afternoon. I want to give you a reward."

5. A perfect ending for a love affair that had lasted nearly 60 years.

V. Respond to each of the following statements.

1. The heart that loves is always young.

2. True love is immortal.

3. In today's cynical world, the foundation for many marriages is not on selfless love.

4. Love is the attachment that results from deeply appreciating another's goodness.

5. Persistence can make a miracle!

VI. Provide a text which can support your viewpoint on one of the statements in *Exercise V*. Make your comments on the text you choose.

Unit Seven

Text A

A Conversation with a Cat
H. Belloc

《和一只猫的对话》类似于中国古人偷得浮生半日闲的境界，反映出一个人生孤独的主题，将对于生命的思考借对一只猫的自语道出。读来亲切又令人伤感。

The other day I went into the bar of a railway station, taking a glass of beer, sat down at a little table by myself to <u>meditate</u> upon the necessary but tragic isolation of the human soul. I began my meditation by consoling myself with the truth that something in common runs through all nature, but I went on to consider that this <u>cut no ice</u>, and that the heart needed something more. I might by long research have discovered some third term a little less <u>hackneyed</u> than these two, when fate, or some fostering star, sent me a <u>tawny</u> silky, long-haired cat.

If it be true that nations have the cats they deserve, then the English people deserve well in cats, for there are none so prosperous or so friendly in the world. But even for an English cat this cat was exceptionally friendly and fine—especially friendly. It leapt at one graceful bound into my lap, nestled there, put out an engaging right front paw to touch my arm with a pretty timidity by way of introduction, rolled up at me an eye of bright but innocent affection, and then smiled a secret smile of approval.

No man could be so timid after such an approach as not to make some manner of response. So did I. I even took the liberty of stroking Amathea (for by that name did I receive this vision), and though I began this gesture in a respectful fashion, after the best models of polite <u>deportment</u> with strangers, I was soon leading it some warmth, for I was touched to find that I had a friend; yes,

meditate /ˈmedɪteɪt/ v. **a.** to engage in contemplation or reflection; **b.** to engage in mental exercise (as concentration on one's breathing or repetition of a mantra) for the purpose of reaching a heightened level of spiritual awareness
cut no ice (*colloq.*) don't work, have no effect
hackney /ˈhækni/ v. **a.** to make common or frequent use of; **b.** to make trite, vulgar, or commonplace
tawny /ˈtɔːni/ *adj.* of a warm sandy color
deportment /dɪˈpɔːtmənt/ *n.* the manner in which one conducts oneself

even here, at the ends of the tubes in S. W. 99. I proceeded (as is right) from caress to speech, and said, "Amathea, most beautiful of cats, why have you deigned to single me out for so much favour? Did you recognize in me a friend to all that breathes, or were you yourself suffering from loneliness (though I take it you are near your own dear home), or is there pity in the hearts of animals as there is in the hearts of some humans? What, then, was your motive? Or am I, indeed, foolish to ask, and not rather to take whatever good comes to me in whatever way from the gods?"

caress /kəˈres/ *n.* a. an act or expression of kindness or affection, endearment; b. a light stroking, rubbing, or patting; c. kiss

deign /deɪn/ *v.* to condescend reluctantly and with a strong sense of the affront to one's superiority

dissension /dɪˈsenʃən/ *n.* disagreement; esp. partisan and contentious quarreling

bestow /bɪˈstəʊ/ *v.* a. to put to use, apply; b. to put in a particular or appropriate place; c. to convey as a gift—usu used with on or upon

disdain /dɪsˈdeɪn/ *n.* a feeling of contempt for someone or sth regarded as unworthy or inferior.

ful *adj.* full of or expressing disdain

beatitude /bi(ː)ˈætitjuːd/ *n.* a state of utmost bliss

repose /rɪˈpəʊz/ *n.* a. a state of resting after exertion or strain; esp. rest in sleep; b. eternal or heavenly rest; c. peace, tranquility; d. composure of manner, poise

To these questions Amathea answered with a loud purring noise, expressing with closed eyes of ecstasy her delight in encounter.

"I am more than flattered, Amathea," said I, by way of answer; "I am consoled. I did not know that there was in the world anything breathing and moving, let alone so tawny-perfect, who would give companionship for its own sake and seek out, through deep feeling, some one companion out of all living kind. If you do not address me in words I know the reason and I commend it; for in words lie the seeds of all dissension, and love at its most profound is silent. At least, I read that in a book, Amathea; yes, only the other day. But I confess that the book told me nothing of those gestures which are better than words, or of that caress which I continue to bestow upon you with all the gratitude of my poor heart."

To this Amathea made a slight gesture of acknowledgement—not disdainful—wagging her head a little, and then setting it down in deep content.

"Oh, beautiful-haired Amathea, many have praised you before you found me to praise you, and many will praise you, some in your own tongue, when I am no longer held in the bonds of your presence. But none will praise you more sincerely. For there is not a man living who knows better than I that the four charms of a cat lie in its closed eyes, its long and lovely hair, its silence, and even its affected love."

But at the word affected Amathea raised her head, looked up at me tenderly, once more put forth her paw to touch my arm, and then settled down again to purring beatitude.

"You are secure," said I sadly; "mortality is not before you. There is in your complacency no foreknowledge of death nor even of separation. And for that reason, Cat, I welcome you the more. For if there has been given to your kind this repose in common living, why, then we men also may find it by following your example and not considering too much what may be to come and not remembering too much what has been and will never return. Also, I thank you, for this, Amathea, my sweet Euplokamos" (for I was becoming a little familiar through an acquaintance of a full five minutes and from the absence of all recalcitrance), " that you have reminded me of my youth, and in a

recalcitrant /rɪ'kælsɪtrənt/ adj. a. difficult to manage or operate; b. not responsive to treatment; c. resistant. recalcitrance n.

enmity /'enmɪti/ n. positive, active, and typically mutual hatred or ill will

plaint /pleɪnt/ n. protest, complaint

treason /'triːzən/ n. a. the betrayal of a trust; b. the offense of attempting by overt acts to overthrow the government of the state

confer /kən'fɜː/ v. a. to give from or as if from a position of superiority; b. to give (as a property or characteristic) to someone or sth

beholden /bɪ'həʊldən/ adj. being under obligation for a favor or gift

sort of shadowy way, a momentary way, have restored it to me. For there is an age, a blessed youthful age (O my cat) even with the miserable race of men, when all things are consonant with the life of the body, when sleep is regular and long and deep, when enmities are either unknown or a subject for rejoicing and when the whole of being is lapped in hope as you are now lapped on my lap, Amathea. Yes, we also, we of the doomed race, know peace. But whereas you possess it from blind kittenhood to that last dark day so mercifully short with you, we grasp it only for a very little while. But I would not sadden you by the mortal plaint. That would be treason indeed, and a vile return for your goodness. What! When you have chosen me out of seven London millions upon whom to confer the tender solace of the heart, when you have proclaimed yourself so suddenly to be my dear, shall I introduce you to the sufferings of those of whom you know nothing save that they feed you, house you and pass you by? At least you do not take us for gods, as do the dogs, and the more am I humbly beholden to you for this little service of recognition—and something more."

Amathea slowly raised herself upon her four feet, arched her back, yawned, looked up at me with a smile sweeter than ever and then went round and round, preparing for herself a new couch upon my coat, whereon she settled and began once more to purr in settled ecstasy.

Already had I made sure that a rooted and anchored affection had come to me from out the emptiness and nothingness of the world and was to feed my soul henceforward; already had I changed the mood of long years and felt a conversion towards the life of things, an appreciation, a cousinship with the created light—and all that through one new link of loving kindness—when whatever it is that dashes the cup of bliss from the lips of mortal man (Tupper) up and dashed it good and hard. It was the Ancient Enemy who put the fatal sentence into my heart, for we are the playthings of the greater powers, and surely some of them are evil.

"You will never leave me, Amathea," I said; "I will respect your sleep and we will sit here together through all uncounted time, I holding you in my arms and you dreaming of fields of Paradise. Nor shall anything part us, Amethea; you are my cat and I am your human. Now and onwards into the fullness of peace."

discreet /dɪsˈkriːt/ *adj.* having or showing discernment or good judgment in conduct and esp. in speech
sacrament /ˈsækrəmənt/ *n.* a. a Christian rite (as baptism or the Eucharist) that is believed to have been ordained by Christ and that is held to be a means of divine grace or to be a sign or symbol of a spiritual reality; b. a religious rite or observance comparable to a Christian sacrament. sacramental *adj.*

Then it was that Amathea lifted herself once more, and with delicate, discreet, unweighted movement of perfect limbs leapt lightly to the floor as lovely as a wave. She walked slowly away from me without so much as looking back over her shoulder; she had another purpose in her mind; and as she so gracefully and so majestically neared the door which she was seeking, a short, unpleasant man standing at the bar said, "Puss, Puss, Puss!" and stooped to scratch her gently behind the ear. With what a wealth of singular affection, pure and profound, did she not gaze up at him, and then rub herself against his leg in token and external expression of a sacramental friendship that should never die.

Cultural Notes

Hilaire Belloc (1870—1953)—Born in 1870 in a village a dozen miles from Paris a few days before the start of the Franco-Prussian war. Because of the war, he and his sister were taken to England and when the family returned to their home at the end of the war, they found it utterly vandalized by the occupying German troops. This in some measure explains his life-long hostility to all things German. He returned to England and was educated at the Oratory School Birmingham, under Cardinal Newman, and later at Balliol College, Oxford, but before Balliol he went back to France to honor what he saw as an obligation to do his military service there, though he was not legally required to. His experience in the artillery influenced him strongly and, like another of his great loves, the sea never seems far from his mind in his writings. At Oxford, Belloc was famed both for brilliance in debate and high energy. He became President of the Oxford Union, but probably because of his decided, and not always, fashionable views, failed to be elected a don after graduating, and this remained a permanent disappointment and a grievance for him. His first book was a small volume of verse, published in 1896, and from then on a torrent of books, pamphlets, letters etc. poured from his pen. It astonishes, not only in its bulk but in its diversity; French and British history, military strategy, satire, comic and serious verse, literary criticism, topography and travel, transla-tions, religious, social and political commentary, long-running controversies with such opponents as H.G. wells and Dr. G.G. Coulton, and hundreds of essays, fill over one hundred and fifty volumes. It is little wonder that A.P. Herbert described him as "the man who wrote a library". During the 1914—1918 war he added greatly to his already huge work-load by his immensely detailed and authoritative war commentaries, each week filling much of the journal *Land and Water* which was dedicated to news of the war. *The Times* paid high tribute to Belloc's amazing powers in the field, drawing attention to his article in *London Magazine,* over 2 and a half years before the start of the war "in which he predicted, with the most extraordinary accuracy, the proceedings of the Germans at Liege as they have happened at the opening of the present war". *The Times* described this as "one of the most astonishingly accurate prophecies of a great war in the history of journalism." In that war, Belloc lost his son, Louis; then another son, Peter, died on active service in the war of 1939—1946, so Belloc would certainly have recalled the saying of Herodotus that "In pace sons bury their fathers; in war fathers bury their sons". It was after that third great loss in 1940 (his wife, Elodie, had died in 1910) that his health began to fail. He suffered a stroke, and although he lived until 1953, wrote virtually no more. Both during his lifetime and since, Belloc's refusal to tone down his views, and his contempt for the political, literary and social establishments of the day, militated against recognition of him as a major writer and thinker. Nor was he helped by the range of his work; critics like to pigeon-hole a writer as poet, historian, playwright, or novelist, and they could not cope with his diversity, huge output, and his overwhelming ebullience. They resented him. Even today, that fear and resentment is to be seen in the dismissive little articles and reviews, but slowly the truth is emerging that Hilaire Belloc is among the great writers of English prose and that the best of his verse is of equally high quality. More importantly, he was a thinker of power, significance and integrity. As Robert Speaight says in his biography of the Catholic author, "Men who had not always agreed with what Belloc said admired the way that he had said it." Perhaps more importantly, "no man of our time has fought so consistently for the good things." Hilaire Belloc was a big, turbulent and complicated man, and no subject for hagiography.

Amathea—Also called Amalthea. In Greek mythology, it was the she-goat (or, according to some, Nymph) nurse of the infant god Zeus who nourished him with her milk in a cave on Mount Ida after his mother had him sent to Crete so his father would not eat him. When the god reached maturity he created his thunder-shield from her hide. The goat later broke a horn, and Zeus filled it with the fruits of the harvest.   So the Horn of Amalthea became the symbol of plenty, and whoever had it in his or her possession would never starve.

Created light—According to the Bible, in the beginning of creation, when God made heaven and earth, the earth was without form and void, with darkness over the face of the abyss,   and a mighty wind that swept over the surface of the waters. God said, 'Let there be light', and there was light; and God saw that the light was good, and he separated light from darkness. He called the light day, and the darkness night. So evening came, and morning came, the first day.

Tupper (1810—1889)—Martin Farquhar Tupper, English writer, the author of Proverbial Philosophy, was born in London on the 17th of July 1810. He was the son of Martin Tupper, a doctor, who came of an old Huguenot family. He was educated at Charterhouse and at Christ Church, Oxford, where he gained a prize for a theological essay, Gladstone being second to him. He was called to the bar at Lincoln's Inn,   but never practised.   He began a long career of authorship in 1832 with Sacra Poesis,   and in 1838 he published Geraldine,   and other Poems, and for fifty years was fertile in producing both verse and prose;   but his name is indissolubly connected with his long series of didactic moralisings in blank verse, the Proverbial Philosophy (1838—1867), which for about twenty-five years enjoyed an extraordinary popularity that has ever since been the cause of persistent satire. The first part was, however, a comparative failure, and N. P. Willis, the American author,   took it to be a forgotten work of the 17th century.   The commonplace character of Tupper's reflections is indubitable,   and his blank verse is only prose cut up into suitable lengths; but the Proverbial Philosophy was full of a perfectly genuine moral and religious feeling,   and contained many apt and striking expressions.   By these qualities it appealed to a large and uncritical section of the public. A genial, warm-hearted man, Tupper's humane instincts prompted him to espouse many reforming movements; he was an early supporter of the Volunteer movement,   and did much to promote good relations with America.   He was also a mechanical inventor in a small way.   In 1886 he published *My Life* as an Author;   and on the 29th of November 1889 he died at Albury, Surrey.

Ancient Enemy—It refers to SATAN in the Bible.   As it is told in Genesis 2, God created Adam and Eve as the first people in the world and let them live in the Garden of Eden.   God told Adam that he was free to eat from every tree in the garden, except the tree of knowledge of good and evil. Later, Satan, speaking through a serpent, deceived Eve to eat the fruit. She then took the fruit to Adam and he ate it knowing he was doing the wrong thing. Because they disobeyed what God had explicitly told them and chose to believe Satan, they began to experience spiritual death, and soon physical death. God expelled them from the garden. No longer would it be easy to harvest fruit. Thorns and weeds would make planting and harvesting hard labor. Men would have to work to eat. Women would give birth in pain. Animals became dangerous and carnivorous. Satan, also known as the devil, is mentioned frequently in the Bible. Most conservative Christian churches teach beliefs that Satan is a profoundly evil, fallen angel who is totally dedicated to the destruction of everyone's lives. He is a supernatural being who "walketh about, seeking whom he may devour," and is aided by countless demons. He and his demons are all pervasive. They engage in world-wide "spiritual warfare," and are a continual threat to all. There are many popular ideas about this evil spirit being. Some think that Satan is not real, but is rather a personification of the wickedness that abides in the world. Others admit that the devil exists, but presume that he is now confined in the fiery pits of an ever burning hell. Still others believe that Satan is free and actively promoting sinfulness in our world today.

sacrament—It's a Latin word, meaning something holy, or an outward sign of something sacred. In Christianity, a sacrament is commonly defined as having been instituted by Jesus and consisting of a visible sign of invisible grace. Christianity is divided as to the number and operation of sacraments. The traditional view held by Orthodox, Roman Catholics, and certain Anglicans counts the sacraments as seven—Eucharist, baptism, confirmation, penance, anointing of the sick, matrimony, and holy orders. These are held to produce grace in the soul of the recipient by the very performance of the sacramental act; the recipient need only have the right intention. Most Protestant denominations recognize two sacraments—baptism and communion, or the Lord's Supper. Protestants hold generally that it is the faith of the participant, itself a gift of God, rather than the power of the sacramental act that produces grace. A conventional division of the seven sacraments sets apart the "sacraments of the dead," i.e. baptism and penance, because they are for souls in a state of sin; the rest, "sacraments of the living," are conferred on souls in a state of grace.

Exercises

I. Answer the following questions based on the text.

1. Why did the speaker think the isolation of the human soul was necessary but tragic?
2. Why did the speaker welcome the cat so much?
3. What stopped the conversion towards the life of things that the man felt in his heart?
4. How do you understand the affection of the cat for the man?
5. What kind of people do you think the speaker is?

II. Text review. Write T for true and F for false in the bracket before the statement.

(   ) 1. The cat annoyed the speaker much with its purring.
(   ) 2. The speaker called the cat Amathea to show his contempt for its timidity.
(   ) 3. There is pity in the heart of the cat as in those of human beings.
(   ) 4. The cat was pleased at the encounter with the speaker.
(   ) 5. The speaker thinks that the best communication is in words.
(   ) 6. Amathea acknowledged the man's caress by wagging her head slightly.
(   ) 7. Mortality is the source of woe to humans according to the author.
(   ) 8. Even in the youth, human beings as the doomed race, cannot enjoy peace.
(   ) 9. Cats take people for gods as much as dogs do.
(   ) 10. The man felt reassured when he saw Amathea gazing at another man with much affection.

III. Paraphrase the following sentences in English.

1. I might by long research have discovered some third term a little less hackneyed than these two, when fate, or some fostering star, sent me a tawny silky, long-haired cat.
2. No man could be so timid after such an approach as not to make some manner of response.
3. For if there has been given to your kind this repose in common living, why, then we men also may find it by following your example and not considering too much what may be to come and not remembering too much what has been and will never return.

4. Already had I made sure that a rooted and anchored affection had come to me from out the emptiness and nothingness of the world and was to feed my soul henceforward...

5. Then it was that Amathea lifted herself once more, and with delicate, discreet, unweighted movement of perfect limbs leapt lightly to the floor as lovely as a wave.

IV. Translate the following sentences into Chinese.

1. I began my meditation by consoling myself with the truth that something in common runs through all nature, but I went on to consider that this cut no ice, and that the heart needed something more.

2. If it be true that nations have the cats they deserve, then the English people deserve well in cats, for there are none so prosperous or so friendly in the world.

3. But I confess that the book told me nothing of those gestures which are better than words, or of that caress which I continue to bestow upon you with all the gratitude of my poor heart.

4. For there is an age, a blessed youthful age (O my cat) even with the miserable race of men, when all things are consonant with the life of the body, when sleep is regular and long and deep, when enmities are either unknown or a subject for rejoicing and when the whole of being is lapped in hope as you are now lapped on my lap, Amathea.

5. With what a wealth of singular affection, pure and profound, did she not gaze up at him, and then rub herself against his leg in token and external expression of a sacramental friendship that should never die.

V. Respond to each of the following statements.

1. In words lie the seeds of all dissension, and love at its most profound is silent.

2. If we do not consider too much what the future holds for us, nor do we remember too much what has been and will never return, we men also may find a peaceful mind.

3. We are the playthings of the greater powers, some of which are evil.

4. The human soul is suffering from some kind of loneliness which is necessary but tragic.

5. There is an age even with the miserable race of men, when all things are consonant with the life, when enmities are either unknown or a subject for rejoicing and when the whole of being is lapped in hope.

VI. Provide a text which can support your viewpoint on one of the statements in *Exercise V*. Make your comment on the text you choose.

Text B

Listening

Eudora Welty

《倾听》本文以一位作者的口吻,叙述童年时代对于成人之间谈话的倾听和感受,怀着一种回忆的温馨娓娓道来那段经历对于自己写作生涯的影响。让我们的耳畔似乎也响起小时候那些熟悉的声音。

In that vanished time in small-town Jackson, most of the ladies I was familiar with, the mothers of my friends in the neighborhood, were busiest when they were sociable. In the afternoons there was regular visiting up and down the little grid of residential streets. Everybody had calling cards, even certain children; and newborn babies themselves were properly announced by sending out their tiny engraved calling cards attached with a pink or blue bow to those of their parents. Graduation presents to high-school pupils were often "card cases". On the hall table in every house the first thing you saw was a silver tray waiting to receive more calling cards on top of the stack already piled up like jackstraws; they were never thrown away.

My mother let none of this idling, as she saw it, pertain to her. She went her own way with or without her calling cards, and though she was fond of her friends and they were fond of her, she had little time for small talk. At first, I hadn't known what I'd missed.

When we at length bought our first automobile, one of our neighbors was often invited to go with us on the family Sunday afternoon ride. In Jackson it was counted an affront to the neighbors to start out for anywhere with an empty seat in the car. My mother sat in the back with her friend, and I'm told that as a small child I would ask to

grid /grɪd/ *n.* a network of uniformly spaced horizontal and perpendicular lines (as for locating points on a map); also sth resembling such a network

jackstraws *n.* (*pl.*) **a.** a game in which a set of straws or thin strips is let fall in a heap with each player in turn trying to remove one at a time without disturbing the rest; **b.** one of the pieces used in the game jackstraws

pertain /pəˈteɪn/ *v.* **a.** to belong as a part, member, accessory, or product; **b.** to belong as a duty or right; **c.** to be appropriate to sth

affront /əˈfrʌnt/ *n.* a deliberate offense, insult

sit in the middle, and say as we started off, "Now talk."

There was dialogue throughout the lady's accounts to my mother. "I said"..."He said"... "And I'm told she very plainly said"... "it was midnight before they finally heard, and what do you think it was."

What I loved about her stories was that everything happened in scenes. I might not catch on to what the root of the trouble was in all that happened, but my ear told me it was dramatic. Often she said, "The crisis had come."

This same lady was one of Mother's callers on the telephone who always talked a long time. I knew who it was when my mother would only reply, now and then, "Well, I declare," or "you don't say so," or "Surely not." She'd be standing at the wall telephone, listening against her will, and I'd sit on the stairs close by her. Our telephone had a little bar set into the handle which had to be pressed and held down to keep the connection open, and when her friend had said goodbye, my mother needed me to prize her fingers loose from the little bar; her grip had become paralyzed. "What did she say?" I asked.

"She wasn't saying a thing in this world," sighed my mother. "She was just ready to talk, that's all."

My mother was right. Years later, beginning with my story "Why I live at the P.O.", I wrote reasonably often in the form of a monologue that takes possession of the speaker. How much more gets told besides!

This lady told everything in her sweet, marveling voice, and meant every word of it kindly. She enjoyed my company perhaps even more than my mother's. She invited me to catch her doodlebugs; under the trees in her backyard were dozens of their holes. When you stuck a broom straw down one and called, "Doodlebug, doodlebug, your house is on fire and all your children are burning up," she believed this is why the doodlebug came running out of the hole. This was why I loved to call up her doodlebugs instead of ours.

My mother could never have told me her stories, and I think I knew why even then: my mother didn't believe them. But I could listen to this murmuring lady all day. She believed everything she heard, like the doodlebug. And so did I.

This was a day when ladies' and children's clothes were very often made at home. My mother cut out all the dresses and her little boys' rompers, and a sewing woman would come and spend the day upstairs in the sewing room fitting and stitching them all. This was Fannie. This old black sewing woman,

dialogue /'daɪəlɒg/ n. a. a conversation between two or more persons; also a similar exchange between a person and sth else (as a computer); b. an exchange of ideas and opinions; c. a discussion between representatives of parties to a conflict that is aimed at resolution

doodlebug /'duːdlbʌg/ n. a. the larva of an ant lion; also any of several other insects; b. a device (as a divining rod) used in attempting to locate underground gas, water, oil, or ores

romper /'rɒmpə/ n. a jumpsuit for infants—often used in plural

along with her speed and dexterity, brought along a great provision of up-to-the-minute news. She spent her life going from family to family in town and worked right in its bosom, and nothing could stop her. My mother would try, while I stood being pinned up. "Fannie, I'd rather Eudora didn't hear that." "That" would be just what I was longing to hear, whatever it was. "I don't want her exposed to gossip" —as if gossip were measles and I could catch it. I did catch some of it but not enough.

dexterity /deks'terɪti/ *n.* a. mental skill or quickness, adroitness; b. readiness and grace in physical activity; esp. skill and ease in using the hands

gossip /'gɒsɪp/ *n.* a. rumor or report of an intimate nature; b. a chatty talk; c. the subject matter of gossip

tantalize /'tæntəlaɪz/ *v.* to tease or torment by or as if by presenting sth desirable to the view but continually keeping it out of reach

worldly /'wɜːldli/ *adj.* a. of, relating to, or devoted to this world and its pursuits rather than to religion or spiritual affairs; b. possessing a practical and often shrewd understanding of human affairs

derogatory /dɪ'rɒgətəri/ *adj.* a. detracting from the character or standing of sth—often used with to, towards, or of; b. expressive of a low opinion

gist /dʒɪst/ *n.* a. the ground of a legal action; b. the main point or part, essence

instinct /'ɪnstɪŋkt/ *n.* a. a natural or inherent aptitude, impulse, or capacity; b. a largely inheritable and unalterable tendency of an organism to make a complex and specific response to environmental stimuli without involving reason

"Mrs. O'Neil's oldest daughter she had her wedding dress tried on, and all her fine underclothes featherstitched and ribbon run in and then—" "I think that will do, Fannie," said my mother. It was tantalizing never to be exposed long enough to hear the end.

Fannie was the worldliest old lady to be imagined. She could do whatever her hands were doing without having to stop talking, and she could speak in a wonderfully derogatory way with any number of pins stuck in her mouth. Her hands steadied me like claws as she stumped on her knees around me, tacking me together. The gist of her tale would be lost on me, but Fannie didn't bother about the ear she was telling it to; she just liked telling. She was like an author. In fact, for a good deal of what she said, I daresay she was the author.

Long before I wrote stories, I listened for stories. Listening for them is something more acute than listening to them. I suppose it's an early form of participation in what goes on. Listening children know that stories are there. When their elders sit and begin, children are just waiting and hoping for one to come out, like a mouse from its hole.

It was taken entirely for granted that there wasn't any lying in our family, and I was advanced in adolescence before I realized that in plenty of homes where I played with schoolmates and went to parties, children lied to their parents and parents lied to their children and to each other. It took me a long time to realize that these very same everyday lies, and the stratagems and jokes and tricks and dares that went with them, were in fact the basis of the scenes I so well loved to hear about and hoped for and treasured in conversation of adults.

My instinct—the dramatic instinct—was to lead me, eventually, on the right track for a storyteller: the scene was full of hints, pointers, suggestions, and promises of things to find out and know about human beings. I had to grow up and learn to listen for the unspoken as well as the spoken—and to know a truth, I also had to recognize a lie.

Cultural Notes

Eudora Welthy (1909—2001)—Born in Jackson, Mississippi, she attended the Mississippi College for Women, graduated from the University of Wisconsin (1929) and studied advertising at Columbia University for a year. Her first short story appeared in 1936, and gradually she began to be published in small, then regional and general circulation magazines. She published collections of her short stories and began publishing novels, as well. Soon after her first novel was published, she stopped writing to care full-time for her family for fifteen years: for two brothers with severe arthritis and her mother who had had a stroke. After her mother died in 1966, she returned to writing. She was a 6-time winner of the O. Henry Award for Short Stories, and her many awards include the National Medal for Literature, the American Book Award, and, in 1969, a Pulitzer Prize. Welty's memoir (*One Writer's Beginnings*) as well as *A Curtain of Green, The Wide Net, The Golden Apples*, and *The Bride of the Innisfallen* are included in the Library of America volume. She was also an accomplished and published photographer. But it is for her fiction, usually set in the rural South, that she's known as the First Lady of Southern Literature. She will always be literary voice and soul of the South in America.

Jackson—Jackson County was established at the same time as Hancock County, December 14, 1812. The county was named for President Andrew Jackson. Its largest town and county seat is Pascagoula, formerly Scranton, located on the Pascagoula Bay and river. The folks who live here pride themselves with the fact that their city of less than half a million people is rich in cultural offerings. With a city orchestra, opera and two ballet companies, visitors can indulge in fine arts in the comfort of a smaller setting. In addition to literary stories, there is the great oral tradition here in Jackson, and the city abounds with storytellers.

Calling card—The first visiting cards appeared in France during the reign of Louis XIV. As an adoption from French court etiquette, visiting cards came to America and Europe. They included refined engraved ornaments and fantastic coat of arms. Visiting cards, or calling cards, were an essential accessory to any 19th century middle class lady or gentleman. In the United States there was a rigid distinction between business and visiting cards. The visiting cards served as tangible evidence of meeting social obligations, as well as a streamlined letter of introduction. The stack of cards in the card tray in the hall was a handy catalog of exactly who had called and whose calls might need to be returned. They did smack of affectation however, and were not generally used among country folk or working class Americans. Business cards on the other hand, were widespread among men and women, of all classes with a business to promote. It was considered to be in very poor taste to use a business card when making a social call. A business card, left with the servants, could imply that you had called to collect a bill. Ladies' and gentlemen's Calling Cards were to be exchanged according to the existing etiquette rules, such as,

- On making a first call you must have a card for each lady of the household.
- On making a call leave your card to the servant. You will be allowed to see the hostess only after she examines your card.
- On the hall table in every house, there should be a small silver, or other card tray, a pad and a pencil.
- When the door-bell rings, the servant on duty should have the card tray ready to present, on the palm of the left hand.
- A gentleman should carry them loose in a convenient pocket; but a lady may use a card case.
- Do not examine the cards in the card-basket. You have no right to investigate as to who calls on a lady.
- A young lady can have a card of her own after having been in society a year.
- American gentleman should never fold the corner of his card, despite of the temporary fashion. Some European gentlemen, on the contrary, fold the upper right corner to indicate that they've delivered it themselves (the servant should never hand his master's card folded).
- Fold the card in the middle if you wish to indicate that the call is on several, or all of the members of the family.

Small talk—In most English-speaking countries, it is normal and necessary to make "small talk" in certain situations. Small talk is a casual form of conversation that "breaks the ice" or fills an awkward silence between people. Even though you may feel shy using your second language, it is sometimes considered rude to say nothing. People with many different relationships use small talk. The most common type of people to use small talk are those who do not know each other at all. It is also common for people who are only acquaintances, often called a "friend of a friend", to use small talk. Other people who have short casual conversations are office employees who may not be good friends but work in the same department. Customer service representatives, waitresses, hairdressers and receptionists often make small talk with customers. There are certain "safe" topics that people usually make small talk about. The weather is probably the number one thing that people who do not know each other well discuss. Sometimes even friends and family members discuss the weather when they meet or start a conversation. Another topic that is generally safe is current events. As long as you are not discussing a controversial issue, such as a recent law concerning equal rights, it is usually safe to discuss the news. Sports news is a very common topic, especially if a local team or player is in a tournament or play-off or doing extremely well or badly. Entertainment news, such as a celebrity who is in town, is another good topic. If there is something that you and the other speaker has in common, that may also be acceptable to talk about. There are also some subjects that are not considered acceptable when making small talk. Discussing personal information such as salaries or a recent divorce is not done between people who do not know each other well. Compliments on clothing or hair are acceptable; however, you should never say something (good or bad) about a person's body. Private issues or negative comments about another person not involved in the conversation are also not acceptable. People make small talk just about anywhere, but there are certain places where it is very common. Most often, small talk occurs in places where people are waiting for something. For example, you might chat with another person who is waiting for the bus to arrive, or to the person beside you waiting to get on an aeroplane. People also make small talk in a doctor's or dentist's waiting room, or in queues at the grocery store. Just remember, in an English-speaking environment it is often better to make a few mistakes than to say nothing at all!

Exercises

I. Answer the following questions based on the text.

1. What kind of picture was described in the first paragraph?
2. What does the author mean by the word "scenes"?
3. Why did the author recite the rhyme for catching doodlebugs here?
4. Did the two "catch"s have the same meaning in "as if gossip were measles and I could *catch* it. I did *catch* some of it"?
5. How did the girl feel like listening to the adults' talks?

II. Text review. Write T for true and F for false in the bracket before the statement.

( ) 1. At that time in Jackson everyone had calling cards except newborn babies.

( ) 2. Mother didn't use calling cards because they were not important in people's social life.

( ) 3. The girl could remember clearly the stories told by the neighbor lady in their car.

( ) 4. Mother was fond of listening to the murmuring of her friend, though she had a lot of things to do.

( ) 5. The lady liked to tell stories because she believed everything she heard.

( ) 6. The sewing woman did the cutting, fitting and stitching for everyone in the family.

( ) 7. Mother asked her daughter to learn how to make clothes from the black woman.

( ) 8. Fannie kept on telling all kinds of stories about people, much being created by herself.

( ) 9. It seems that lies exist in every family and is a necessary part of daily life.

( ) 10. The scenes in story-telling have much to do with the nature of human beings.

III. Paraphrase the following sentences in English.

1. My mother let none of this idling, as she saw it, pertain to her.

2. I might not catch on to what the root of the trouble was in all that happened, but my ear told me it was dramatic.

3. I wrote reasonably often in the form of a monologue that takes possession of the speaker.

4. It was tantalizing never to be exposed long enough to hear the end.

5. Long before I wrote stories, I listened for stories.

IV. Translate the following sentences into Chinese.

1. On the hall table in every house the first thing you saw was a silver tray waiting to receive more calling cards on top of the stack already piled up like jack-straws.

2. In Jackson it was counted an affront to the neighbors to start out for anywhere with an empty seat in the car.

3. My mother sat in the back with her friend, and I'm told that as a small child I would ask to sit in the middle, and say as we started off, "Now talk."

4. This old black sewing woman, along with her speed and dexterity, brought along a great provision of up-to-the-minute news.

5. It took me a long time to realize that these very same everyday lies, and the stratagems and jokes and tricks and dares that went with them, were in fact the basis of the *scenes* I so well loved to hear about and hoped for and treasured in conversation of adults.

V. Respond to each of the following statements.

1. Listening *for* stories is something more acute than listening *to* them.

2. The lies, jokes and tricks that are prevalent in people's everyday conversation consist of the basis of stories.

3. Writing requires listening for the unspoken as well as the spoken.

4. Great literature is simply language charged with meaning to the utmost possible degree.

5. Literature is a kind of intellectual light, which, like the sunlight, may sometimes enable us to see what we do not like.

VI. Provide a text which can support your viewpoint on one of the statements in *Exercise V*. Make your comment on the text you choose.

Unit Eight

The Oval Portrait

Edgar Allen Poe

《椭圆画像》艾德加·艾伦·坡的小说一直以怪异荒诞驰名,本文通过死者还魂的故事,展现了这一特点。该主题是坡的小说中一个反复出现的主题。

THE CHATEAU into which my valet had ventured to make forcible entrance, rather than permit me, in my desperately wounded condition, to pass a night in the open air, was one of those piles of commingled gloom and grandeur which have so long frowned among the Appennines, not less in fact than in the fancy of Mrs. Radcliffe. To all appearance it had been temporarily and very lately abandoned. We established ourselves in one of the smallest and least sumptuously furnished apartments. It lay in a remote turret of the building. Its decorations were rich, yet tattered and antique. Its walls were hung with tapestry and bedecked with manifold and multiform armorial trophies, together with an unusually great number of very spirited modern paintings in frames of rich golden arabesque. In these paintings, which depended from the walls not only in their main surfaces, but in very many nooks which the bizarre architecture of the chateau rendered necessary—in these paintings my incipient delirium, perhaps, had caused me to take deep interest; so that I bade Pedro to close the heavy shutters of the room-since it was already night-to light

commingle /kə'mɪŋgəl/ *v.* a. to blend thoroughly into a harmonious whole; b. to combine (funds or properties) into a common fund or stock.

sumptuous /'sʌmptjuəs/ *adj.* extremely costly, rich, luxurious, or magnificent

turret /'tʌrɪt/ *n.* a little tower; specifically an ornamental structure at an angle of a larger structure

tattered /'tætəd/ *adj.* a. worn to shreds; or wearing torn or ragged clothing; b. ruined or disrupted

bedeck /bɪ'dek/ *v.* decorate

arabesque /ˌærə'besk/ *n.* a. an ornament or style that employs flower, foliage, or fruit and sometimes animal and figural outlines to produce an intricate pattern of interlaced lines; b. a posture (as in ballet) in which the body is bent forward from the hip on one leg with one arm extended forward and the other arm and leg backward; c. an elaborate or intricate pattern

incipient /ɪn'sɪpiənt/ *adj.* only partly in existence; imperfectly formed

delirium /dɪ'lɪriəm/ *n.* a. state of violent mental agitation; b. a usually brief state of excitement and mental confusion often accompanied by hallucinations

the tongues of a tall candelabrum which stood by the head of my bed—and to throw open far and wide the fringed curtains of black velvet which enveloped the bed itself. I wished all this done that I might resign myself, if not to sleep, at least alternately to the contemplation of these pictures, and the perusal of a small volume which had been found upon the pillow, and which purported to criticise and describe them.

Long—long I read—and devoutly, devotedly I gazed. Rapidly and gloriously the hours flew by and the deep midnight came. The position of the candelabrum displeased me, and outreaching my hand with difficulty, rather than disturb my slumbering valet, I placed it so as to throw its rays more fully upon the book.

But the action produced an effect altogether unanticipated. The rays of the numerous candles (for there were many) now fell within a niche of the room which had hitherto been thrown into deep shade by one of the bed-posts. I thus saw in vivid light a picture all unnoticed before. It was the portrait of a young girl just ripening into womanhood. I glanced at the painting hurriedly, and then closed my eyes. Why I did this was not at first apparent even to my own perception. But while my lids remained thus shut, I ran over in my mind my reason for so shutting them. It was an impulsive movement to gain time for thought—to make sure that my vision had not deceived me—to calm and subdue my fancy for a more sober and more certain gaze. In a very few moments I again looked fixedly at the painting.

That I now saw aright I could not and would not doubt; for the first flashing of the candles upon that canvas had seemed to dissipate the dreamy stupor which was stealing over my senses, and to startle me at once into waking life.

The portrait, I have already said, was that of a young girl. It was a mere head and shoulders, done in what is technically termed a vignette manner; much in the style of the favorite heads of Sully. The arms, the bosom, and even the ends of the radiant hair melted imperceptibly into the vague yet deep shadow which formed the back-ground of the whole. The frame was oval, richly gilded and filigreed in Moresque. As a thing

candelabrum /kændɪ'lɑːbrəm/ n. branched ornamental candlestick having several lights

fringe /frɪndʒ/ n. an ornamental border consisting of short straight or twisted threads or strips hanging from cut or raveled edges or from a separate band

peruse /pə'ruːz/ v. a. to examine or consider with attention and in detail, study; b. to look over or through in a casual or cursory manner; c. read; esp. to read over in an attentive or leisurely manner. perusal n.

purport /pɜː'pɒt/ v. a. to have the often specious appearance of being, intending, or claiming (sth implied or inferred); claim; b. intend, purpose

devout /dɪ'vaʊt/ adj. a. expressing devotion or piety; b. devoted to a pursuit, belief, or mode of behavior, earnest; c. warmly sincere

niche /nɪtʃ/ n. a. a recess in a wall esp. for a statue; b. sth that resembles a niche

hitherto /ˌhɪðə'tuː/ adv. used to describe a situation that has existed up to this point or up to the present time

aright /ə'raɪt/ adv. in a correct manner

dissipate /'dɪsɪpeɪt/ v. a. to break up and drive off (as a crowd); b. to cause to spread thin or scatter and gradually vanish; c. to spend or use up wastefully or foolishly

stupor /'stjuːpə/ n. a. the feeling of distress and disbelief that you have when sth bad happens accidentally; b. marginal consciousness

filigree /'filɪgriː/ n. delicate and intricate ornamentation (usually in gold or silver or other fine twisted wire)

of art nothing could be more admirable than the painting itself. But it could have been neither the execution of the work, nor the immortal beauty of the countenance, which had so suddenly and so vehemently moved me. Least of all, could it have been that my fancy, shaken from its half slumber, had mistaken the head for that of a living person. I saw at once that the peculiarities of the design, of the vignetting, and of the frame, must have instantly dispelled such idea—must have prevented even its momentary entertainment. Thinking earnestly upon these points, I remained, for an hour perhaps, half sitting, half reclining, with my vision riveted upon the portrait. At length, satisfied with the true secret of its effect, I fell back within the bed. I had found the spell of the picture in an absolute life-likeliness of expression, which, at first startling, finally confounded, subdued, and appalled me. With deep and reverent awe I replaced the candelabrum in its former position. The cause of my deep agitation being thus shut from view, I sought eagerly the volume which discussed the paintings and their histories. Turning to the number which designated the oval portrait, I there read the vague and quaint words which follow:

"She was a maiden of rarest beauty, and not more lovely than full of glee. And evil was the hour when she saw, and loved, and wedded the painter. He, passionate, studious, austere, and having already a bride in his Art; she a maiden of rarest beauty, and not more lovely than full of glee; all light and smiles, and frolicsome as the young fawn; loving and cherishing all things; hating only the Art which was her rival; dreading only the pallet and brushes and other untoward instruments which deprived her of the countenance of her lover. It was thus a terrible thing for this lady to hear the painter speak of his desire to portray even his young bride. But she was humble and obedient, and sat meekly for many weeks in the dark, high turret-chamber where the light dripped upon the pale canvas only from overhead. But he, the painter, took glory in his work, which went on from hour to hour, and from day to day. And he was a passionate, and wild, and moody man, who became lost in reveries; so that he would not see that the light which fell so ghastly in that lone turret withered the health and the spirits of his bride, who pined visibly to all but him. Yet she smiled on and still on, uncomplainingly, because she saw that the painter (who had high renown) took a fervid and burning pleasure in his task, and wrought day and night to depict her who so loved

countenance /'kaʊntɪnəns/ n. a. the appearance conveyed by a person's face; b. the human face

confound /kən'faʊnd/ v. to throw (a person) into confusion or perplexity

subdue /sʌb'djuː/ v. a. put down by force or intimidation; b. hold within limits and control; c. get on top of; deal with successfully

appall /ə'pɔːl/ v. to overcome with shock or dismay

quaint /kweɪnt/ adj. a. unusual or different in character or appearance, odd; b. pleasingly or strikingly old-fashioned or unfamiliar

glee /gliː/ n. exultant high-spirited joy

austere /ɔː'stɪə/ adj. a. stern and cold in appearance or manner; b. somber, grave

frolicsome /'frɒlɪksəm/ adj. full of gaiety, playful

pallet /'pælɪt/ n. board that provides a flat surface on which artists mix paints and the range of colors used

untoward /ˌʌntə'wɔːd/ adj. difficult to guide, manage, or work with

him, yet who grew daily more dispirited and weak. And in sooth some who beheld the portrait spoke of its resemblance in low words, as of a mighty marvel, and a proof not less of the power of the painter than of his deep love for her

surpassing /səːˈpɑːsɪŋ/ *adj.* greatly exceeding others, of a very high degree
surpassingly *adv.*
pallid /ˈpælɪd/ *adj.* a. deficient in color, wan; b. lacking sparkle or liveliness, dull
aghast /əˈgɑːst/ *adj.* struck with terror, amazement, or horror, shocked

whom he depicted so surpassingly well. But at length, as the labor drew nearer to its conclusion, there were admitted none into the turret; for the painter had grown wild with the ardor of his work, and turned his eyes from canvas merely, even to regard the countenance of his wife. And he would not see that the tints which he spread upon the canvas were drawn from the cheeks of her who sat beside him. And when many weeks had passed, and but little remained to do, save one brush upon the mouth and one tint upon the eye, the spirit of the lady again flickered up as the flame within the socket of the lamp. And then the brush was given, and then the tint was placed; and, for one moment, the painter stood entranced before the work which he had wrought; but in the next, while he yet gazed, he grew tremulous and very pallid, and aghast, and crying with a loud voice, 'This is indeed life itself!' turned suddenly to regard his beloved: —She was dead!"

Cultural Notes

Edgar Allen Poe (1809—1849)—Born on 19 January 1809 in Boston, Massachusetts, the son of actors Elizabeth Arnold Hopkins (1787—1811) and David Poe (1784—1810). He had a brother named William Henry (1807—1831) and sister Rosalie (1811—1874). After the death of his parents Edgar was taken in by John Allan, a wealthy merchant in Richmond, Virginia. Young Edgar traveled with the Allans to England in 1815 and attended school in Chelsea. In 1820 he was back in Richmond where he attended the University of Virginia and studied Latin and poetry and also loved to swim and act. While in school he became estranged from his foster father after accumulating gambling debts. Unable to pay them or support himself, Poe left school and enlisted in the United States Army where he served for two years. He had been writing poetry for some time and in 1827 *"Dreams"—Oh! that my young life were a lasting dream!* first appeared in the Baltimore North American, the same year his first book *Tamerlane and Other Poems* was published, at his own expense. Poe enlisted in the West Point Military Academy but was dismissed a year later. In 1829 his second book *Al Aaraaf, Tamerlane and Minor Poems* was published. The same year *Poems* (1831) was published Poe moved to Baltimore to live with his aunt Maria Clemm, mother of Virginia Eliza Clemm (1822—1847) who would become his wife at the age of thirteen. His brother Henry was also living in the Clemm household but he died of tuberculosis soon after Edgar moved in. In 1833, *the Baltimore Saturday Visiter* published some of his poems and he won a contest in it for his story "MS found in a Bottle". In 1835 he became editor and contributor of *the Southern Literary Messenger.* Though not without his detractors and troubles with employers, it was the start of his career as respected critic and essayist. Other publications which he contributed to were Burton's *Gentleman's Magazine* (1839—1840), Graham's *Magazine* (1841—1842), *Evening Mirror,* and Godey's *Lady's Book.* As an important American poet, critic, short story writer, and author of such macabre works as *The Fall of the House of Usher* (1840), Edgar Poe contributes greatly to the genres of horror and science fiction and is now considered the father of the modern detective story. He is especially highly lauded as a poet. Poe's psychologically thrilling tales examining the depths of the human psyche earned him much fame during his lifetime and after his death. His own life was marred by tragedy at an early age (his parents died before he was three years old) and in his oft-quoted works we can see his darkly passionate sensibilities—a tormented and sometimes neurotic obsession with death and violence and overall appreciation for the beautiful yet tragic mysteries of life. Poe's literary criticisms of poetry and the art of short story writing include *The Poetic Principal* and *The Philosophy of Composition.* There have been numerous collections of his works published and many of them have been inspiration for popular television and film adaptations including *The Tell-Tale Heart, The Black Cat*, and *The Raven.* He has been the subject of numerous biographers and has significantly influenced many other authors even into the 21st Century.

Mrs. Radcliffe (1764—1823)—Ann Radcliffe, English novelist, born in London. The daughter of a successful tradesman, she married William Radcliffe, a law student who later became editor of the English Chronicle. Her best works, *The Romance of the Forest* (1791), *The Mysteries of Udolpho* (1794), and *The Italian* (1797), give her a prominent place in the tradition of the Gothic romance. Her works were extremely popular among the upper class and the growing middle class, especially among young women. Stylistically, Radcliffe was noted for her vivid descriptions of exotic locales, though in reality the author had rarely or never visited the actual locations. In her tales, scenes of terror and suspense are infused with an aura of romantic sensibility. Her excellent use of landscape to create mood and her sense of mystery and suspense had an enormous influence on later writers and produced many imitators.

vignette—A photographic portrait which is clear in the center, and fades off into the surrounding color at the edges. It's a visual effect of darkened corners used to help frame an image or soften the frame outline. Graphically the term refers to a kind of decorative design usually in books, used both to separate sections or chapters and to decorate borders; these were often based on vine—leaves. It's also used for short descriptive literature focusing on a particular moment or person.

Sully—Thomas Sully, born in Horncastle in Lincolnshire, England, on June 8 (some sources say June 19), 1783, to actors Sarah Chester and Matthew Sully. Thomas Sully emigrated to America with his parents and eight siblings at age nine and lived in Charleston, South Carolina. He received coaching from school friend Charles Fraser, who became Charleston's most famous miniaturist, and from an elder brother, Lawrence Sully, who also painted miniatures. Thomas Sully was best known as a portrait artist who reflected the manners and demeanor of great people of his day. A naturalized American citizen, he preserved for posterity the nation's politicians, military heroes, inventors, actors, and aristocrats as well as European nobles and the queen of England. In the decades preceding the invention of photography, his prolific output of portraits and historic scenes became a storehouse of details from the past. A year after his death on November 5, 1872, in Philadelphia, his heirs published posthumously *Hints to Young Painters and the Process of Portrait-Painting as Practiced by the Late Thomas Sully* (1873). Its explanation of artistic works from the colonial and federal periods retained for history the inside information on color selection, lighting, and technique. His likenesses of 500 historic figures, including Daniel Boone, Benjamin Franklin, and US presidents Thomas Jefferson, James Monroe, and Andrew Jackson, are national treasures.

Moresque—Moors were the Muslim peoples of mixed Arab race who conquered Spain and held power there in the years from 711 to 1492. The term Moresque means an ornament or a decoration in Moorish style or having all the usual qualities of the Moorish style of art or architecture.

Exercises

I. Answer the following questions based on the text.

1. Can you infer what kind of chateau they had entered?

2. Why did the speaker shut his eyes upon the portrait for a few moments?

3. What was so special about the painting that it had absorbed the speaker entirely?

4. Did the painter love his young bride much more than his Art?

5. How do you understand the death of the young lady on the completion of the work by the painter?

II. Text review. Write T for true and F for false in the bracket before the statement.

( ) 1. Many paintings hung from the main walls of the chateau, but nothing in the corners.

( ) 2. He didn't notice the oval portrait at first because it was in the shadow.

( ) 3. He asked his valet to move the position of the candelabrum so as to read the book better.

( ) 4. The speaker took no interest in the pictures because he was wounded and wanted to have a good sleep.

( ) 5. He fixed his eyes on the painting of the young girl once he found it there.

( ) 6. It was the immortal beauty of the countenance that moved him profoundly.

( ) 7. Unable to fall asleep, he eagerly turned to the paged in the book for a detailed explanation of the portrait.

( ) 8. The young lady didn't lead a happy life after wedding the painter.

( ) 9. The bride was happy to act as the model of her husband because she wanted to have more time together with him.

( ) 10. The painter himself was overwhelmed by the power of life in his work.

III. Paraphrase the following sentences in English.

1. To all appearance it had been temporarily and very lately abandoned.

2. …in these paintings my incipient delirium, perhaps, had caused me to take deep interest.

3. …for the first flashing of the candles upon that canvas had seemed to dissipate the dreamy stupor which was stealing over my senses.

4. I had found the spell of the picture in an absolute life-likeliness of expression, which, at first startling, finally confounded, subdued, and appalled me.

5. The cause of my deep agitation being thus shut from view, I sought eagerly the volume which discussed the paintings and their histories.

IV. Translate the following sentences into Chinese.

1. Its walls were hung with tapestry and bedecked with manifold and multiform armorial trophies, together with an unusually great number of very spirited modern paintings in frames of rich golden arabesque.

2. The position of the candelabrum displeased me, and outreaching my hand with difficulty, rather than disturb my slumbering valet, I placed it so as to throw its rays more fully upon the book.

3. It was an impulsive movement to gain time for thought—to make sure that my vision had not deceived me- to calm and subdue my fancy for a more sober and more certain gaze.

4. But it could have been neither the execution of the work, nor the immortal beauty of the countenance, which had so suddenly and so vehemently moved me.

5. Yet she smiled on and still on, uncomplainingly, because she saw that the painter (who had high renown) took a fervid and burning pleasure in his task, and wrought day and night to depict her who so loved him, yet who grew daily more dispirited and weak.

V. Respond to each of the following statements.

1. The eye is the painter and the ear the singer.
2. Death is just a part of life, something we're all destined to do.
3. Life is very nice, but it lacks form. It's the aim of art that gives it some.
4. Good painting is like good cooking; it can be tasted but not explained.
5. Art is long, and time is fleeting.

VI. Provide a text which can support your viewpoint on one of the statements in *Exercise V*. Make your comment on the text you choose.

Text B

A Diagnosis of Death
Ambrose Bierce

在这个故事中,一个人向他的医生讲述他如何开始相信幽灵。这是一个灵异而有趣的话题。

'I am not so superstitious as some of your physicians—men of science, as you are pleased to be called,' said Hawver, replying to an accusation that had not been made.' Some of you—only a few, I confess—believe in the immortality of the soul, and in apparitions which you have not the honesty to call ghosts. I go no further than a conviction that the living are sometimes seen where they are not, but have been-where they have lived so long, perhaps so intensely, as to have left their impress on everything about them. I know, indeed, that one's environment may be so affected by one's personality as to yield, long afterward, an image of one's self to the eyes of another. Doubtless the impressing personality has to be the right kind of personality as the perceiving eyes have to be the right kind of eyes—mine, for example.'

'Yes, the right kind of eyes, conveying sensations to the wrong kind of brains,' said Dr. Frayley, smiling.

'Thank you; one likes to have an expectation gratified; that is about the reply that I supposed you would have the civility to make.'

'Pardon me. But you say that you know. That is a good deal to say, don't you think? Perhaps you will not mind the trouble of saying how you learned.'

'You will call it a hallucination, 'Hawver said,' but that does not matter.' And he told the story.

'Last summer I went, as you know, to pass the hot weather term in the town of Meridian. The relative at whose house I had intended to stay was ill, so I sought other quarters. After some difficulty I succeeded in renting a vacant dwelling that had been occupied by an eccentric doctor of the name of Mannering, who had gone away years before,

diagnosis /ˌdaɪəgˈnəʊsɪs/ *n.* **a.** the art or act of identifying a disease from its signs and symptoms; **b.** the decision reached by diagnosis; **c.** investigation or analysis of the cause or nature of a condition, situation, or problem; **d.** a statement or conclusion from such an analysis

superstition /ˌsuːpəˈstɪʃən/ *n.* **a.** a belief or practice resulting from ignorance, fear of the unknown, trust in magic or chance, or a false conception of causation; **b.** an irrational abject attitude of mind toward the supernatural, nature, or God resulting from superstition.

superstitious *adj.* of, relating to, or swayed by superstition

physician /fɪˈzɪʃən/ *n.* a person skilled in the art of healing; specifically one educated, clinically experienced, and licensed to practice medicine as usually distinguished from surgery

confess /kənˈfes/ *v.* **a.** to tell or make known (as sth wrong or damaging to oneself), admit; **b.** to acknowledge (sin) to God or to a priest

apparition /ˌæpəˈrɪʃən/ *n.* the spirit of a dead person moving in bodily form

conviction /kənˈvɪkʃən/ *n.* **a.** a strong persuasion or belief; **b.** the state of being convinced

perceive /pəˈsiːv/ *v.* to have or come to have knowledge of (sth) through one of the senses (esp. sight) or through the mind; see

convey /kənˈveɪ/ *v.* **a.** to bear from one place to another; esp. to move in a continuous stream or mass; **b.** to impart or communicate by statement, suggestion, gesture, or appearance

gratify /ˈgrætɪfaɪ/ *v.* **a.** to give pleasure and satisfaction to; **b.** to satisfy (a desire)

hallucination /həˌluːsɪˈneɪʃən/ *n.* **a.** perception of objects with no reality usually arising from disorder of the nervous system or in response to drugs (as LSD); **b.** the object so perceived

vacant /ˈveɪkənt/ *adj.* **a.** not lived in; **b.** not put to use; **c.** devoid of thought, reflection, or expression

eccentric /ɪkˈsentrɪk/ *adj.* **a.** deviating from an established or usual pattern or style; **b.** deviating from conventional or accepted usage or conduct esp. in odd or whimsical ways

no one knew where, not even his agent. He had built the house himself and had lived in it with an old servant for about ten years. His practice, never very extensive, had after a few years been given up entirely. Not only so, but he had withdrawn himself almost altogether from social life and become a recluse. I was told by the village doctor, about the only person with whom he held any relations, that during his retirement he had devoted himself to a single line of study, the result of which he had expounded in a book that did not commend itself to the approval of his professional

recluse /rɪ'klu:s/ n. a person who leads a secluded or solitary life

expound /ɪks'paʊnd/ v. a. to explain by setting forth in careful and often e-laborate detail; b. to defend with argument

commend /kə'mend/ v. a. to officially recognize (someone or sth) as being worthy of praise, notice, etc.; speak favourably of (someone or sth); b. to put (someone or sth, esp. oneself) into the care or charge of someone else

sane /seɪn/ adj. a. proceeding from a sound mind, rational; b. mentally sound; esp. able to anticipate and appraise the effect of one's actions; c. healthy in body

forecast /'fɔːkɑːst/ v. a. to calculate or predict (some future event or condi-tion) usu as a result of study and analysis of available pertinent data; espe-cially to predict (weather conditions) on the basis of correlated meteorologi-cal observations; b. to indicate as likely to occur

prognosis /prɒg'nəʊsɪs/ n. a. a doctor's opinion, based on medical experi-ence, of what course a disease will probably take; b. a description of the fu-ture, judgment concerning the course and result of a set of events already begun

melancholy /'melənkəli/ n. a. an abnormal state attributed to an excess of black bile and characterized by irascibility or depression; b. depression of spirits

disposition /dɪspə'zɪʃən/ n. a. prevailing tendency, mood, or inclination; b. temperamental makeup; c. the tendency of sth to act in a certain manner un-der given circumstances

addict /ə'dɪkt/ v. to devote or surrender (oneself) to sth habitually or obses-sively

dejection /dɪ'dʒekʃən/ n. lowness of spirits, sadness

impending /ɪm'pendɪŋ/ adj. (usually of sth unpleasant) about to happen

brethren, who, indeed, considered him not entirely sane. I have not seen the book and cannot now recall the title of it, but I am told that it expounded a rather startling theory. He held that it was possible in the case of many a person in good health to forecast his death with precision, several months in advance of the event. The limit, I think, was eighteen months. There were local tales of his having exerted his powers of prognosis, or perhaps you would say diagnosis; and it was said that in every instance the person whose friends he had warned had died suddenly at the appointed time, and from no assignable cause. All this, however, has nothing to do with what I have to tell; I thought it might amuse a physician.

'The house was furnished, just as he had lived in it. It was a rather gloomy dwelling for one who was neither a recluse nor a student, and I think it gave something of its character to me—perhaps some of its former occupant's character; for always I felt in it a certain melancholy that was not in my natural disposition, nor, I think, due to loneliness. I had no servants that slept in the house, but I have always been, as you know, rather fond of my own society, being much addicted to reading, though little to study. Whatever was the cause, the effect was dejection and a sense of impending evil; this was especially so in Dr. Mannering's study, although that room was the lightest and most airy in the house. The doctor's life-size portrait in oil hung in that room, and seemed completely to dominate it. There was nothing unusual in the picture; the man was evidently rather good looking, about fifty years old, with iron-grey hair, a smooth-shaven face and dark, serious eyes. Something in the picture always drew and held my attention. The man's appearance became familiar to me, and rather "haunted" me.

'One evening I was passing through this room to my bedroom, with a lamp— there is no gas in Meridian. I stopped as usual before the portrait, which seemed in the lamplight to have a new expression, not easily named, but distinctly uncanny. It interested but did not disturb me. I moved the lamp from one side to the other and observed the effects of the altered light. While so engaged I felt an impulse to turn round. As I did so I saw a man moving across the room directly toward me! As soon as he came near enough for the lamplight to illuminate the face I saw that it was Dr. Mannering himself; it was as if the portrait were walking!'

"I beg your pardon," I said, somewhat coldly, "but if you knocked I did not hear."

'He passed me, within an arm's length, lifted his right forefinger, as in warning, and without a word went on out of the room, though I observed his exit no more than I had observed his entrance.

'Of course, I need not tell you that this was what you will call a hallucination and I call an apparition. That room had only two doors, of which one was locked; the other led into a bedroom, from which there was no exit. My feeling on realizing this is not an important part of the incident.

'Doubtless this seems to you a very commonplace "ghost story"—one constructed on the regular lines laid down by the old masters of the art. If that were so I should not have related it, even if it were true. The man was not dead; I met him to-day in Union Street. He passed me in a crowd.'

Hawver had finished his story and both men were silent. Dr. Frayley absently drummed on the table with his fingers.

'Did he say anything to-day?' he asked—'anything from which you inferred that he was not dead?'

Hawver stared and did not reply.

'Perhaps,' continued Frayley, 'he made a sign, a gesture—lifted a finger, as in warning. It's a trick he had—a habit when saying something serious— announcing the result of a diagnosis, for example.'

'Yes, he did—just as his apparition had done. But, good God! Did you ever know him?'

haunt /hɔːnt/ v. a. to have a disquieting or harmful effect on, trouble; b. to recur constantly and spontaneously to; c. to reappear continually in; d. to visit or inhabit as a ghost

uncanny /ʌnˈkæni/ adj. a. seeming to have a supernatural character or origin, eerie, mysterious; b. being beyond what is normal or expected, suggesting superhuman or supernatural powers

impulse /ˈɪmpʌls/ n. a. a sudden spontaneous inclination or incitement to some usually unpremeditated action; b. a propensity or natural tendency usually other than rational

illuminate /ɪˈluːmɪneɪt/ v. a. to supply or brighten with light; b. to make clear; c. to bring to the fore, highlight

commonplace /ˈkɒmənpleɪs/ adj. commonly found or seen, ordinary, unremarkable

Hawver was apparently growing nervous.

'I knew him. I have read his book, as will every physician some day. It is one of the most striking and important of the century's contributions to medical science. Yes, I knew him; I attended him in an illness three years ago. He died.'

> manifest /'mænɪfest/ *adj.* plain to see or clear to the mind. **manifestly** *adv.*
> **disturbed** /dɪs'tɜːbd/ *adj.* having or showing signs of an illness of the mind or the feelings

Hawver sprang from his chair, manifestly disturbed. He strode forward and back across the room; then approached his friend, and in a voice not altogether steady, said: 'Doctor, have you anything to say to me—as a physician?'

'No, Hawver; you are the healthiest man I ever knew. As a friend I advise you to go to your room. You play the violin like an angel. Play it; play something light and lively. Get this cursed bad Business off your mind.'

The next day Hawver was found dead in his room, the violin at his neck, the bow upon the string, his music open before him at Chopin's Funeral March.

Cultural Notes

Ambrose Bierce (1842—1914?)—Bierce was born in a log cabin in Ohio. His family, though strongly religious, provided him with no formal education and he left home in his teens for a military academy in Kentucky. At the outbreak of civil war, he enlisted in the Union Army in which he served with distinction— rising quickly from private to major. At the end of the war, Bierce settled in San Francisco where he began contributing articles to a number of journals. He married in 1971 before heading off to England where he completed three collections of stories. Returning to San Francisco, he worked for several papers, most notably William Randolph Hearst's '*San Francisco Examiner*' where his cynical but popular columns earned him a reputation as the 'literary dictator of the Pacific Coast'. It was also during this period that he completed the two short story collections '*Tales of Soldiers and Civilians*' and '*Can Such Things Be*'. Although a harsh critic of many of the conventions of his day—stating his disapproval of 'human institutions in general, including all forms of government, most laws and customs, and all contemporary literature'—Ambrose Bierce was perhaps most deeply affected by his belief in the waste and futility of war. In 1896 he was set to work on another of Hearst's papers in Washington and the entire capital reportedly 'ran for cover'. But his divorce in 1904 and the deaths of his two sons from suicide and acute alcoholism took their toll. In 1913, at the age of 71, Bierce settled his affairs and headed off to Mexico—the scene of a bloody civil war; he was said to have exclaimed: 'To be a Gringo in Mexico—ah, that is euthanasia'. The exact circumstances of his death remain unknown. His most notable work is *The Devil's Dictionary*.

Exercises

I. Answer the following questions based on the text.

1. How did the author relate the ghost story to us?
2. Did Hawver believe in the startling theory held by the eccentric doctor?
3. How did Hawver feel in the house of Dr. Mannering?
4. How did Hawver react when Dr. Frayley told him he knew Dr. Mannering and confirmed his death to him?
5. What is the diagnosis of death in this story?

II. Text review. Write T for true and F for false in the bracket before the statement.

( ) 1. Hawver was blamed by other physicians for being superstitious.

( ) 2. Hawver only believed that the image of a person may appear again in a place after he has not bee there for a long time.

( ) 3. Last summer Hawver went to Meridian to see one of his relatives who was ill.

( ) 4. The house where Hawver stayed for the summer had been rented by an eccentric doctor with the name of Mannering before.

( ) 5. Dr. Mannering expounded an appalling theory in his book after years of study.

( ) 6. As a recluse, Hawver enjoyed his own society in a room with a lot of books to read.

( ) 7. Hawver hung the doctor's portrait in his bedroom because he was deeply attracted by it.

( ) 8. Hawver was frightened when he saw the apparition of Dr. Mannering walking silently across the room.

( ) 9. Dr. Mannering had the habit of lifting one of his forefingers when announcing his diagnosis to someone.

( ) 10. Dr. Frayley tried to reassure his friend about his health and suggested him to play the violin.

III. Paraphrase the following sentences in English.

1. I know, indeed, that one's environment may be so affected by one's personality as to yield, long afterward, an image of one's self to the eyes of another.

2. One likes to have an expectation gratified; that is about the reply that I supposed you would have the civility to make.

3. During his retirement he had devoted himself to a single line of study, the result of which he had expounded in a book that did not commend itself to the approval of his professional brethren, who, indeed, considered him not entirely sane.

4. I felt in it a certain melancholy that was not in my natural disposition, nor, I think, due to loneliness

5. I observed his exit no more than I had observed his entrance.

IV. Translate the following sentences into Chinese.

1. Some of you—only a few, I confess—believe in the immortality of the soul, and in apparitions which you have not the honesty to call ghosts.

2. Doubtless the impressing personality has to be the right kind of personality as the perceiving eyes have to be the right kind of eyes.

3. He held that it was possible in the case of many a person in good health to forecast his death with precision, several months in advance of the event.

4. I had no servants that slept in the house, but I have always been, as you know, rather fond of my own society, being much addicted to reading, though little to study.

5. Whatever was the cause, the effect was dejection and a sense of impending evil; this was especially so in Dr. Mannering's study, although that room was the lightest and most airy in the house.

V. Respond to each of the following statements.

1. The living are sometimes seen where they are not, but have lived and left impress.

2. It is possible in the case of many a person in good health to forecast his death with precision.

3. The environment where one has lived may lend some character of its former occupant to others.

4. Something that always holds your attention may haunt you in a particular period of time.

5. An apparition may come as a warning, a remembrance or a sign to announce
something terrible.

**VI. Provide a text which can support your viewpoint on one of the statements
in *Exercise V*. Make your comment on the text you choose.**

Unit Nine

Sharing Our Creative Work with Others—Creativity

Linda Dessau

　　具有创造力并创造性的工作是社会的需求，而创造能力的形成需要积累和历练。本文试作如何培养并充分发挥创造力的论述。

In my "Roadblocks to Creativity" e-course, I ask the question:

"What's your first thought if someone hesitates before giving you their opinion about your creative project?"

One artist wrote: "When some one hesitates before giving their opinion of my work, I think it is going to be negative; I recently showed some work to my boss and her criticism was so harsh that I now won't show her anything, but the worse part is—it made me even more conscious of showing my work to others as well. She was going through some hard stuff at the time, so my timing was way off.

I now will show my work if it is something I am really sure of—or to someone that isn't so harsh. When showing some one else my work—if I get a negative response I take it as some thing against me personally. Not too smart."

I replied to this person:

"It's too bad that you had such a negative experience when you showed your work to your boss. It's great that you recognize that she was having a bad day, and that her response had more to do with that than the value of your work. But I hear some distorted thinking that now you can NEVER show her anything ("all or nothing" is a prime example of distorted thinking).

I think you're absolutely wise to protect

roadblock /'rəudblɒk/ *n.* a bar or other object(s) used for closing a road to stop traffic, an enemy, etc.

harsh /hɑːʃ/ *adj.* a. unpleasant in causing pain to the senses; b. (of people, punishments, etc.) which show cruelty or lack of kindness

distort /dɪsˈtɔːt/ *v.* a. to twist out of the true meaning or proportion; b. to twist out of a natural, normal, or original shape or condition; also to cause to be perceived unnaturally

prime /praɪm/ *adj.* first in rank, authority, or significance, principal

your fragile creative projects as they're being brought into the world. There are certain stages of a project when you really should choose very carefully who you share them with."

This correspondence got me thinking about the fragility and sensitivity of the artist soul, the seeming insensitivity of the "real world" and how to bridge the two.

Two of my creativity heroes, Julia Cameron and SARK, each have much to say on the subject.

fragile /'frædʒail/ *adj.* **a.** easily broken or destroyed; **b.** constitutionally delicate, lacking in vigor

dampen /'dæmpən/ *v.* **a.** to check or diminish the activity or vigor of, deaden; **b.** to make damp

fabulous /'fæbjʊləs/ *adj.* **a.** resembling or suggesting a fable, of an incredible, astonishing, or exaggerated nature; **b.** wonderful, marvelous; **c.** told in or based on fable

proactive /ˌprəʊ'æktɪv/ *adj.* **a.** relating to, caused by, or being interference between previous learning and the recall or performance of later learning; **b.** acting in anticipation of future problems, needs, or changes

sabotage /'sæbətɑːʒ/ *n.* **a.** destruction of an employer's property (as tools or materials) or the hindering of manufacturing by discontented workers; **b.** an act or process tending to hamper or hurt; **c.** deliberate subversion

validate /'vælɪdeɪt/ *v.* **a.** to make legally valid; **b.** to support or corroborate on a sound or authoritative basis. **validation** *n.*

Julia Cameron, in the chapter of The Artist's Way titled "Week 12: Recovering a Sense of Faith", describes "Wet Blankets" as those people in our lives who dampen our creative spirit. She suggests that we "move silently among doubters", and that we actually craft lists of who will nourish and support us and those who are sure to act as "Wet Blankets". Then it's up to us to protect our creative dreams by choosing carefully who to share them with.

SARK, in the chapter of Make Your Creative Dreams Real titled "Fabulous Fifth Month: Creative Dreams Support Systems", advises us to be proactive and that we teach our friends and family how best to support us in our creative work. She gives concrete suggestions about what to say and what to ask for. She also gives guidelines for looking outside your regular circle of family and friends and forming a "creative dream team" with other artists for the specific purpose of nurturing each other's creativity.

Julia Cameron also points out that a common self-sabotage mechanism can be running straight to a "Wet Blanket" when we've got something exciting (therefore scary) going on. I've done this myself.

It happens when one of my creative dreams is taking form and shape. This is when I get that feeling of being connected to the Universe, of receiving "divine" inspiration, of really being onto something that feels right for me AND in service to the world at the same time. It's exciting and it's also very scary.

I can take many paths at this point. One path that I sometimes choose is to immediately seek validation, reassurance and support. It's a lifelong habit of not quite trusting myself (and, really, not quite trusting the Universe, which is very silly of me!), and of needing something outside of myself to tell me it's ok (and that I'm ok).

I remember once when I was feeling excited, scared and on the verge of something amazing. I immediately reached for the phone, didn't choose carefully, and opened myself to feedback without requesting the specific type of feedback I was after.

devastate /'devəsteɪt/ *v.* a. to bring to ruin or desolation by violent action; b. to reduce to chaos, disorder, or helplessness, overwhelm

defiant /dɪ'faɪənt/ *adj.* bold, challenging, impudent

see the light a. to be born or come to exist; b. to be made public; c. to understand or accept an idea or the truth of sth

sounding board a. a structure behind or over a pulpit, rostrum, or platform to give distinctness and sonority to sound; b. a device or agency that helps propagate opinions or utterances; c. a person or group on whom one tries out an idea or opinion as a means of evaluating it

When I was told the project wasn't ready, that I needed to do more research, that I shouldn't rush into it and that "this type of thing" hadn't proven to be successful for others, I was crushed and devastated (exactly what that self-sabotaging part of me wanted).

Luckily I am VERY stubborn and defiant (not always my best qualities, but in this situation they actually worked FOR me), and after a couple of days of licking my wounds I was able to build up my hope and faith in the project again, regardless of what that person said.

That project did see the light, and it is bringing success. It feels right for me AND it's serving the world.

Here are some steps to consider BEFORE reaching out and sharing your creative work and dreams— I'll be keeping these in mind as well!

1. Choose carefully. Think about people you've shared with in the past and what kind of responses you got. Think about how it felt to have the conversation and how you felt afterwards—did you feel like you couldn't wait to get back to creating something else or did you feel like hanging it up for good? If it's someone you've never shared your creative work before, imagine having the conversation and what response you might get. Choose the person who will build you up, not tear you down.

2. Consider the timing. The less formed the idea, the more "fragile" it is and the more important it be supported in a non-judgmental and creativity-enhancing way. Are you truly ready to let someone into the process or would it be better to keep it to yourself for a while longer? Be very honest with yourself about this. Get still and quiet and listen closely for the truth when it comes.

3. What do you want? Again, think carefully about this and be honest. Do you want support and validation so that you can be re-fueled in your excitement of the project? Do you want a sounding board so that you can hear yourself think (talking to someone else can be a GREAT idea generator)? Or do you want to invite constructive criticism and suggestions for making the work better?

4. Ask for what you want! The other person can't read your mind and depending on their line of work and their personality type they may instinctively want to give

advice, make suggestions or look for possible reasons why something might not work.

snuff /snʌf/ *v.* a. to extinguish by or as if by the use of a candlesnuffer—often used with *out*; b. to make extinct, put an end to—usully used with *out*; c. kill, execute

Many wonderful creative sparks have been extinguished by conversations that never should have happened. Don't let yours be snuffed out!

Cultural Notes

wet blanket—The basic meaning of it as a noun is a blanket dampened with water so as to extinguish a fire. It also comes as an idiom, deriving from the above, to refer to a person or thing that discourages enthusiasm or enjoyment, especially someone who spoils the pleasure of others, a depressing companion. For example: Nobody asked him to join the group because he's such a wet blanket. Another term for the same meaning is *spoilsport*.

Exercises

I. Answer the following questions based on the text.

1. What do you think the author's job may be?
2. How did the author comment on the first artist in their correspondence?
3. What did SARK suggest us to do to support our creative dreams?
4. What are the steps for us to consider before sharing our creative work with others?
5. In your opinion what is the most essential for one to succeed despite the negative opinions from others?

II. Text review. Write T for true and F for false in the bracket before the statement.

( ) 1. The author emphasizes the importance of choosing who to share the project with for an artist.
( ) 2. The boss criticized the work of the first artist because it's short of creativity.
( ) 3. Julia Cameron refers to "wet blankets" as people who will support our creative ideas.
( ) 4. Both Julia and SARK focused their speeches on how to protect an artist's creative dream.
( ) 5. The author felt so discouraged at the feedback from others about her

project that she finally gave it up.

(　) 6. Julia Cameron offered some steps to overcome the so-called self-sabotage mechanism.

(　) 7. You should follow the steps after you have had some unhappy conversations with your friends.

(　) 8. Different opinions from others will have different consequences on your action.

(　) 9. You should consider the timing for you to tell someone about your project carefully for fear that he should be in a bad temper and gave you a harsh criticism.

(　) 10. At most times you need a sounding-board to hear your own voice.

III. Paraphrase the following sentences in English.

1. She was going through some hard stuff at the time, so my timing was way off.

2. It's great that you recognize that she was having a bad day, and that her response had more to do with that than the value of your work.

3. Julia Cameron also points out that a common self-sabotage mechanism can be running straight to a "Wet Blanket" when we've got something exciting (therefore scary) going on.

4. I immediately reached for the phone, didn't choose carefully, and opened myself to feedback without requesting the specific type of feedback I was after.

5. That project did see the light, and it is bringing success.

IV. Translate the following sentences into Chinese.

1. This correspondence got me thinking about the fragility and sensitivity of the artist soul, the seeming insensitivity of the "real world" and how to bridge the two.

2. She suggests that we "move silently among doubters", and that we actually craft lists of who will nourish and support us and those who are sure to act as "Wet Blankets".

3. This is when I get that feeling of being connected to the Universe, of receiving "divine" inspiration, of really being onto something that feels right for me AND in service to the world at the same time.

4. I immediately reached for the phone, didn't choose carefully, and opened myself to feedback without requesting the specific type of feedback I was after.

5. The other person can't read your mind and depending on their line of work and their personality type they may instinctively want to give advice, make suggestions or look for possible reasons why something might not work.

V. Respond to each of the following statements.

1. It is wise to protect one's creative projects as they are being brought into the world.

2. Once we have taken our way, we should go along it no matter what others say about it.

3. Many people have a lifelong habit of not quite trusting themselves.

4. Talking to someone else can be a great idea generator.

5. Many wonderful creative sparks have been extinguished by conversations that never should have happened.

VI. Provide a text which can support your viewpoint on one of the statements in *Exercise V*. Make your comment on the text you choose.

Text B

Why Management Kills Creativity

Anonymous

经营管理能力与创造力之间的关系耐人寻味，企业管理者如何才能最大限度地激发员工的创造力呢？本文读罢会略解此惑。

Ten or so years ago, an international consultant, specializing in employee involvement and team development, published a story relating to workplace communication that is heart-warming and damning at the same time.

In 1981, Peter Grazer was working as the project engineer on a construction project to modernize a silicon manufacturing facility in St. Louis, Missouri. A crew of ironworkers had been assigned a particularly daunting task of erecting some structural steel in a difficult to reach area of the plant.

Unfazed by the complexity of the assignment, the ironworkers completed the work weeks ahead of schedule, well under budget, and without safety problems. Grazer and his colleagues of the management team resolved to express their appreciation to the crew in an unmistakable, tangible way.

damning /'dæmɪŋ/ *adj.* causing or leading to condemnation or ruin

daunting /'dɔːntɪŋ/ *adj.* tending to overwhelm or intimidate

faze /feɪz/ *v.* to disturb the composure of, disconcert, daunt

They sent letters to the Homes of the workers, thanking them for their outstanding work and inviting them and their wives to a dinner in their honor at a fancy hotel in St. Louis.

camaraderie /ˌkæməˈrɑːdəriː/ *n.* a spirit of friendly good-fellowship
unduly /ʌnˈdjuːli/ *adv.* in an undue manner, excessively
budding /ˈbʌdɪŋ/ *adj.* being in an early stage of development
wrangle /ˈræŋgəl/ *v.* a. to obtain by persistent arguing or maneuvering; b. to herd and care for (livestock and esp. horses) on the range
strangle /ˈstræŋgəl/ *v.* a. to choke to death by compressing the throat with sth (as a hand or rope), throttle; b. to suppress or hinder the rise, expression, or growth of

The dinner was a memorable occasion, enjoyed to the full by both management and the workers in a spirit of camaraderie. A couple of days later, Grazer was walking around the site when he came upon one of the crew members.

Jerry was in his fifties and was usually loud and jovial. Moreover, he was naturally hardened from his years of working with steel, and not the type to get unduly emotional over anything.

The project engineer was a little taken aback to see Jerry so quiet and deep in thought on this particular morning, especially so soon after the dinner. He anxiously asked Jerry if anything was wrong.

"You remember those letters you sent to our homes?" he asked. "When I arrived Home that day my wife was waiting for me at the door—with the letter in her hands and tears in her eyes. And she said to me: 'Jerry, you've been an ironworker for 30 years, and nobody's ever thanked you for anything.'"

No thanks in 30 years?

Jerry paused, and both he and the project engineer stood there quietly for a moment. "How is it possible," thought Grazer, "that somebody could work for thirty years and not be thanked for anything he did?"

Dr. Roger Firestien, a noted expert on creative problem solving techniques, quotes this article of Peter Grazer's in his book *Leading on the Creative Edge*.

The need to be recognized is clearly one of our most sophisticated drives and one of the most difficult to achieve. The problem is that we are wholly dependent upon others for its satisfaction.

From a purely pragmatic standpoint, lack of recognition can have a profoundly negative impact on productivity. Studies show that encouragement and recognition play a major role in stimulating creativity in research and development organizations.

In a magazine article a few years back, writer Arthur Gordon gave an almost frightening example of how far this can go.

At the University of Wisconsin, a group of budding writers, said to be brilliant boys with real literary talent among them, once formed a club to discuss their literary efforts.

Wranglers vs. Stranglers

At each meeting, one of them would read something he had written and submit it to the criticism of the others. No one pulled any punches here; in fact, the critiques were so brutal that the club members dubbed themselves "The Stranglers".

Meanwhile, on the other side of campus, a group of women had also come together for the same purpose. The women called their little group "The Wranglers." They also took turns to read their manuscripts aloud.

punch /pʌntʃ/ *n.* a. a quick blow with or as if with the fist; b. effective energy or forcefulness
pull punches (also pull a punch) to refrain from using all the force at one's disposal
feeble /'fiːbəl/ *adj.* a. markedly lacking in strength; b. indicating weakness; c. deficient in qualities or resources that indicate vigor, authority, force, or efficiency
bevy /'bevi/ *n.* a large group or collection
gravitate /'græviteɪt/ *v.* a. to move toward sth; b. to be drawn or attracted esp. by natural inclination
premise /'premɪs/ *n.* a. a proposition antecedently supposed or proved as a basis of argument or inference; b. sth assumed or taken for granted, presupposition
hopper /'hɒpə/ *n.* a usually funnel-shaped receptacle for delivering material (as grain or coal); also any of various other receptacles for the temporary storage of material

But here the similarity between the two groups ended, for the Wranglers would go out of their way to say kind things about each other. Far from sowing the seeds of self-doubt, they actively supported each other, and encouraged all literary efforts, however feeble.

And the payoff came about twenty years later.

Gordon asserts that for all the sparkling talent residing in the Stranglers at the time, not one member of the band achieved any kind of literary reputation. From the Wranglers, on the other hand, emerged a bevy of highly successful writers, led by Marjorie Kennan Rawlings who wrote "The Yearling."

Dr. Firestien adds that his experience in Business suggests that most organizations more closely follow the Stranglers' pattern than the Wranglers'.

"Why do we naturally gravitate towards the negative?" he asks, and then answers his own question: "I think the primary reason may be that we haven't been taught to look first at the strengths of an idea."

As if to prove his premise, Firestien shows participants in his seminars a picture of an odd-looking wheelbarrow with a very large hopper, a short handle, and a single wheel behind the hopper. He then calls for comments on its design.

Typical comments include: "The hopper is too big", "The handle is too short", "The wheel's in the wrong place", or "Go back to the drawing board, Roger!" Of course, all these "comments" are criticisms.

In real life, he then explains, this wheelbarrow is used for high-rise construction, and there's an important reason for each design element.

"Ah, but you set us up!" is the standard, indignant response. "You didn't give us all the information on it."

To which the presenter politely replies by pointing out that most new ideas look like that when they're first proposed. Often, you don't have all the info on a new idea on hand when you first see it.

Not so fast, please!

But why jump the gun by killing it on the spot? Firestien contends that this is, in fact, the knee-jerk reaction of many people to all new ideas.

jump the gun to start sth (like a race) too soon

contend v. /kən'tend/ a. maintain, assert; b. to struggle for, contest

What's the solution?

Let's say someone proposes an idea. (That "someone" could be another party: your boss, your subordinate, your colleague, friend or spouse; but it could also be YOU—your inner, creative, "real" self!) If you're at all "normal", your natural urge will be to tear the concept to pieces.

But stop! Don't let your passions get the better of you! If Dr. Firestien had re-drawn his wheelbarrow to fit in with all the comments he received, he would have come back to the same wheelbarrow that has been in use for thousands of years.

Defer your judgment, just for a while. Has the idea no strengths at all? Focus on these first, and the drawbacks afterwards.

The fruits of your efforts may surprise you.

Cultural Notes

St. Louis—St. Louis is the second largest city in Missouri. Located at the confluence of the Mississippi and Missouri rivers, St. Louis is near the geographic center of the United States. Its modified continental climate is characterized by four seasons without prolonged periods of extreme heat or high humidity. Alternate invasions of moist air from the Gulf of Mexico and cold air masses from Canada produce a variety of weather conditions. Winters are brisk and seldom severe; annual snowfall averages about eighteen inches. Hot days with temperatures of 100 degrees or higher occur on the average of five days per year. Severe storms are often accompanied by hail and damaging winds, and tornadoes have caused destruction and loss of life. Since its founding St. Louis has undergone several significant stages of development, which parallel the nation's westward expansion, symbolized by the city's famous Gateway Arch. St. Louis enjoys a rich and culturally diverse life and a revitalized downtown commercial district. As one of the first regions in the country to confront defense cutbacks in the 1990s and develop plans for dealing with them, the St. Louis area has emerged as a national laboratory for the post-Cold-War economy.

Missouri—Missouri became the 24th state of the United States on August 10, 1821. Two of this country's greatest waterways, the Mississippi River on the state's eastern border, and the Missouri River, which winds across the state, helped Missouri become a supply center for many of the westward-bound settlers of the nation's early years. Shipping along the navigable rivers boosted the state's status as an agricultural supplier. Barges and steamboats used the water ways to move goods and people. River towns boomed. Railroads continued to fuel the growth of Missouri as a large transportation center. Today more than a dozen major railroads carry goods through the state, and transcontinental airlines keep passengers and cargo on the move. People who live in Missouri or who come from Missouri are called Missourians.

Exercises

I. Answer the following questions based on the text.

1. How did the management team decide to express their appreciation to the crew?
2. Why was Jerry deep in thought on the morning when Peter Grazer met him?
3. What does Peter Grazer's article indicate in your opinion?
4. What is the relationship between recognition and creativity?
5. What did Dr. Firestien aim at by presenting the example of a wheelbarrow in his seminars?

II. Text review. Write T for true and F for false in the bracket before the statement.

( ) 1. An international consultant published a story about employee involvement 10 years ago.
( ) 2. Peter Grazer was assigned a daunting task of erecting some structural steel in a short period of time.
( ) 3. The assignment was completed well in advance, although it was very complex.
( ) 4. Everyone was satisfied with the dinner except Jerry, who felt disappointed at the management.
( ) 5. The group of women called themselves "the Wranglers" because they always argued heatedly with each other about the manuscript.
( ) 6. The Wranglers and the Stranglers had absolutely different results because of their contrasting attitudes towards others' literary efforts.
( ) 7. The business organizations had nothing in common with the two literary groups on the campus.
( ) 8. People in the seminars made no affirmative comments on the picture of the wheelbarrow presented to them.
( ) 9. It doesn't matter if our immediate reaction to a new idea is negative, because all normal people do that.

( ) 10. Before making our judgment, we should consider the drawbacks of an idea first.

III. Paraphrase the following sentences in English.

1. The project engineer was a little taken aback to see Jerry so quiet and deep in thought on this particular morning, especially so soon after the dinner.

2. No one pulled any punches here; in fact, the critiques were so brutal that the club members dubbed themselves "The Stranglers".

3. Gordon asserts that for all the sparkling talent residing in the Stranglers at the time, not one member of the band achieved any kind of literary reputation.

4. "Ah, but you set us up!" is the standard, indignant response.

5. Firestien contends that this is, in fact, the knee-jerk reaction of many people to all new ideas.

IV. Translate the following sentences into Chinese.

1. A crew of ironworkers had been assigned a particularly daunting task of erecting some structural steel in a difficult to reach area of the plant.

2. Moreover, he was naturally hardened from his years of working with steel, and not the type to get unduly emotional over anything.

3. Far from sowing the seeds of self-doubt, they actively supported each other, and encouraged all literary efforts, however feeble.

4. To which the presenter politely replies by pointing out that most new ideas look like that when they're first proposed.

5. If Dr. Firestien had redrawn his wheelbarrow to fit in with all the comments he received, he would have come back to the same wheelbarrow that has been in use for thousands of years.

V. Respond to each of the following statements.

1. The need to be recognized is one of our most sophisticated drives to achieve.

2. We are dependent too much upon others for the satisfaction of the need to be recognized.

3. We haven't been taught to look first at the strengths of an idea.

4. Most new ideas look odd when they're first proposed.

5. The staff's creativity will be killed if the management of the business makes no recognition of their work.

VI. Provide a text which can support your viewpoint on one of the statements in *Exercise V*. Make your comment on the text you choose.

Unit Ten

How to Escape out of Thought Traps?

Anonymous

每个人都会面临精神和思维的困境,在当今社会如何脱离它尤其成为人们研究和论争的焦点问题,本文通过对于困境的分析试图找出一条对症的解决办法。

Have you ever been really sure about something, only to find out you were mistaken? Did you notice how you operated "as if" you were correct? You may have even seen, heard, touched, tasted, or smelled the world in a way to support your stance. And perhaps you felt you had solid logic to support this position.

So how did the possibility of an opposite opinion make its way through your logic and basically the reality as you knew it, to get you to change your mind? Did you fight hard to stay where you were? Did you go through so called "denial"? Did you lock in to your position, and build up a wall to prevent entry of any contrary thought?

Now the question I have for you is, "Were you keeping them out or were you trapping yourself in?"

In sales, a prospect may be dead-set in his view about a particular product or service. Now the sales rep may know that the prospect does not have all the facts yet, so he sets out trying to convey this to the prospect.

One of two things can result. One the prospect tightens the grip on his view or two he begins to shift his perception. Now this of course depends on the rapport and sales strategy used by the sales professional to enter into the prospect's "thought blockade" and free him from that "one"

stance /stæns/ *n.* **a.** a way of standing or being placed, posture; **b.** intellectual or emotional attitude

sales rep means "sales representative", whose job is to sell some product to customers

rapport /ræˈpɔː/ *n.* relation; esp. relation marked by harmony, conformity, accord, or affinity

blockade /blɒˈkeɪd/ *n.* **a.** the isolation by a warring nation of an enemy area (as a harbor) by troops or warships to prevent passage of persons or supplies; broadly a restrictive measure designed to obstruct the commerce and communications of an unfriendly nation; **b.** sth that blocks

perspective. Listen to the conversations around you, perhaps even the words coming out of your own mouth, are you building your own thought blockade or "thought trap"?

If so, how do you get out? Then (If so desired!) how do you get others out?

congruent /ˈkɒŋgruənt/ *adj.* **a.** being in agreement, harmony, or correspondence; **b.** conforming to the circumstances or requirements of a situation, appropriate

intellect /ˈɪntɪlekt/ *n.* **a.** the power of knowing as distinguished from the power to feel and to will, the capacity for knowledge; **b.** the capacity for rational or intelligent thought esp. when highly developed; **c.** a person with great intellectual powers

validate /ˈvælɪdeɪt/ *v.* **a.** to support or corroborate on a sound or authoritative basis; **b.** to recognize, establish, or illustrate the worthiness or legitimacy of

validation *n.* an act, process, or instance of validating

crap /kræp/ *n.* **a.** (usually vulgar) feces; **b.** (usually vulgar) the act of defecating; **c.** (sometimes vulgar) nonsense rubbish

Recognize The Traps!

Let's start by looking at the traps of the intellectual mind, the one who weaves such wonderful webs of logic that leaves us feeling good while keeping us quite stuck.

Trap One: Being Right

I often tell the couples I work with, "Do you want to be happy or do you want to be right?" Surprisingly, I see quite a lot of incongruent responses. It is like they know they should say "be happy" and (that's why they do), but in fact, they really want to say "be right". Now the real interesting thing is that the intellect wants to be right, regardless of you being right or not. Confused?

Then let's make an important distinction.

You are not your intellect! You the being (soul) are much, much more! The intellect's limitations are not your limitations to the degree that you can separate your "self" (soul) from the intellect. Recognizing these traps and how to avoid them will help in that separation process.

Trap Two: Validation

The intellect seeks constant validation. It is constantly saying recognize me, notice me, "Hey! I'm over here!" Whether it is validation from authorities or peers, this need for validation becomes a crucial trap to avoid. Kids learn this early on. A child comes Home with their report card in hand and an eager look of anticipation, waiting for those few key words, "Oh honey, you did great!" Yeah! The kids can now feel worthy. Now imagine what happens when this is compounded over a few decades. Pretty soon we are all looking for validation in every direction.

Trap Three: Sharing

I've just got to tell you about this one. Oh you won't believe it. The intellect likes to share things. Through sharing it can feel more validated and of course be right. Ever felt like crap and wanted to let others know that you felt that way? Did you hope they would sympathize with your story and tell you how right you are in feeling this way? Hoping they would validate your stance? If so, then you fell into another trap to feed the intellect while starving your real self.

Trap Four: Safety

As the intellect spins its logic, forming a thought blockade, it is also creating a sense of safety. If it constructs well-thought-out logic that sounds reasonable, it is safe from any challenges. So what happens when a contrary idea comes knocking on the door? The intellect's internal safety procedure is kicked in. You may have seen the behaviors that go along with such an internal process if you have ever challenged someone's "sacred cow."

A woman called me up a few weeks back and wanted me to see her son because he was very messy. She asked if I could hypnotize him to always clean up after himself. I told her that it certainly was possible; however I wanted to know a few things first. So I asked her what happens to her when she sees that he hasn't cleaned up after himself? She replied with great tension in her voice, "Well that just makes my blood boil!" So I asked if it always made her blood boil. She stammered, "Yes!"

Then I asked her what she thought about her response she had to his messiness. I asked her what kinds of effects she thinks this may be having on her own body, her health. I continued by saying, what if she could see a messy room and her blood not boil. Talk about running full force right into a sacred cow. (Moooove!)

Her intellect's safety alerts kicked in immediately. She got very defensive and went on tirade about how she was right, and no one could see all that she went through day in and day out, raising three kids while working, and if her blood didn't boil she would become just as lazy as her son, and the whole house would be a wreck. Then she ended the call by saying that she was perfectly fine, and it was her son who had the problem.

Now how many of you identified with her story, sympathized with her stance? Did you get sucked into the trap? Did you let her logical retort validate your own stance?

Go back and read it again. What did she do? How did she trap herself? Her intellect screamed bloody murder the moment we came up on her sacred cow of cleanliness.

It started by building a logical argument around why she was right and he (or me, for challenging her) was in the wrong. She used that along with the lack of validation and recognition from everyone else to validate her logic. And finally, she felt compelled to share it with me to externalize the trap and

sacred cow one that is often unreasonably immune from criticism or opposition

messy /'mesi/ *adj.* a. marked by confusion, disorder, or dirt; b. lacking neatness or precision; c. extremely unpleasant or trying

hypnotize /'hɪpnətaɪz/ *v.* a. to induce hypnosis in; b. to dazzle or overcome by or as if by suggestion

tension /'tenʃən/ *n.* a feeling of nervous anxiety, worry, pressure

make one's blood boil make someone greatly and suddenly angry .

stammer /'stæmə/ *v.* to make involuntary stops and repetitions in speaking

tirade /taɪ'reɪd/ *n.* a long very angry scolding speech

retort /rɪ'tɔːt/ *n.* a quick, rather angry, often amusing answer

external /ɪk'stɜːnl/ *adj.* a. capable of being perceived outwardly; b. of, relating to, or connected with the outside or an outer part

externalize *v.* to make external

<u>manifest</u> it into reality.

By sharing, the logic is not just a construct in her mind anymore. Adding

manifest /ˈmænɪfest/ *v.* to make evident or certain by showing or displaying
seductive /sɪˈdʌktɪv/ *adj.* having alluring or tempting qualities

voice and breath to it begins to give it a life of its own. This is where the pointing begins. And remember whenever there is one finger pointing outwards, there are three fingers pointing back to the person doing the pointing.

Getting Out of the Trap

Now that you know what to look out for, you can begin using the tools below to stay out as well as help others to stay out of those thought traps. Remember this takes practice. The hardest step is to recognize it. The moment you do recognize it you are in a sense already on your way out. But then it is about freeing yourself from the logic that the intellect has spun around the trap. Even then you may find it is easier to spot other people's traps quicker than your own. And the reason for that is because your own logic is most <u>seductive</u> to you not to others. So while they may be seduced by their logic, you can clearly see through it. And it certainly works the other way around as well. So go slowly with this at first. You don't want to find yourself at the end of the week with no friends because you challenged all their sacred cows without maintaining rapport.

Cultural Notes

sacred cow—Figuratively, it refers to anything that is beyond criticism. For example, "That housing project is a real sacred cow: the city council won't hear of abandoning it." It's an English-language formulation of the Hindu principle of the sanctity of all life, including animal life and especially that of the cow, which is accorded veneration. In India, followers of Hinduism consider cows sacred and do not eat them because they believe the animals contain the souls of dead persons.

Exercises

I. Answer the following questions based on the text.

1. How do you understand "prospect" in the fourth paragraph?

2. How do you know you are building a thought blockade for yourself?

3. What is the purpose of the author to mention the woman and her son?

4. What is "sacred cow", according to your understanding?

5. What did the author suggest us to do to stay out of a thought blockade?

II. Text review. Write T for true and F for false in the bracket before the statement.

( ) 1. Even what you are sure about may turn out to be incorrect in reality.

( ) 2. If you fight hard against whatever thought contrary to you, you may get stuck in a thought trap.

( ) 3. The being of a person cannot be separated from the intellect although they are often inconsistent with each other.

( ) 4. Children suffer from more thinking traps than adults.

( ) 5. The intellect needs to share feeling with others so as to validate the person's stance.

( ) 6. A woman visited the author and complained a lot about her son's messiness.

( ) 7. The internal safety procedure shelters one from one's own defects.

( ) 8. You should never point your fingers at others no matter how angry you are.

( ) 9. Once you know what the traps are, you'll easily escape out of them.

( ) 10. You should point out the others' thought traps as soon as you've found them.

III. Paraphrase the following sentences in English.

1. Let's start by looking at the traps of the intellectual mind, the one who weaves such wonderful webs of logic that leaves us feeling good while keeping us quite stuck.

2. If so, then you fell into another trap to feed the intellect while starving your real self.

3. Did you let her logical retort validate your own stance?

4. Her intellect screamed bloody murder the moment we came up on her sacred cow of cleanliness.

5. And finally, she felt compelled to share it with me to externalize the trap and manifest it into reality.

IV. Translate the following sentences into Chinese.

1. You may have even seen, heard, touched, tasted, or smelled the world in a way to support your stance.

2. So how did the possibility of an opposite opinion make its way through your logic and basically the reality as you knew it, to get you to change your mind?

3. You may have seen the behaviors that go along with such an internal process if you have ever challenged someone's "sacred cow."

4. The moment you do recognize it you are in a sense already on your way out.

5. But then it is about freeing yourself from the logic that the intellect has spun around the trap.

V. Respond to each of the following statements.

1. Seeing is believing.

2. You are not your intellect! You the being (soul) are much, much more!

3. The intellect's need for validation is a crucial trap to avoid.

4. Whenever there is one finger pointing outwards, there are three fingers pointing back to the person doing the pointing.

5. You may find it is easier to spot other people's traps quicker than your own.

VI. Provide a text which can support your viewpoint on one of the statements in *Exercise V*. Make your comment on the text you choose.

Text B

Motivated by All the Wrong Reasons
Teresa Franklyn

这是一种"反其道"的论述，但是揭示了生活中的真理：我们并不是只受正面因素的影响，而如何利用和对待负面影响是每个人都应该重视的。

Sometimes trying to be spiritual holds us back from actually living the spiritual life we want. In our quest to live such spiritual and good lives, we often avoid the stuff that makes us seem unspiritual, even if that very stuff can move us toward our own spiritual growth.

Spiritual seekers are well aware of the power of intention. We know that it is the thought behind the action that is more important than the action itself. We know if we are motivated by fear and take action based on that fear, the results can be limiting and work against us.

Because of this, we try to align our intentions with that of love, abundance and wholeness. Unfortunately, for many of us, when we go within to explore our motivation, seeking

quest /kwest/ *n.* an act or instance of seeking
motivate /ˈməʊtɪveɪt/ *v.* to provide with a motive, impel
align /əˈlaɪn/ *v.* a. to bring into line or alignment; b. to array on the side of or against a party or cause

that deeper answer to why we want something, we sometimes end up no deeper than where we began. We might tell ourselves we really want to do or get something in order to help humanity or some other noble reason to make us feel better about ourselves, but in reality, we may simply be motivated by money, greed, fame, power, etc.

> **catalyst** /'kætlɪst/ n. a. a substance that enables a chemical reaction to proceed at a usually faster rate or under different conditions (as at a lower temperature) than otherwise possible; b. an agent that provokes or speeds significant change or action
> **destiny** /'destɪni/ n. a. sth to which a person or thing is destined, fortune; b. a predetermined course of events often held to be an irresistible power or agency
> **alcoholic** /ˌælkə'hɒlɪk/ a. adj. of, relating to, or caused by alcohol; b. adj. affected with alcoholism; c. n. a person affected with alcoholism
> **anonymous** /ə'nɒnɪməs/ adj. a. not named or identified; b. of unknown authorship or origin
> **ego** /'iːgəʊ/ n. the self, esp. as seen in relation to other selves or to the outside world

Upon discovering this, we then sit around telling ourselves we don't want to do something unless we are doing it for the right reasons. So we sit, and sit, and sit. Years pass and we're still sitting, waiting for that right reason to come, that spiritual, pure and noble reason.

While it is noble to want to act out of the right reasons, sometimes the wrong reasons can be just the catalyst we need in order to take action and find the right reasons.

It is through the process of pursuing our destiny that we create our destiny and discover who we truly are and what we're all about. If we sit around waiting to be noble and whole before we act toward nobility and wholeness, we will never get there.

When I was 19, I dated a recovering alcoholic. He was in Alcoholics Anonymous and suggested that I go to Al-Anon (for family & friends of alcoholics) to better understand him. He also knew that my father happened to drink quite a bit and thought it would be good for me to understand more about alcoholism in general. For no other reason than to please him and be a "good" girlfriend, I went. I certainly didn't think I needed to go, not for me, for him, or for my father.

Now we all know that people-pleasing, an ego-driven motive, is not a spiritually good reason to do something. But was it the right reason for me? Yes. And here's why.

In those meetings, I learned about the true nature of alcoholism. I learned that I

am not to blame for my father's drinking (I didn't even know I had been blaming myself). I learned that I am worthy, valuable and important. I learned to trust in a Higher Power, have faith that the Universe is in order and most importantly, I learned to trust and believe in myself.

All of this came out of my ego's desire to please someone else, to make them think that I am a "good" girlfriend and therefore, a "good" person.

Had I refused to go because my intentions

weren't pure and spiritually driven, who knows how many more years I would have lived in blame, shame and denial.

My point is, don't sit around and wait for the right reasons to motivate you. Sometimes the right reasons come disguised as the wrong reasons. If greed is the only thing that will motivate you to get up off that couch and take action toward your dreams, I say go for it! Use whatever you have currently available to you, right or wrong, good or bad, to start the process.

If you have searched within and cannot seem to find the right reasons, use those "wrong" reasons to catapult you into action toward fulfilling your life's purpose. Somewhere along the way, the right reasons will emerge and make themselves very clear to you. Often we think we want something for a certain reason and when we get it, or while in the process of getting it, we discover the true meaning behind our motivations. Or our reasons change, our intentions and motivation changes as we learn and grow.

I have a friend who started a business years ago strictly to make money. Her husband left her and she had to find a way to not only support herself, but also to prove to him that she didn't need him. It was part necessity, part revenge. Actually, to be quite honest, it was mostly revenge. She could have easily taken an office job to support herself since her previous employer before she married had offered her old job back. But she refused. She wanted to make lots of money and become a successful Business woman to spite her ex-husband.

Two years into the business, she discovered that she loved working for herself. She loved the independence and satisfaction that creating her own income generated inside her. Her business transformed as she transformed. She found that she loved seeing her customers happy and began focusing a big part of her Business toward customer satisfaction. She discovered that she had a lot of strength and courage and didn't need to depend on anyone else for her well-being.

Motivated initially by revenge, she soon learned that it didn't matter what he thought. In fact, to this day, she has no idea if he knows about her success and she could care less. She is happy, confident and leads a joyous and full life. She is no longer motivated by revenge, spite or ego-driven desires.

Like me, had she not taken action and instead sat around waiting for more noble intentions, it is uncertain where she would be today.

So go out and live your dreams. Lead your spiritual life by accepting and embracing seemingly unspiritual

denial /dɪ'naɪəl/ n. refusal to satisfy a request or desire

disguise /dɪs'gaɪz/ v. a. to change the customary dress or appearance of; b. to furnish with a false appearance or an assumed identity

catapult /'kætəpʌlt/ v. to throw or launch by or as if by a catapult

fulfill /fʊl'fil/ v. a. to put into effect, execute; b. to meet the requirements of (a business order)

revenge /rɪ'vendʒ/ n. action taken in return for an injury or offense

spite /spaɪt/ v. annoy, offend

joyous /'dʒɔɪəs/ adj. joyful

embrace /ɪm'breɪs/ v. a. to clasp in the arms, hug; b. cherish, love; c. encircle, enclose; d. to take up esp. readily or gladly

things. Go after your goals, no matter how un-spiritually motivated they may be. If this is the only way to get you moving, it doesn't matter if you are doing it for money, revenge, greed, power, attention, glory, <u>martyrdom</u>, <u>sainthood</u>

martyrdom /'mɑːtədəm/ *n.* the suffering of death on account of adherence to a cause and esp. to one's religious faith
sainthood /'semthʊd/ *n.* the quality or state of being a saint

or any other ego-driven desire. Along the way, you'll find your true self and all those "wrong" reasons will fall away and be replaced by more pure and noble reasons. If it takes a wrong reason to turn your life around toward wholeness, it must not be so "wrong" after all.

Cultural Notes

Al-Anon—Al-Anon offers understanding and support for families and friends of problem drinkers, whether the alcoholic is still drinking or not. Alateen, a part of Al-Anon, is for young people aged 12—17 (inclusive) who have been affected by someone else's drinking, usually that of a parent. The parents, children, wives, husbands, friends and colleagues of alcoholics could all be helped by Al-Anon and Alateen whether or not the drinker in their lives recognises that a problem exists. At Al-Anon group meetings members receive comfort and understanding and learn to cope with their problems through the exchange of experience, strength and hope. The sharing of problems binds individuals and groups together in a bond that is protected by a policy of anonymity. Members learn that there are things they can do to help themselves and indirectly to help the problem drinker. Changed attitudes, which come from greater understanding of the illness, may result in the drinker seeking help. Al-Anon is self-supporting through members' voluntary contributions and the sale of its literature. The groups are non-professional and have no religious or other affiliations and no opinions on outside issues. Al-Anon is based on the Twelve Steps and Twelve Traditions adapted from Alcoholics Anonymous; it is non-professional, self-supporting, non-religious, non-political and multi-racial.

Exercises

I. Answer the following questions based on the text.

1. What is the meaning of "spiritual" in the first paragraph?
2. How can the wrong reasons be the catalyst we need to find the right ones?

3. How do you understand "wrong reasons" in the text?

4. How did the author convey her idea to us?

5. What is the main idea of the text?

II. Text review. Write T for true and F for false in the bracket before the statement.

(　) 1. We are always in the quest of noble motivations for doing things.

(　) 2. Only when we act out of right reasons can we live spiritual lives.

(　) 3. Most of us are deceitful to say that we want to get something in order to help humanity.

(　) 4. We should sit around waiting for the coming of the right reasons.

(　) 5. The author's father had been in Al-Anon for some years.

(　) 6. The author regretted having been to the meetings of Al-Anon in order to please her boyfriend.

(　) 7. The right reasons may come in disguise of the wrong ones.

(　) 8. Mostly for the sake of money, the author's friend started her own business after being deserted by her husband.

(　) 9. The woman leads a joyous life in the revenge of her ex-husband.

(　) 10. The writer was not sure whether her friend, without a noble intention, should take action or not.

III. Paraphrase the following sentences in English.

1. Sometimes trying to be spiritual holds us back from actually living the spiritual life we want.

2. Because of this, we try to align our intentions with that of love, abundance and wholeness.

3. For no other reason than to please him and be a "good" girlfriend, I went.

4. People-pleasing, an ego-driven motive, is not a spiritually good reason to do something.

5. In fact, to this day, she has no idea if he knows about her success and she could care less.

IV. Translate the following sentences into Chinese.

1. In our quest to live such spiritual and good lives, we often avoid the stuff that makes us seem unspiritual, even if that very stuff can move us toward our own spiritual growth.

2. While it is noble to want to act out of the right reasons, sometimes the wrong

reasons can be just the catalyst we need in order to take action and find the right reasons.

3. Had I refused to go because my intentions weren't pure and spiritually driven, who knows how many more years I would have lived in blame, shame and denial.

4. If you have searched within and cannot seem to find the right reasons, use those "wrong" reasons to catapult you into action toward fulfilling your life's purpose.

5. Along the way, you'll find your true self and all those "wrong" reasons will fall away and be replaced by more pure and noble reasons.

V. Respond to each of the following statements.

1. It is the thought behind the action that is more important than the action itself.

2. When we go within to explore our motivation to actions, we sometimes end up no deeper than where we began.

3. It is through the process of pursuing our destiny that we create our destiny and discover who we truly are and what we're all about.

4. Sometimes the right reasons of doing things come in disguise of the wrong ones.

5. In order to get ourselves in action, we need to be motivated by a wrong reason sometimes.

VI. Provide a text which can support your viewpoint on one of the statements in *Exercise V*. Make your comment on the text you choose.

Unit Eleven

Text A

On Life

Percy Bysshe Shelley

Life and the world, or whatever we call that which we are and feel, is an astonishing thing. The mist of familiarity obscures from us the wonder of our being. We are struck with admiration at some of its transient modifications, but it is itself the great miracle.

What are changes of empires, the wreck of dynasties, with the opinions which supported them; what is the birth and the extinction of religious and of political systems to life? What are the revolutions of the globe which we inhabit, and the operations of the elements of which it is composed, compared with life? What is the universe of stars, and suns, of which this inhabited earth is one, and their motions, and their destiny, compared with life? Life, the great miracle, we admire not, because it is so miraculous. It is well that we are thus shielded by the familiarity of what is at once so certain and so unfathomable, from an astonishment which would otherwise absorb and overawe the functions of that which is its object.

If any artist, I do not say had executed, but had merely conceived in his mind the system of the sun, and the stars, and planets, they not existing, and had painted to us in words, or

obscure /əb'skjuə/ a. *adj.* dark; hidden; not clearly seen or understood; b. *adj.* not well known; c. *v.* make obscure

transient /'trænziənt/ a. *adj.* lasting for a short time only; brief; b. (*US*) guest (in a hotel, boarding house, etc.) who is not a permanent resident

modification /ˌmɔdɪfi'keɪʃən/ *n.* change or alteration

extinction /ɪks'tɪŋkʃən/ *n.* a. making, being, becoming extinct; b. act of extinguishing.

religious /rɪ'lɪdʒəs/ a. *adj.* of religion; b. *adj.* (of a person) devout; god fearing; c. *adj.* of a monastic order; d. *adj.* scrupulous; conscientious; e. *n.* person bound by monastic vows; monk or nun

shield /ʃiːld/ *n.* a. piece of armor (metal, leather, wood) carried on the arm, to protect the body when fighting; representation of a shield, e.g. carved on a stone gateway, showing a person's coat of arms; b. (*fig.*) person or thing that protects.

unfathomable /ʌn'fæðəməbəl/ *adj.* so deep that can not be reached; (*fig.*) too strange or difficult to be understood

overawe /'əuvər'ɔː/ *v.* awe completely; awe through great respect, etc.

execute /'eksɪkjuːt/ *v.* a. carry out (what one is asked or told to do); b. (*legal*) give effect to; c. (*legal*) make legally binding; d. carry out punishment by death on (sb); e. perform on the stage, at a concert, etc.

upon canvas, the spectacle now afforded by the nightly cope of heaven, and illustrated it by the wisdom of astronomy, great would be our admiration. Or had he imagined the scenery of this earth, the mountains, the seas, and the rivers; the grass, and the flowers, and the variety of the forms and masses of the leaves of the woods, and the colours which attend the setting and the rising sun, and the hues of the atmosphere, turbid or serene, these things not before existing, truly we should have been astonished, and it would not have been a vain boast to have said of such a man, Non merita nome di creatore, se non Iddio ed il Poeta. But now these things are looked on with little wonder, and to be

canvas /'kænvəs/ *n.* strong, coarse cloth used for tents, sails, bags, etc. and by artists for oil-painting
spectacle /'spektəkəl/ *n.* a. public display, procession, etc, esp. one with ceremony; b. sth seen; sth taking place before the eyes, esp. sth fine, remarkable or noteworthy
astronomy /ə'strɒnəmɪ/ *n.* science of the son, moon, stars and planets
turbid /'tɜːbɪd/ *adj.* a. (of liquids) thick; muddy; not clear; b. (*fig.*) disordered, confused
non merita nome di creatore, se non Iddio ed il Poeta none deserves the name of Creator but God and the Poet
fragment /'frægmənt/ a. *n.* part broken off; separate or incomplete part; b. *v.* break into fragments
commencement /kə'mensmənt/ *n.* a. beginning; b. (in US universities, and at Cambridge and Dublin) ceremony at which degrees are conferred
abstraction /æb'strækʃən/ *n.* a. abstracting or being abstracted; b. absent-mindedness; c. visionary idea; idea of a quality apart from its material accompaniments
convict /kən'vɪkt/ *n.* person convicted of crime and undergoing punishment
dogmatism /'dɒɡmətɪzəm/ *n.* the quality of being dogmatic; being dogmatic

conscious of them with intense delight is esteemed to be the distinguishing mark of a refined and extraordinary person. The multitude of men care not for them. It is thus with Life—that which includes all.

What is life? Thoughts and feelings arise, with or without our will, and we employ words to express them. We are born, and our birth is unremembered, and our infancy remembered but in fragments; we live on, and in living we lose the apprehension of life. How vain is it to think that words can penetrate the mystery of our being! Rightly used they may make evident our ignorance to ourselves, and this is much. For what are we? Whence do we come? and whither do we go? Is birth the commencement, is death the conclusion of our being? What is birth and death?

The most refined abstractions of logic conduct to a view of life, which, though startling to the apprehension, is, in fact, that which the habitual sense of its repeated combinations has extinguished in us. It strips, as it were, the painted curtain from this scene of things. I confess that I am one of those who are unable to refuse my assent to the conclusions of those philosophers who assert that nothing exists but as it is perceived.

It is a decision against which all our persuasions struggle, and we must be long convicted before we can be convinced that the solid universe of external things is 'such stuff as dreams are made of.' The shocking absurdities of the popular philosophy of mind and matter, its fatal consequences in morals, and their violent dogmatism concerning the source of all things, had early conducted me to materialism. This materialism is a seducing system to young and superficial minds. It allows its disciples to talk, and dispenses them from thinking. But I was discontented with such a view of things as it afforded; man is a being of high aspirations, 'looking both before and after,' whose 'thoughts wander through eternity,' disclaiming alliance with transience and decay; incapable of imagining to himself annihilation; existing but in the future and the past; being, not what he is, but what he has been and shall be. Whatever may be his true and final destination, there is a spirit within him at enmity with nothingness and dissolution. This is the character of all life and being. Each is at once the centre and the circumference; the point to which all things are referred, and the line in which all things are contained. Such contemplations as these, materialism and the popular philosophy of mind and matter alike forbid; they are only consistent with the intellectual system.

It is absurd to enter into a long recapitulation of arguments sufficiently familiar to those inquiring minds, whom alone a writer on abstruse subjects can be conceived to address. Perhaps the most clear and vigorous statement of the intellectual system is to be found in Sir William Drummond's Academical Questions.

After such an exposition, it would be idle to translate into other words what could only lose its energy and fitness by the change. Examined point by point, and word by word, the most discriminating intellects have been able to discern no train of thoughts in the process of reasoning, which does not conduct inevitably to the conclusion which has been stated.

What follows from the admission? It establishes no new truth, it gives us no additional insight into our hidden nature, neither its action nor itself. Philosophy, impatient as it may be to build, has much work yet remaining, as pioneer for the overgrowth of ages. It makes one step towards this object; it destroys error, and the roots of error. It leaves, what it is too often the duty of the reformer in political and ethical questions to leave, a vacancy.

It reduces the mind to that freedom in

disciple /dɪ'saɪpəl/ n. follower of any leader of religious thought, art, learning, etc.

dispense /dɪs'pens/ v. a. deal out; distribute; administer; b. mix; prepare, give out (medicines); c. do without; d. render unnecessary

disclaim /dɪs'kleɪm/ v. say that one does not own, that one has no connection with

alliance /ə'laɪəns/ n. a. association or connection; b. union of persons, families, e.g. by marriage, or states (by treaty)

transience /'trænzɪəns/ n. lasting for a short time only; briefness

annihilation /ə,naɪə'leɪʃən/ n. complete destruction (of military or naval forces etc.)

dissolution /dɪsə'luːʃən/ n. breaking up; undoing or ending (of a marriage, partnership etc.)

circumference /sə'kʌmfərəns/ n. line that marks out a circle or other curved figure; distance round sth

contemplation /,kɒntəm'pleɪʃən/ n. deep thought; intention; expectation

consistent /kən'sɪstənt/ adj. (of a person, his behavior, principles, etc.) confirming to a regular pattern or style; regular

recapitulation /riːkəpɪtjʊ'leɪʃ(ə)n/ n. repeating; going through again the main points of sth (that has been told, discussed, argued about, etc.)

abstruse /əb'struːs/ adj. whose meaning or answer is hidden or difficult to understand; profound

vigorous /'vɪɡərəs/ adj. strong; energetic

discriminating /dɪ'skrɪmɪneɪtɪŋ/ adj. a. able to see or make small differences; b. giving special or different treatment to certain people, countries, etc.; differential

vacancy /'veɪkənsi/ n. a. condition of being empty or unoccupied; b. unoccupied space; blank; c. lack of ideas or intelligence; d. position in business, etc. for which sb is needed

which it would have acted, but for the misuse of words and signs, the instruments of its own creation. By signs, I would be understood in a wide sense, including what is properly meant by that term, and what I peculiarly mean. In this latter sense, almost all familiar objects are signs, standing, not for themselves, but for others, in their capacity of suggesting one thought which shall lead to a train of thoughts. Our whole life is thus an education of error.

Let us recollect our sensations as children. What a distinct and intense appreh-ension had we of the world and of ourselves! Many of the circumstances of social life were then important to us which are now no longer so. But that is not the point of comparison on

sensation /sen'seɪʃən/ *n.* a. ability to feel; feeling; b. (instance of sth that causes a) quick and excited reaction

constitute /'kɒnstɪtjuːt/ *v.* a. give (sb) authority to hold (a position, etc.); b. establish; give legal authority to (a committee, etc.); c. make up (a whole); amount to; be the components of

reverie /'revəri/ *n.* a. (instance/occasion of a) condition of being lost in dreamy, pleasant thoughts; b. piece of dreamy music

entangle /ɪn'tæŋgəl/ *v.* a. catch in a snare or among obstacles; b. (*fig.*) put or get into difficulties, in unfavorable circumstances

reiteration /riː,tə'reɪʃən/ *n.* a. act of reiterating; b. instance of repetition

deduction /dɪ'dʌkʃən/ *n.* taking away (an amount or a part)

nominal /'nɒmɪnəl/ *adj.* a. existing in name or word only, not in fact; b. of little importance or value; c. (gram) of a noun or nouns; d. of, or bearing a name

vulgarly /'vʌlgəli/ *adv.* ill mannered, in bad taste

subsist /səb'sɪst/ *v.* exist; be kept in existence on

assemblage /ə'semblɪdʒ/ *n.* bringing or coming together; assembly (now the usual word)

which I mean to insist. We less habitually distinguished all that we saw and felt, from ourselves. They seemed as it were to constitute one mass. There are some persons who, in this respect, are always children. Those who are subject to the state called reverie, feel as if their nature were dissolved into the surrounding universe, or as if the surrounding universe were absorbed into their being. They are conscious of no distinction. And these are states which precede, or accompany, or follow an unusually intense and vivid apprehension of life. As men grow up this power commonly decays, and they become mechanical and habitual agents. Thus feelings and then reasonings are the combined result of a multitude of entangled thoughts, and of a series of what are called impressions, planted by reiteration.

The view of life presented by the most refined deductions of the intellectual philosophy, is that of unity. Nothing exists but as it is perceived. The difference is merely nominal between those two classes of thought, which are vulgarly distinguished by the names of ideas and of external objects. Pursuing the same thread of reasoning, the existence of distinct individual minds, similar to that which is employed in now questioning its own nature, is likewise found to be a delusion. The words I, YOU, THEY, are not signs of any actual difference subsisting between the assemblage of thoughts thus indicated, but are merely marks employed to denote the different modifications of the one mind.

Cultural Notes

Percy Bysshe Shelley (1792—1822)—Percy Bysshe Shelley was one of the major English Romantic poets and is widely considered to be among the finest lyric poets of the English language. He is perhaps most famous for such anthology pieces as *Ozymandias, Ode to the West Wind, To a Skylark, and The Masque of Anarchy.* However, his major works were long visionary poems including *Alastor, Adonais, The Revolt of Islam, Prometheus Unbound* and the unfinished *The Triumph of Life.*

Percy Bysshe Shelley, born at Field Place near Horsham in 1792, was the son of Sir Timothy Shelley, the M.P. for New Shoreham. Shelley was educated at Eton and Oxford University. At university Shelley began reading books by radical political writers such as William Godwin. He also wrote The Necessity of Atheism, a pamphlet that attacked the idea of compulsory Christianity. Oxford University was shocked when they discovered what Shelley had written and on 25th March 1811, he was expelled. Shelley eloped to Scotland with Harriet Westbrook, a sixteen-year-old daughter of a coffeehouse keeper. Shelley moved to Ireland where he made revolutionary speeches on religion and politics. He also wrote a political pamphlet *A Declaration of Rights,* on the subject of the French Revolution, but it was considered to be too radical for distribution in Britain. Percy Bysshe Shelley returned to England where he became involved in radical politics. In 1817 he wrote the pamphlet *A Proposal for Putting Reform to the Vote Throughout the United Kingdom.* In the pamphlet Shelley suggested a national referendum on electoral reform and improvements in working class education.

In 1822, Shelley moved to Italy with Leigh Hunt and Lord Byron where they published the journal *The Liberal.* By publishing it in Italy the three men remained free from prosecution by the British authorities. The first edition of *The Liberal* sold 4,000 copies. Soon after its publication, Percy Bysshe Shelley was lost at sea on 8th July, 1822, while sailing to meet Leigh Hunt.

Sir William Drummond—He is a distinguished scholar and philosopher. The date of his birth seems not to be ascertained, nor does any memoir of which we are aware, describe his early education. In 1805, his *Academical Questions* appeared, the first work in which he put forward claims to be esteemed a metaphysician. Although in this work he talks of the dignity of philosophy with no little enthusiasm, and gives it a preference to other subjects, more distinct than many may now admit; yet his work has certainly done more for the demolition of other systems than for instruction in any he has himself propounded. He perhaps carried the skeptical philosophy of Hume a little beyond its first bounds, by showing that we cannot comprehend the idea of simple substance.

Exercises

I. Answer the following questions based on the text.

1. Do you think life is a miracle compared with the planets and stars of the universe? Are you satisfied with your own life?
2. In what does the greatness of life lie since it is of such transience?
3. The text suggests that nothing exists but as it is perceived. Is it against your own belief?
4. How can we understand that all familiar objects are only signs, standing not for themselves but for others?
5. I, You, and They are only different modifications of one mind. What does this sentence mean?

II. Text Review. Write T for true and F for false in the brackets before each of the following statements.

( ) 1. According to the text, when people get into closer connection with each other, the familiarity will get rid of the mist between each other.

( ) 2. People think the world we are in is a great wonder and they look on it with awe and intense delight.

( ) 3. Thoughts and feelings arise with our will as we are human beings.

( ) 4. The author agrees with the conception that nothing exists except what is perceived.

( ) 5. In a sense, our life is made up of the past and future, the being is so transient and impossible to catch.

( ) 6. Everybody has definitely one life, and he could choose to have his life in the center—and then it would be in the center only.

( ) 7. As the text suggests, many of the circumstances of social life were then important to people but not all the way so.

( ) 8. Reverie is a state in which people feel as if they were dissolved into the surrounding universe because the universal beauty is so intense.

( ) 9. People are aware that they are different and that everything around is distinguished with its own characteristics.

( ) 10. Entangled thoughts combine to produce feelings and reasonings and impressions.

III. Paraphrase the following sentences in English.

1. What are changes of empires, the wreck of dynasties, with the opinions that supported them; what is the birth and the extinction of religious and of political systems to life?

2. The most refined abstractions of logic conduct to a view of life, which, though startling to the apprehension, is, in fact, that which the habitual sense of its repeated combinations has extinguished in us.

3. It is a decision against which all our persuasions struggle, and we must be long convicted before we can be convinced that the solid universe of external things is 'such stuff as dreams are made of.'

4. It reduces the mind to that freedom in which it would have acted, but for the misuse of words and signs, the instruments of its own creation.

5. We less habitually distinguished all that we saw and felt, from ourselves. They seemed as it were to constitute one mass.

IV. Translate the following sentences into Chinese.

1. Life and the world, or whatever we call that which we are and feel, is an astonishing thing. The mist of familiarity obscures from us the wonder of our being.

2. It is well that we are thus shielded by the familiarity of what is at once so certain and so unfathomable, from an astonishment which would otherwise absorb and overawe the functions of that which is its object.

3. We are born, and our birth is unremembered, and our infancy remembered but in fragments; we live on, and in living we lose the apprehension of life. How vain is it to think that words can penetrate the mystery of our being!

4. This is the character of all life and being. Each is at once the centre and the circumference; the point to which all things are referred, and the line in which all things are contained.

5. Nothing exists but as it is perceived. The difference is merely nominal between those two classes of thought, which are vulgarly distinguished by the names of ideas and of external objects.

V. Respond to each of the following statements.

1. We are becoming more and more lost in life though we thought we are more understanding and seeing more thoroughly the nature.

2. Science could never solve the problems of life though people believe with it we are "stronger" in a sense.

3. The philosophical state of our existence is that we see less about what we think most familiar to us.

4. Poets are those who look into the nature and express what he sees there.

5. Different people interpret life differently. Some think it is like wine, but some think life is suffering.

VI. Provide a text which can support your viewpoint on one of the statements in *Exercise V*. Make your comment on the text you choose.

Text B

The Rhythm of Life

Alice Meynell

If life is not always poetical, it is at least metrical. Periodicity rules over the mental experience of man, according to the path of the orbit of his thoughts. Distances are not gauged, ellipses not measured, velocities not ascertained, times not known. Nevertheless, the recurrence is sure. What the mind suffered last week, or last year, it does not suffer now; but it will suffer again next week or next year. Happiness is not a matter of events; it depends upon the tides of the mind. Disease is metrical, closing in at shorter and shorter periods towards death, sweeping abroad at longer and longer intervals towards recovery. Sorrow for one cause was intolerable yesterday, and will be intolerable to-morrow; today it is easy to bear, but the cause has not passed. Even the burden of a spiritual distress unsolved is bound to leave the heart to a temporary peace;

periodicity /ˌpɪərɪəˈdɪsɪti/ *n.* the quality, state, or fact of being regularly recurrent or having periods

orbit /ˈɔːbɪt/ *n.* path followed by a heavenly body, e.g. a planet, the moon, or a manmade object

gauge /ɡeɪdʒ/ *n. a.* standard measure; extent; *b.* distance between rails; *c.* thickness of wire, sheet-metal, etc.; diameter of a bullet, etc.; *d.* instrument for measuring, e.g. rainfall, strength of wind, size, diameter, etc., of tools, wire, etc.

ellipse /ɪˈlɪps/ *n.* regular oval

velocity /vɪˈlɒsɪti/ *n. a.* speed; quickness; *b.* rate of motion

ascertain /ˌæsəˈteɪn/ *v.* find out (in order to be certain about)

interval /ˈɪntəvəl/ *n. a.* time (between two events or two parts of an action); (esp.) time between two acts of a play, two parts of a concert, etc.; *b.* space between (two objects or points); *c.* (*music*) difference of pitch between two notes on a given scale

intolerable /ɪnˈtɒlərəbəl/ *adj.* that cannot be tolerated or endured

temporary /ˈtempərəri/ *adj.* lasting for, designed to be used for, a short time only

and remorse itself does not remain—it returns.

Gaiety takes us by a dear surprise. If we had made a course of notes of its visits, we might have been on the watch, and would have had an expectation instead of a discovery. No one makes such observations; in all the diaries of students of the interior world, there have never come to light the records of the Kepler of such cycles. But Thomas e Kempis knew of the recurrences, if he did not measure them. In his cell alone with the elements—"What wouldst thou more than these? for out of these were all things made"—he learnt the stay to be found in the depth of the hour of bitterness, and the remembrance that restrains the soul at the coming of the moment of delight, giving it a more conscious welcome, but presaging for it an inexorable flight. And "rarely, rarely comest thou," sighed Shelley, not to Delight merely, but to the Spirit of Delight.

Delight can be compelled beforehand, called, and constrained to our service—Ariel can be bound to a daily task; but such artificial violence throws life out of metre, and it is not the spirit that is thus compelled. THAT flits upon an orbit elliptically or parabolically or hyperbolically curved, keeping no man knows what trysts with Time.

remorse /rɪˈmɔːs/ n. a. deep, bitter regret for wrong-doing; b. compunction
gaiety /ˈɡeɪəti/ n. a. being gay; cheerfulness; b. merrymaking; joyful, festive occasions
interior /ɪnˈtɪəriə/ adj. a. situated inside; of the inside; b. inland; away from the coast; c. home or domestic (contrasted with foreign)
presage /ˈpresɪdʒ/ n. (formal) presentiment; sign looked upon as a warning
inexorable /ɪnˈeksərəbəl/ adj. relentless; unyielding
constrain /kənˈstreɪn/ v. make sb do sth by using force or strong persuasion
elliptically /ɪˈlɪptɪkəli/ adv. omitting from a sentence of words needed to complete the construction or meaning
parabolically /ˌpærəˈbɒlikəli/ adv. of, like, a parabola (a plane curve formed by cutting, a cone on a plane parallel to its side, so that the two arms get father away from one another)
hyperbolically /ˌhaɪpəˈbɒlikli/ adv. using exaggerated statements
tryst /traɪst/ n. (archaic) (time and place for, agreement to have, a) meeting, esp. between lovers
infraction /ɪnˈfrækʃən/ n. a. breaking of a rule, law, etc; b. instance of this
Eppur si muove this is what Galileo is alleged to have said on going into house arrest: "but it does move."
flux /flʌks/ n. continuous succession of changes
reflux /ˈriːflʌks/ n. flowing back; ebb
impetus /ˈɪmpɪtəs/ n. a. force with which a body moves; b. impulse; driving force

It seems fit that Shelley and the author of the "Imitation" should both have been keen and simple enough to perceive these flights, and to guess at the order of this periodicity. Both souls were in close touch with the spirits of their several worlds, and no deliberate human rules, no infractions of the liberty and law of the universal movement, kept from them the knowledge of recurrences. Eppur si muove. They knew that presence does not exist without absence; they knew that what is just upon its flight of farewell is already on its long path of return. They knew that what is approaching to the very touch is hastening towards departure. "O wind," cried Shelley, in autumn,

O wind,
If winter comes can spring be far behind?

They knew that the flux is equal to the reflux; that to interrupt with unlawful recurrences, out of time, is to weaken the impulse of onset and retreat; the sweep and impetus of movement. To live in constant efforts after an equal life, whether the equality

subjection /səb'dʒekʃən/ *n.* getting or being brought under control

desolation /ˌdesə'leɪʃən/ *n.* making or being desolated

rejoice /rɪ'dʒɔɪs/ *v.* a. make glad; cause to be happy; b. feel great joy; show signs of great happiness

uncovenanted /ʌn'kʌvənəntid/ opposite of "covenanted" (meaning promised, pledged)

beatitude /bi(ː)'ætitjuːd/ *n.* great happiness; blessedness

forsaken /fə'seɪkən/ *v.* give up; break away from; desert

docile /'dəʊsaɪl/ *adj.* easily trained or controlled

irrevocable /ɪ'revəkəbəl/ *adj.* final and unalterable; that cannot be revoked

irrigate /'ɪrɪgeɪt/ *v.* supply with water

Indo-Germanic /'ɪndəʊʒəː'mænik/ relevant with India and German

lapse /læps/ *n.* a. slight error in speech or behavior; slip of the memory; tongue or pen; b. falling away from what is right; c. (of time) passing away; interval; (*legal*) ending of a right, etc. from failure to use it or ask for its renewal

ebb /eb/ *v.* a. (of the tide) flow back from the land to the sea; b. grow less; become weak or faint; c. the flowing out of the tide; d. (*fig.*) low state; decline or decay

cumulative /'kjuːmjʊlətɪv/ *adj.* increasing in amount by one addition after another

be sought in mental production, or in spiritual sweetness, or in the joy of the senses, is to live without either rest or full activity. The souls of certain of the saints, being singularly simple and single, have been in the most complete subjection to the law of periodicity. Ecstasy and desolation visited them by seasons. They endured, during spaces of vacant time, the interior loss of all for which they had sacrificed the world. They rejoiced in the uncovenanted beatitude of sweetness alighting in their hearts. Like them are the poets whom, three times or ten times in the course of a long life, the Muse has approached, touched, and forsaken. And yet hardly like them; not always so docile, nor so wholly prepared for the departure, the brevity, of the golden and irrevocable hour. Few poets have fully recognized the metrical absence of their muse. For full recognition is expressed in one only way—silence.

It has been found that several tribes in Africa and in America worship the moon, and not the sun; a great number worship both; but no tribes are known to adore the sun, and not the moon. On her depend the tides; and she is Selene, mother of Herse, bringer of the dews that recurrently irrigate lands where rain is rare. More than any other companion of earth is she the Measurer. Early Indo-Germanic languages knew her by that name. Her metrical phases are the symbol of the order of recurrence. Constancy in approach and in departure is the reason of her inconstancies. Juliet will not receive a vow spoken in invocation of the moon; but Juliet did not live to know that love itself has tidal times—lapses and ebbs which are due to the metrical rule of the interior heart, but which the lover vainly and unkindly attributes to some outward alteration in the beloved. For man—except those elect already named—is hardly aware of periodicity. The individual man either never learns it fully, or learns it late. And he learns it so late, because it is a matter of cumulative experience upon which cumulative evidence is long lacking. It is in the after-part of each life that the law is learnt so definitely as to do away with the hope or fear of continuance. That young sorrow comes so near to despair is a result of this young ignorance. So is the early hope of great achievement.

Life seems so long, and its capacity so great, to one who knows nothing of all the intervals it needs must hold—intervals between aspirations, between actions, pauses as inevitable as the pauses of sleep. And life looks impossible to the young unfortunate, unaware of the inevitable and unfailing refreshment. It would be for their peace to learn that there is a tide in the affairs of men, in a sense more subtle—if it is not too audacious to add a meaning to Shakespeare—than the phrase was meant to contain. Their joy is flying away from them on its way home; their life will wax and wane; and if they would be wise, they must wake and rest in its phases, knowing that they are ruled by the law that commands all things—a sun's revolutions and the rhythmic pangs of maternity.

audacious /ɔːˈdeɪʃəs/ *adj.* a. daring; bold; b. foolishly bold; c. impudent
rhythmic /ˈrɪðmɪk/ *adj.* marked by rhythm; having rhythm
maternity /məˈtɜːnɪti/ *n.* being a mother

Cultural Notes

Alice Meynell (1847—1922)—Alice Meynell was an English writer, editor, critic, and suffragist, now remembered mainly as a poet. Alice Meynell was born in Barnes of wealthy parents and was educated privately by her father. She spent much of her early life in Italy and converted to Catholicism on reaching her majority. She married Wilfrid Meynell in 1877, working with him on his periodical, *Merry England.* In addition to writing numerous poems and critical essays, Alice Meynell was one of the leading literary figures of her era, editing anthologies and opening her home for literary gatherings. She was twice nominated as Poet Laureate. Her poems, most of which are fairly short, display a purity and sensitivity reflecting her strong religious beliefs. *Preludes* (1875) was her first poetry collection.

Kepler (1571—1630)—Kepler was a German astronomer who discovered how the planets move around the sun. These principles are known as Kepler's Laws, and they greatly influenced the work of Sir Isaac Newton.

Thomas e Kempis (1380—1471)—Thomas e Kempis was a German monk who is believed to have written *The Imitation of Christ.*

Selene—She was an archaic lunar deity and the daughter of the titans Hyperion and Theia. In Roman mythology the moon goddess is called Luna, Latin for "moon". Like most moon deities, Selene plays a fairly large role in her pantheon. However, Selene was eventually largely supplanted by Artemis, and Luna by

Diana. In the collection known as the Homeric hymns, there is a *Hymn to Selene* (xxxii), paired with the hymn to Helios; in it Selene is addressed as "far-winged", an epithet ordinarily applied to birds. The etymology of Selene is uncertain, but if the word is of Greek origin, it is likely connected to the word selas, meaning "light". In post-renaissance art, Selene is generally depicted as a beautiful woman with a pale face, riding a silver chariot pulled by a yoke of oxen or a pair of horses. Often, she has been shown riding a horse or bull, wearing robes and a half-moon on her head and carrying a torch. Essentially, Selene is the moon goddess but is literally defined as "the moon".

Herse—She is a figure in Greek mythology, daughter of Cecrops (or, according to Pausanias, of Actaeus), sister to Aglaulus and Pandrosus. According to Apollodorus, when Hephaestus unsuccessfully attempted to rape Athena, she wiped his semen off her leg with wool and threw it on the ground, impregnating Gaia. Athena wished to make the resulting infant Erichthonius immortal and to raise it, so she gave it to three sisters: Herse, Aglaulus and Pandrosus in a basket and warned them never to open it. Aglaulus and Herse opened the basket which contained the infant and future king, Erichthonius, who was somehow mixed or intertwined with a snake. The sight caused Herse and Aglaulus to go insane and they jumped to their deaths off the Acropolis. Shrines were constructed for Herse and Aglaulus on the Acropolis.

Exercises

I. Answer the following questions based on the text.

1. Why does the text insist that if life is not always poetical, it is at least metrical?
2. What does "presence does not exist without absence" mean? Do you think it is contradictive?
3. Why is the famous line about the west wind by Shelley is quoted here?
4. Please tell the reason why several tribes in Africa and in America worship the moon rather than the sun.
5. In what way is man similar to that of nature?

II. Text Review. Write T for true and F for false in the brackets before each of the following statements.

( ) 1. We could only expect the visit of joy rather than go and find it: it is so indefinite for us human beings.

(　) 2. Happiness is something we can make—for example, we can get more happiness if we earn more money.

(　) 3. Young sorrow and the early hope of great achievement come so near to despair is a result of young ignorance.

(　) 4. The law of periodicity is most deeply rooted in the souls of certain of the saints, singularly simple and single.

(　) 5. Ecstasy and desolation will visit people in turn, just like the rising and falling ides, and different seasons.

(　) 6. Generally speaking, people in their latter life will know better about the truth of it.

(　) 7. Poets could write masterpieces when they have the interval sparkles of gift.

(　) 8. In fact, few people could make a course of notes of the visits of happy moods.

(　) 9. Ordinary men rarely learn periodicity on time, they could only learn it partly or too late.

(　) 10. Poetic souls can be in closer connection with the periodicity of the social world.

III. Paraphrase the following phrases or sentences in English.

1. If life is not always poetical, it is at least metrical. Periodicity rules over the mental experience of man, according to the path of the orbit of his thoughts.

2. Delight can be compelled beforehand, called, and constrained to our service.

3. It seems fit that Shelley and the author of the "Imitation" should both have been keen and simple enough to perceive these flights.

4. They knew that the flux is equal to the reflux; that to interrupt with unlawful recurrences, out of time, is to weaken the impulse of onset and retreat.

5. Constancy in approach and in departure is the reason of her inconstancies.

IV. Translate the following sentences into Chinese.

1. Life seems so long, and its capacity so great, to one who knows nothing of all the intervals it needs must hold—intervals between aspirations,   between actions, pauses as inevitable as the pauses of sleep.

2. It has been found that several tribes in Africa and in America worship the moon, and not the sun; a great number worship both; but no tribes are known to adore the sun, and not the moon.

3. The individual man either never learns it fully, or learns it late. And he learns it so late, because it is a matter of cumulative experience upon which cumulative evidence is long lacking.

4. Sorrow for one cause was intolerable yesterday, and will be intolerable tomorrow; today it is easy to bear, but the cause has not passed

5. Both souls were in close touch with the spirits of their several worlds, and no deliberate human rules, no infractions of the liberty and law of the universal movement, kept from them the knowledge of recurrences.

V. Respond to each of the following statements.

1. Different people have different attitudes towards the world—though the world itself is same.

2. Sensitive minds have greater possibility to perceive the beauty of the world.

3. Poems and verses generally have metrical features as a rule.

4. What is just upon its flight of farewell is already on its long path of return.

5. Love, like the tide, has its own metric, so just take it easy.

VI. Provide a text which can support your viewpoint on one of the statements in *Exercise V*. Make your comments on the text you choose.

Unit Twelve

Love

Ralf Waldo Emerson

Every promise of the soul has innumerable fulfillments; each of it. Nature, <u>uncontainable</u>, flowing, <u>forelooking</u>, in the first <u>sentiment</u> of kindness anticipates already a benevolence which shall lose all particular regards in its general light. The introduction to this <u>felicity</u> is in a private and tender relation of one to one, which is the <u>enchantment</u> of human life; which, like a certain divine rage and enthusiasm, seizes on man at one period, and works a revolution in his mind and body; unites him to his race, pledges him to the domestic and <u>civic</u> relations, carries him with new sympathy into nature, <u>enhances</u> the power of the senses, opens the imagination, adds to his character heroic and sacred attributes, establishes marriage, and gives <u>permanence</u> to human society.

The natural association of the sentiment of love with the <u>heyday</u> of the blood seems to require, that in order to portray it in vivid tints, which every youth and maid should confess to be true to their <u>throbbing</u> experience, one must not be too old. The delicious fancies of youth reject the least <u>savour</u> of a mature philosophy, as chilling with age and <u>pedantry</u> their purple bloom. And, therefore, I know I incur the <u>imputation</u> of unnecessary hardness and stoicism

uncontainable /ˌʌnkənˈteɪməbəl/ *adj.* unable to keep in control

forelooking /fɔːˈlukɪŋ/ *n.* foreseeing

sentiment /ˈsentɪmənt/ *n.* a. mental feeling, the total of what one thinks and feels on a subject; b. (tendency to be moved by) (display of) tender feeling contrasted with reason; c. expression of feeling; opinions or points of view

felicity /fɪˈlɪsɪti/ *n.* a. (*formal*) great happiness or contentment; b. pleasing manner of speaking or writing

enchantment /ɪnˈtʃɑːntmənt/ *n.* being charmed or delighted

civic /ˈsɪvɪk/ *adj.* of the official and affairs of a town or a citizen

enhance /ɪnˈhɑːns/ *v.* add to (the value, attraction, powers, price, etc.)

permanence /ˈpɜːmənəns/ *n.* a. state of being permanent; b. permanent thing, person or position

permanent /ˈpɜːmənənt/ *adj.* not expected to change; going on for a long time; intended to last

heyday /ˈheɪdeɪ/ *n.* time of greatest prosperity or power

throb /θrɒb/ *v.* (of the heart, pulse, etc.) beat esp. beat more rapidly than usual

savor /ˈseɪvə/ *n.* taste or flavor (of sth); suggestion of a quality

pedantry /ˈpedəntrɪ/ *n.* tiresome and unnecessary display of learning; too much insistence upon formal rules

imputation /ˌɪmpjuː(ː)ˈteɪʃən/ *n.* a. considering as the act, quality, or outcome of; b. accusation, or suggestion of wrong doing

from those who compose the Court and Parliament of Love. But from these formidable censors I shall appeal to my seniors. For it is to be considered that this passion of which we speak, though it begin with the young, yet forsakes not the old, or rather suffers no one who is truly its servant to grow old, but makes the aged participators of it, not less than the tender maiden, though in a different and nobler sort. For it is a fire that, kindling its first embers in the narrow nook of a private bosom, caught from a wandering spark out of another private heart, glows and enlarges until it warms and beams upon multitudes of men and women, upon the universal heart of all, and so lights up the whole world and all nature with its generous flames.

formidable /'fɔːmɪdəbəl/ *adj.* a. causing fear or dread; b. requiring great effort to deal with or overcome

censor /'sensə/ *n.* official with authority to examine letters, books, periodicals, plays, films, etc. and to cut out anything regarded as immortal or in other ways undesirable, or in time of war, helpful to the enemy

multitude /'mʌltɪtjuːd/ *n.* a. great number (esp. of people gathered together); b. greatness of number

adherence /əd'hɪərəns/ *n.* a. sticking fast to; b. remaining faithful to; supporting firmly

deface /dɪ'feɪs/ *v.* spoil the appearance of; make engraved lettering illegible

disfigure /dɪs'fɪɡə/ *v.* spoil the appearance or shape of

nourishment /'nʌrɪʃmənt/ *n.* keeping (sb) alive and well with food; making well and strong; improving (land) with manure, etc.

compunction /kəm'pʌŋkʃən/ *n.* uneasiness of conscience; feeling of regret for one's action

embitter /ɪm'bɪtə/ *v.* arouse bitter feelings in

melancholy /'melənkəli/ *n.* a. sadness; low spirits; b. *adj.* sad; low spirited; causing sadness or low spirits

hilarity /hɪ'lærɪti/ *n.* noisy merriment; loud laughter

It matters not, therefore, whether we attempt to describe the passion at twenty, at thirty, or at eighty years. He who paints it at the first period will lose some of its later, he who paints it at the last, some of its earlier traits. Only it is to be hoped that, by patience and the Muses' aid, we may attain to that inward view of the law, which shall describe a truth ever young and beautiful, so central that it shall commend itself to the eye, at whatever angle beholden.

And the first condition is, that we must leave a too close and lingering adherence to facts, and study the sentiment as it appeared in hope and not in history. For each man sees his own life defaced and disfigured, as the life of man is not, to his imagination. Each man sees over his own experience a certain stain of error, whilst that of other men looks fair and ideal. Let any man go back to those delicious relations which make the beauty of his life, which have given him sincerest instruction and nourishment, he will shrink and moan. Alas! I know not why, but infinite compunctions embitter in mature life the remembrances of budding joy, and cover every beloved name. Every thing is beautiful seen from the point of the intellect, or as truth. But all is sour, if seen as experience. Details are melancholy; the plan is seemly and noble. In the actual world—the painful kingdom of time and place—dwell care, and canker, and fear. With thought, with the ideal, is immortal hilarity, the rose of joy. Round it all the Muses sing. But grief cleaves to names, and persons, and the partial interests of today and yesterday. The strong bent of nature is seen in the proportion which this topic of personal relations usurps in the conversation of society.

civility /sɪ'vɪlɪti/ *n.* politeness; (*pl.*) polite acts
rustic /'rʌstɪk/ a. *adj.* (in a good sense) characteristic of country people; unaffected; b. rough; unrefined; c. of rough workmanship
satchel /'sætʃəl/ *n.* small bag for carrying light articles, esp. school books
coquetry /'kɒkɪtri/ *n.* a. flirting; b. instance of this
reverence /'revərə ns/ *n.* deep respect; feeling of wonder and awe

What do we wish to know of any worthy person so much, as how he has sped in the history of this sentiment? What books in the circulating libraries circulate? How we glow over these novels of passion, when the story is told with any spark of truth and nature! And what fastens attention, in the intercourse of life, like any passage betraying affection between two parties? Perhaps we never saw them before, and never shall meet them again. But we see them exchange a glance, or betray a deep emotion, and we are no longer strangers. We understand them, and take the warmest interest in the development of the romance. All mankind love a lover. The earliest demonstrations of complacency and kindness are nature's most winning pictures. It is the dawn of civility and grace in the coarse and rustic. The rude village boy teases the girls about the school-house door; —but today he comes running into the entry, and meets one fair child disposing her satchel; he holds her books to help her, and instantly it seems to him as if she removed herself from him infinitely, and was a sacred precinct. Among the throng of girls he runs rudely enough, but one alone distances him; and these two little neighbours, that were so close just now, have learned to respect each other's personality. Or who can avert his eyes from the engaging, half-artful, half-artless ways of school-girls who go into the country shops to buy a skein of silk or a sheet of paper, and talk half an hour about nothing with the broad-faced, good-natured shop-boy. In the village they are on a perfect equality, which love delights in, and without any coquetry the happy, affectionate nature of woman flows out in this pretty gossip. The girls may have little beauty, yet plainly do they establish between them and the good boy the most agreeable, confiding relations, what with their fun and their earnest, about Edgar, and Jonas, and Almira, and who was invited to the party, and who danced at the dancing-school, and when the singing-school would begin, and other nothings concerning which the parties cooed. By and by that boy wants a wife, and very truly and heartily will he know where to find a sincere and sweet mate, without any risk such as Milton deplores as incident to scholars and great men.

I have been told, that in some public discourses of mine my reverence for the intellect has made me unjustly cold to the personal relations. But now I almost shrink at the remembrance of such disparaging words. For persons are love's world, and the coldest philosopher cannot recount the debt of the young soul wandering here in nature to the power of love, without being tempted to unsay, as treasonable to nature, aught

celestial /sɪˈlestɪəl/ *adj.* a. of the sky; of heaven; b. divinely good or beautiful

rapture /ˈræptʃə/ *n.* ecstatic delight

visitation /ˌvɪzɪˈteɪʃən/ *n.* a. visit; esp. one of an official nature or one made by a bishop or priest; b. trouble, disaster, looked upon as punishment from God

trivial /ˈtrɪvɪəl/ *adj.* a. of small value or importance; b. commonplace; humdrum; c. (of a person) trifling; lacking seriousness; superficial

amber /ˈæmbə/ *n.* hard, clear yellowish-brown gum used for making ornaments, etc.

derogatory to the social instincts. For, though the celestial rapture falling out of heaven seizes only upon those of tender age, and although a beauty overpowering all analysis or comparison, and putting us quite beside ourselves, we can seldom see after thirty years, yet the remembrance of these visions outlasts all other remembrances, and is a wreath of flowers on the oldest brows. But here is a strange fact; it may seem to many men, in revising their experience, that they have no fairer page in their life's book than the delicious memory of some passages wherein affection contrived to give a witchcraft surpassing the deep attraction of its own truth to a parcel of accidental and trivial circumstances. In looking backward, they may find that several things which were not the charm have more reality to this groping memory than the charm itself which embalmed them. But be our experience in particulars what it may, no man ever forgot the visitations of that power to his heart and brain, which created all things new; which was the dawn in him of music, poetry, and art; which made the face of nature radiant with purple light, the morning and the night varied enchantments; when a single tone of one voice could make the heart bound, and the most trivial circumstance associated with one form is put in the amber of memory.

Cultural Notes

Ralph Waldo Emerson (1803—1882)—Ralph Waldo Emerson is one of the most famous American essayists, poets and philosophers. He was born on May 25, 1803, the fourth of eight children. Waldo entered Harvard at 14. He began then to keep a journal, a practice he continued for the rest of his life, later calling its volumes—all long since published—his "savings bank." His early writings contain much poetry. In October, 1826, Emerson was licensed to preach by the Middlesex Association of Ministers. In 1836 he published his first book, *Nature*. He began his career as a Unitarian minister but went on, as an independent man of letters, to become the preeminent lecturer, essayist and philosopher of 19th century America. Emerson was a key figure in the "New England Renaissance," as an author and also through association with the Transcendental Club, many writers, notably Henry David Thoreau, Bronson Alcott and Margaret Fuller, gathered around him at his home in Concord, Massachusetts. Late in life his home was a kind of shrine students and aspiring writers visited, as on a pilgrimage.

He and other transcendentalists did much to open Unitarians and the liberally religious to science, eastern religions and a naturalistic mysticism. His main themes are individualism, independent thinking, self-reliance, idealism and the worship of nature. His works include *Nature, Self-reliance, American Scholar, Overlord and may other essays and poems.*

Exercises

I. Answer the following questions based on the text.

1. Do you agree with the author that love is so powerful that it can work a revolution in a person's mind and body?

2. Do you think that it is self-contradictory when the author said that the delicious fancies of youth reject the least savor of a mature philosophy, as chilling with age and pedantry their purple bloom, and that though it (love) begin with the young, yet forsakes not the old?

3. How do you understand the author's opinion when he mentioned that he who paints it at the first period will lose some of its later, he who paints it at the last, some of its earlier traits?

4. Do you agree with Dorothy Parker's saying that love is like quicksilver in the hand, leave the fingers open and it stays; clutch it, and it darts away?

5. Make a comment on the opinion that love has no awareness of merit or demerit; it has no scale. Love loves; this is its nature.

II. Text Review. Write T for true and F for false in the brackets before each of the following statements.

( ) 1. Only the youth are able to portray love in vivid color, therefore, the old have no such passion.

( ) 2. We want to know of a famous person, while we are not interested in his love stories.

( ) 3. A beauty can last in one's life, and the memory of love can outlast that of other things.

( ) 4. According to the author, if a man is asked to recall his love stories, he would like to try to avoid it.

( ) 5. Love is so great that it can cause a man change a lot mentally but not physically.

( ) 6. The author thinks that love is human nature, and that it needs no affectation, but true emotion.

(   )   7. In the author's opinion, a man tends to view himself as one with many errors. He would think of himself with a derogatory impression.

(   )   8. If he is a servant of the strong passion, a man will stay young forever both in mind and body.

(   )   9. Everything is beautiful, seen from the point of the intellect, as truth. But all is sour, if seen as experience. Therefore, experience is no better than truth.

(   ) 10. Because of love, a girl is a beauty for his beloved one, although she is very plain.

III. Paraphrase the following sentences in English.

1. The strong bent of nature is seen in the proportion which this topic of personal relations usurps in the conversation of society.

2. All mankind love a lover. The earliest demonstrations of complacency and kindness are nature's most winning pictures.

3. For it is to be considered that this passion of which we speak, though it begin with the young, yet forsakes not the old, or rather suffers no one who is truly its servant to grow old.

4. I know not why, but infinite compunctions embitter in mature life the remembrances of budding joy, and cover every beloved name.

5. But be our experience in particulars what it may, no man ever forgot the visitations of that power to his heart and brain...

IV. Translate the following sentences into Chinese.

1. The introduction to this felicity is in a private and tender relation of one to one, which is the enchantment of human life; which, like a certain divine rage and enthusiasm, seizes on man at one period, and works a revolution in his mind and body.

2. The natural association of the sentiment of love with the heyday of the blood seems to require, that in order to portray it in vivid tints, which every youth and maid should confess to be true to their throbbing experience, one must not be too old.

3. For it is a fire that, kindling its first embers in the narrow nook of a private bosom, caught from a wandering spark out of another private heart, glows and enlarges until it warms and beams upon multitudes of men and women, upon the universal heart of all, and so lights up the whole world and all nature with its generous flames.

4. For each man sees his own life defaced and disfigured, as the life of man is not, to his imagination. Each man sees over his own experience a certain stain of

error, whilst that of other men looks fair and ideal.

5. For persons are love's world, and the coldest philosopher cannot recount the debt of the young soul wandering here in nature to the power of love, without being tempted to unsay,　as treasonable to nature,　aught derogatory to the social instincts.

V. Respond to each of the following statements.

1. Being loved doesn't necessarily lead to loving others.

2. We can observe that love does exist everywhere when and only when we get rid of the negative emotions against others.

3. Our life divides at the very moment we take our outlook, both towards life itself and the people around us.

4. Love is prevailing everywhere in nature, and hatred does exist in nature, too.

5. What do you think the relationships between love and evil?

VI. Provide a text which can support your viewpoint on one of the statements in *Exercise V*. Make your comment on the text you choose.

Text B

Of Friendship

Francis Bacon

IT HAD been hard for him that spake it to have put more truth and untruth together in few words,　than in that speech, Whatsoever is delighted in solitude,　is either a wild beast or a god.　For it is most true,　that a natural and secret hatred,　and aversation towards society, in any man, hath somewhat of the savage beast;　but it is most untrue,　that it should have any character at all, of the divine nature;　except it proceed, not out of a pleasure in solitude,　but out of a love and desire to sequester a man's self,　for a higher conversation:　such as is found to have been falsely and feignedly in some of the heathen;　as Epimenides the Candian, Numa the Roman,

solitude /'sɒlɪtjuːd/ *n.* being without companions; lonely

aversation /ə'vɜːsʃən/ *n.* =aversion a. a feeling of stong dislike or unwillingness; b. a person or thing that casues this feeling

sequester /sɪ'kwestə/ *v.* keep sb away or apart from other people; withdraw to a quiet place

feignedly /'feɪnɪdli/ *adv.* pretendingly

heathen /'hiːðən/ *n.* a. one who adheres to the religion of a people or nation that does not acknowledge the God of Judaism, Christianity, or Islam; b. such persons considered as a group; the unconverted

Empedocles the Sicilian, and Apollonius of Tyana; and truly and really, in divers of the ancient hermits and holy fathers of the church. But little do men perceive what solitude is, and how far it extendeth. For a crowd is not company; and faces are but a gallery of pictures; and talk but a tinkling cymbal, where there is no love. The Latin adage meeteth with it a little: Magna civitas, magna solitudo; because in a great town friends are scattered; so that there is not that fellowship, for the most part, which is in less neighborhoods. But we may go further, and affirm most truly, that it is a mere and miserable solitude to want true friends; without which the world is

hermit /'hɜːmɪt/ n. person (esp. man in early Christian times) living alone

cymbal /'sɪmbəl/ n. one of a pair of round brass plates struck together to make chanting sounds

adage /'ædɪdʒ/ n. old and wise saying; proverb

Magna civitas, magna solitudoa (*Latin proverb*) a large city is a great place to be alone

suffocation /ˌsʌfəˈkeɪʃən/ n. a. causing or having difficulty in breathing; b. killing, choking by making breathing impossible

sarza /sarˈsa/ n. a kind of prescription in medieval, used to cure rheumatic disease

spleen /spliːn/ n. bodily organ in the abdomen which causes changes in the blood

sulphur /'sʌlfə/ n. light yellow non-metallic element (symbol S)

hazard /'hæzəd/ a. n. risk; danger; b. n. game at dice, with complicated chances; c. v. take the risk of; expose to danger; d. n. venture to make

thereof /ðeərˈɒv/ adv. (*formal*) of that; from that source

privadoes a Spanish term, referring to a private friend; a confidential friend; a confidant

participes curarum partners of cares

but a wilderness; and even in this sense also of solitude, whosoever in the frame of his nature and affections, is unfit for friendship, he taketh it of the beast, and not from humanity.

A principal fruit of friendship, is the ease and discharge of the fulness and swellings of the heart, which passions of all kinds do cause and induce. We know diseases of stoppings, and suffocations, are the most dangerous in the body; and it is not much otherwise in the mind; you may take sarza to open the liver, steel to open the spleen, flowers of sulphur for the lungs, castoreum for the brain; but no receipt openeth the heart, but a true friend; to whom you may impart griefs, joys, fears, hopes, suspicions, counsels, and whatsoever lieth upon the heart to oppress it, in a kind of civil shrift or confession.

It is a strange thing to observe, how high a rate great kings and monarchs do set upon this fruit of friendship, whereof we speak: so great, as they purchase it, many times, at the hazard of their own safety and greatness. For princes, in regard of the distance of their fortune from that of their subjects and servants, cannot gather this fruit, except (to make themselves capable thereof) they raise some persons to be, as it were, companions and almost equals to themselves, which many times sorteth to inconvenience. The modern languages give unto such persons the name of favorites, or privadoes; as if it were matter of grace, or conversation. But the Roman name attaineth the true use and cause thereof, naming them participes curarum; for it is that which tieth the knot.

And we see plainly that this hath been done, not by weak and passionate princes only, but by the wisest and most politic that ever reigned; who have oftentimes joined to themselves some of their servants; whom both themselves have called friends, and allowed other likewise to call them in the same manner; using the word which is received between private men.

Certainly, if a man would give it a hard phrase, those that want friends, to open themselves unto, are carnnibals of their own hearts. But one thing is most admirable (wherewith I will conclude this first fruit of friendship), which is, that this communicating of a man's self to his friend, works two contrary effects; for it redoubleth joys, and cutteth griefs in halves. For there is no man, that imparteth his joys to his friend, but he joyeth the more; and no man that imparteth his griefs to his friend, but he grieveth the less. So that it is in truth, of operation upon a man's mind, of like virtue as the alchemists use to attribute to their stone, for man's body; that it worketh all contrary effects, but still to the good and benefit of nature. But yet without praying in aid of alchemists, there is a manifest image of this, in the ordinary course of nature. For in bodies, union strengtheneth and cherisheth any natural action; and on the other side, weakeneth and dulleth any violent impression: and even so it is of minds.

The second fruit of friendship, is healthful and sovereign for the understanding, as the first is for the affections. For friendship maketh indeed a fair day in the affections, from storm and tempests; but it maketh daylight in the understanding, out of darkness, and confusion of thoughts. Neither is this to be understood only of faithful counsel, which a man receiveth from his friend; but before you come to that, certain it is, that whosoever hath his mind fraught with many thoughts, his wits and understanding do clarify and break up, in the communicating and discoursing with another; he tosseth his thoughts more easily; he marshalleth them more orderly, he seeth how they look when they are turned into words: finally, he waxeth wiser than himself; and that more by an hour's discourse, than by a day's meditation. It was well said by Themistocles, to the king of Persia, That speech was like cloth of Arras, opened and put abroad; whereby the imagery doth appear in figure; whereas in thoughts they lie but as in packs. Neither is this second fruit of friendship, in opening the understanding, restrained only to such friends as are able to give a man counsel; (they indeed are best;) but even without that, a man learneth of himself,

alchemist /'ælkɪmɪst/ n. a person who studied or practiced alchemy

manifest /'mænɪfest/ a. adj. clear and obvious; b. v. show clearly; c. v. give signs of; d. v. (reflex) come to light; appear

cherisheth /'tʃəːmjus/ a. n. care for tenderly; b. v. keep alive (hope, ambition, feelings, etc.) in one's heart

sovereign /'sɒvrɪn/ n. a. (of power) highest; without limit; (of a nation, state, power) having sovereign power; b. excellent; effective; c. ruler, e.g. a king, queen or an emperor; d. British gold coin not in circulation now (face value one pound)

tempest /'tempɪst/ n. violent storm; (fig.) violent agitation

clarify /'klærɪfaɪ/ make or become clear; make (a liquid, etc.) free from impurities

discourse /'dɪskɔːs/ n. a. speech; lecture; sermon; treatise; b. (formal) talk preach or lecture upon (usu. at length)

marshalleth /'maːʃəlɪŋ/ n. a. an officer of highest rank; official responsible for important public events or ceremonies, e.g. one who accompanies a High Court judge; an officer of the royal household; b. v. arrange in proper order; c. guide or lead (sb) with ceremony

counsel /'kaʊnsəl/ n. group of persons appointed, elected or chosen to give advice, make rules and carry out plans, manage affairs, etc., esp. of government

and bringeth his own thoughts to light, and whetteth his wits as against a stone, which itself cuts not. In a word, a man were better relate himself to a statua, or picture, than to suffer his thoughts to pass in smother. Add now, to make this second fruit of friendship complete, that other point, which lieth more open, and falleth within vulgar observation; which is faithful counsel from a friend. Heraclitus saith well in one of his enigmas, Dry light is ever the best. And certain it is, that the light that a man receiveth by counsel from another, is drier and purer, than that which cometh from his own understanding and judgment; which is ever infused, and drenched, in his affections and customs.

whet /wet/ *v.* sharpen (a knife, axe, etc); (*fig.*) sharpen or excite (the appetite; a desire)

smother /'smʌðə/ *v.* a. cause the death of, by stopping the breath of or by keeping air from, kill by suffocation; b. put out (a fire); keep (a fire) down; c. cover; wrap up, overwhelm with

enigma /ɪ'nɪgmə/ *n.* question, person, thing, circumstance, that is puzzling

infuse /ɪn'fjuːz/ *v.* a. (*formal*) put, pour (a quality, etc. into); b. pour (hot) liquid on (leaves, herbs, etc.) to flavor it to extract its constituents; c. undergo infusion

drench /drentʃ/ *v.* make wet all over, right through

flatter /'flætə/ *v.* a. praise too much, praise insincerely (in order to please); b. give a feeling of pleasure to

preservative /prɪ'zɜːvətɪv/ *n.* subsistence used for preserving

admonition /ædmə'nɪʃən/ *n.* (*formal*) warning

pierce /'pɪəs/ *v.* a. (of sharp-pointed instruments) go into or through; b. (fig. of cold, pain, sounds, etc.) force a way into or through; affect deeply; c. penetrate

corrosive /kə'rəʊsɪv/ *adj.* substance that wears away, destroys slowly by chemical action or disease; being worn away thus

absurdity /əb'sɜːditi/ *n.* state of being ridiculous; unreasonableness

So as there is as much difference between the counsel, that a friend giveth, and that a man giveth himself, as there is between the counsel of a friend, and of a flatterer. For there is no such flatterer as is a man's self; and there is no such remedy against flattery of a man's self, as the liberty of a friend. Counsel is of two sorts: the one concerning manners, the other concerning business. For the first, the best preservative to keep the mind in health, is the faithful admonition of a friend. The calling of a man's self to a strict account, is a medicine, sometime too piercing and corrosive. Reading good books of morality, is a little flat and dead. Observing our faults in others, is sometimes improper for our case. But the best receipt (best, I say, to work, and best to take) is the admonition of a friend. It is a strange thing to behold, what gross errors and extreme absurdities many (especially of the greater sort) do commit, for want of a friend to tell them of them; to the great damage both of their fame and fortune: for, as St. James saith, they are as men that look sometimes into a glass, and presently forget their own shape and favor.

Cultural Notes

Lord Francis Bacon (1561—1626)—Lord Francis Bacon is the father of experimental philosophy, whose father had been Lord Keeper, and he himself was a great many years Lord Chancellor under King James I. Nevertheless, amidst the intrigues of a Court, and the affairs of his exalted employment (Because of bribery and extortion he was sentenced by the House of Lords to pay a fine of about four hundred thousand French livers, to lose his peerage and his dignity of Chancellor.), was enough to engross his whole time, he yet found so much leisure for study as to make himself a great philosopher, a good historian, and an elegant writer. A more surprising circumstance is that he lived in an age in which the art of writing justly and elegantly was little known, much less true philosophy. Lord Bacon, as is the fate of man, was more esteemed after his death than in his lifetime. His enemies were in the British Court, and his admirers were foreigners.

Epimenides the Candian—He is a semi-legendary Cretan poet, prophet, and wonder-worker, variously dated to between 600 and 500 BC, and credited with remarkable longevity, with wandering out of the body and with a miraculous sleep of 57 years. He was a Cretan by birth, of the city of Cnossus.

Numa the Roman— He is the legendary king of Rome, successor to Romulus. His consort, the nymph Egeria, was said to have aided him in his rule. The origin of Roman ceremonial law and religious rites was ascribed to him. Among other achievements, he was supposedly responsible for the pontifices, flamens (sacred priests), vestal virgins, worship of Terminus (the god of landmarks), the building of the temple of Janus, and the reorganization of the calendar into days for business and holidays.

Empedocles the Sicilian (493 BC—444 BC)—Empedocles is the Greek philosopher, poet, and scientist. He propounded a pluralist cosmological scheme in which fire, air, water, and earth mingled and separated under the compulsion of love and strife. Empedocles was born of a noble family in the Sicilian city of Acragas (modern Agrigento).

Apollonius of Tyana—He is a Greek philosopher, and he lived in 1st century AD. As a philosopher of the Neo-Pythagorean school, he traveled widely and became famous for his wisdom and reputed magical powers. He was accused of treason by both Nero and Domitian, but escaped by supposedly magical means. A record of his travels, based on the journal of his companion, Damis, and written (216 AD) by Flavius Philostratus, is a mixture of truth and romantic fiction. Some critics have denounced it for its similarity to the Christ story, but others, such as Voltaire and Charles Blount, have championed the doctrines of

Apollonius. He died, supposedly at age 100, after setting up a school in Ephesus.

Heraclitus—Heraclitus, the son of Vloson, was born about 535 BC in Ephesos, the second great Greek Ionian city. Scholars place his death at about 475 BC. He was a man of strong and independent philosophical spirit. Unlike the Milesian philosophers whose subject was the material beginning of the world, Heraclitus focused instead on the internal rhythm of nature which moves and regulates things, namely, the Logos (Rule). Heraclitus is the philosopher of the eternal change. He expresses the notion of eternal change in terms of the continuous flow of the river which always renews itself. Heraclitus accepted only one material source of natural substances, the Pyr (Fire). This Pyr is the essence of Logos which creates an infinite and uncorrupted world, without beginning. It converts this world into various shapes as a harmony of the opposites. The composition of opposites sustains everything in nature. "Good" and "bad" are simply opposite sides of the same thing.

Exercises

I. Answer the following questions based on the text.

1. Why is friendship so difficult to describe in words?
2. Do you think the kings and emperors can also be true in friendship? What for?
3. What do you think about friendship in your own opinion?
4. What's your opinion on the statement: Whatsoever is delighted in solitude, is either a wild beast or a god?
5. What do you think about the second fruits of friendship mentioned in the text?

II. Text Review. Write T for true and F for false in the brackets before each of the following statements.

( ) 1. If a person is among the crowds, he will not feel lonely.

( ) 2. The friends in a small town are closer than those in the big cities.

( ) 3. According to the author, people don't understand what solitude is, and what its scope is.

( ) 4. The nature of human beings tends to look for the friendship, which is different from that of the animals.

( ) 5. Nothing can open the heart of a person, but a true friend.

( ) 6. In human history, only the weak and passionate princes would seek for friendship in their subjects and servants.

( ) 7. The kings and monarchs had joined some of their servants to themselves in order to build a solid foundation for their rule.

( ) 8. There are many ways to keep the mind in health, such as taking medicine, reading good books. Of all them the best one is the friend counsel.

( ) 9. Birds of a feather flock together. An evil person can't make friends with a noble man.

( ) 10. Communicating can help to clarify one's mind, make one wiser, therefore, communicating is always far better than meditation.

III. Paraphrase the following sentences in English.

1. For a crowd is not company; and faces are but a gallery of pictures; and talk but a tinkling cymbal, where there is no love.

2. But we may go further, and affirm most truly, that it is a mere and miserable solitude to want true friends; without which the world is but a wilderness.

3. A principal fruit of friendship, is the ease and discharge of the fulness and swellings of the heart, which passions of all kinds do cause and induce.

4. For there is no man, that imparteth his joys to his friend, but he joyeth the more; and no man that imparteth his griefs to his friend, but he grieveth the less.

5. The second fruit of friendship, is healthful and sovereign for the understanding, as the first is for the affections.

IV. Translate the following sentences into Chinese.

1. It is a strange thing to observe, how high a rate great kings and monarchs do set upon this fruit of friendship, whereof we speak: so great, as they purchase it, many times, at the hazard of their own safety and greatness.

2. But one thing is most admirable (wherewith I will conclude this first fruit of friendship), which is, that this communicating of a man's self to his friend, works two contrary effects; for it redoubleth joys, and cutteth griefs in halves.

3. For there is no such flatterer as is a man's self; and there is no such remedy against flattery of a man's self, as the liberty of a friend.

4. Reading good books of morality, is a little flat and dead. Observing our faults in others, is sometimes improper for our case. But the best receipt (best, I say, to work, and best to take) is the admonition of a friend.

5. For friendship maketh indeed a fair day in the affections, from storm and tempests; but it maketh daylight in the understanding, out of darkness, and confusion of thoughts.

V. Respond to each of the following statements.

1. Sometimes we do like praise, but faithful counsel from our close friends is important to all of us.

2. As human beings are the social animals, seeking for true friendship is part of one's life.

3. One's own understanding and judgment is usually influenced by his affections and the customs. It has its own limitations.

4. True friendship is beyond time. One does not need to see each other often. The thread may be picked up instantaneously, even after many years.

5. We cannot assume a sense of superiority over a friend without undermining a core attribute of friendship.

VI. Provide a text which can support your viewpoint on one of the statements in *Exercise V.* Make your comment on the text you choose.